MEAN STREETS

D1649099

'I offer fair challenge,' said the Dethak.

Chris stood silent for a moment. Then he said mildly, 'How can the challenge be fair? I have no sword.'

The Dethak threw him one of the swords. Chris caught it by the hilt and studied it curiously. It was beautifully balanced, relatively short, slightly curved and razor-sharp.

The Dethak bowed and stepped back a few paces, remaining sword held high. 'Fight!'

'Sorry,' said Chris. He tossed the sword to the ground, and plunged his hand back into his pocket.

'Then die!' The Dethak sprang, curved blade held high.

THE NEW
ADVENTURES

MEAN STREETS

Terrance Dicks

First published in Great Britain in 1997 by
Virgin Publishing Ltd
332 Ladbroke Grove
London W10 5AH

Bernice Summerfield originally created by Paul Cornell

Cover illustration by Fred Gambino

ISBN 0 426 20519 7

Typeset by Galleon Typesetting, Ipswich
Printed and bound in Great Britain by
Mackays of Chatham PLC

PROLOGUE IN MEGACITY

'Kill them. Kill them both.'

The speaker stood at the picture window of the penthouse, gazing out over Megacity. Gazing, rather, at the fog of pollution which roofed the city. Only the tallest towers in Megacity pierced through the perpetual murk. Only the very rich and the very powerful ever saw Megerra's feeble red sun.

The man hovering anxiously by the door was massive, with a scarred, weathered face and hands the size of shovels. He could have killed the neat, plump little man by the window with a single blow. All the same, he was afraid.

He gulped and licked dry lips, nerving himself to question the order. When he spoke his voice had a rough, gravelly quality. 'That might not be wise, Chief . . .'

The little man frowned. 'And why not?'

'Well, if they really are Pinks . . .'

'We've no proof of that.'

'Garshak is usually reliable. And you know what Pinkertons say, boss.'

'Do I?'

'They never let the death of an operative go unsolved – or unpunished. They'll flood the planet with agents, ask all kinds of questions.'

'I can handle Pinkertons . . .'

Sure you can, you arrogant little shit, thought the big man. The biggest, most effective private-investigation agency in this sector of the galaxy, but you can handle them. Out loud he said deferentially, 'Pinkertons are very big and very persistent. They could give us a lot of trouble – especially now.'

'Why especially now?'

'Well, what with the Project under way . . .'

'And exactly how much do you know about the Project?'

The voice was mild and enquiring but the big man felt a sudden chill. In his peculiar job, to know too little was dangerous. To know too much could be fatal.

He kept his voice calm. 'Just what everyone knows, that it exists, and that it's big.'

The little man nodded. 'Quite so. When you need to know more you'll be told.' He frowned suddenly. 'You say *everyone* knows this much?'

'Well, everyone seems to be talking about it. Barmen, hovercabbies, petty grafters. So if this is a sensitive time, maybe the Pinks should be handled with discretion. It's your decision, Chief.'

The man by the window watched the sun touch the cloud banks of smog with a faint pink glow. Quite a pretty effect, he thought.

He turned away from the window.

'Very well. A good beating, just as a warning. See to it.'

'Right away.'

The big man turned to go.

'Just a moment.'

He waited. 'Chief?'

'All this gossip about the Project . . . I don't like it, I want it stopped.'

'How, Chief? You can't stop people talking.'

'You can discourage them. Kill a few of the chattier ones, for an example to the rest.' He raised an eyebrow. 'I take it you don't object to killing a few barmen and hovercabbies?'

'They're scum,' said the big man simply. 'No one's going to worry about them.'

2

'Very well. And once that's done, arrange a few more beatings for the rest. Spread the word. Tell the usual sources to contact us direct if they hear anything dangerous.' He smiled complacently. 'People can think what they like – but teach them that talking about the Project, even if it's gossip or guesswork, just isn't healthy.'

The big man nodded. 'I'll get on to it today. First, we'll deal with those two nosy Pinks.'

Roz Forrester wasn't much worried when four burly miners swaggered drunkenly into the sleazy downtown beer hall. It was early in the day to be drunk, but Megerra's miners worked and played in shifts that ignored the clock.

She wasn't even concerned when her cop instincts told her the four weren't nearly as drunk as they pretended to be, and that they were taking a particular interest in her and her companion – a massive fair-haired young man with sleepy blue eyes.

Roz Forrester and Chris Cwej were hunting a planet-hopping serial killer called the Ripper as a favour to an old friend.

They were using fake credentials to pose as Pinks – agents of the Interplanetary Pinkerton Bureau – and they'd been warned that Megacity was an unhealthy place for investigators. The place was so corrupt that everyone had something to hide.

'Over there, by the door,' she said quietly.

Chris glanced up at the miners. 'Half drunk. Looking for trouble.'

'Looking for us.'

Chris yawned. 'Same thing. Want another beer?'

'Why not?'

Chris moved over to the bar, leaving Roz alone and apparently unprotected. He smiled at the idea of Roz Forrester ever being unprotected. Chris was bored, and a good bar-room fight was just what he needed.

This one didn't last long.

When Chris moved away, the four miners moved in on Roz. After a few predictable sexual innuendos, the biggest grabbed her by the arm, pulled her to her feet and released her with a scream when her knee slammed into his groin.

Chris crossed the bar in a few long strides, grabbed two of the remaining miners by the back of the neck, and slammed their shaven skulls together with a deeply satisfying clopping sound that echoed around the bar.

Dropping the two dazed miners, Chris swung hopefully round on the fourth, but he was already heading for the door with Roz's victim hobbling painfully after him.

Chris sighed and went back to the bar, returning a moment later with two more beers. Ignoring the unconscious miners, they finished their beers and wandered outside.

Despite the early hour the street was hot and murky, lit by flickering neon.

Chris yawned and stretched. 'What now? Hit a few more joints?'

Roz shook her head. 'You can if you like. My back teeth are floating already. I'm going back to the hotel for a shower and a sleep. After that we'll hit the nightspots. I reckon the Ripper's probably a night person anyway. Your average murdering fiend doesn't care for the daylight.'

'This planet doesn't have any daylight,' grumbled Chris. 'Still, suit yourself. I'll get you a hovercab. Let's try our old friend again.'

'Must we?'

'Better the rat you know . . . Besides, I like to think we're developing a good relationship.'

He crossed to the comm unit by the bar door and shoved a disc into the slot.

The unit crackled into life. 'Hovercab seventy-nine, wha' you wan'?'

'Pick-up at . . .' Chris glanced up at the sputtering neon sign. 'Pick-up at the Dirty Digger, right away.'

'Nah, try someone else, I'm just knocking off.'

'If you don't get your furry ass and your clapped-out

4

hovercab here in two minutes, I'll come and find you and strangle you with your own tail!'

'Hey, that you, boss?' said the voice delightedly. 'Big fair guy with the little dark dame?'

'That's us.'

'Thass me you see turning the corner!'

There was another crackle and the disc popped out of the unit.

Chris pocketed it, grinning at Roz. 'See? I told you we had a good relationship!'

A few minutes later a battered hovercab lurched round the corner and plopped down in front of them, sending up a fountain of dust and debris. The driver, a ratlike life form in a leather jerkin, stuck his head out of the window, flashing rows of long sharp teeth in a maniacal grin.

'OK, where to? You wanna go back to the cop shop?'

Chris handed Roz into the hovercab and shoved a handful of Megacity credits through the driver's window.

'Take the lady back to Megotel One, straight there, shortest route. Don't ask her for any more credits, or I'll have you stuffed for a souvenir.' He leant through the still-open passenger door. 'I'll check out a few more joints, Roz, meet you in the hotel for dinner.'

'Go easy on the beer. We've got a long night's drinking ahead.'

Chris closed the door and stepped back, and the hovercab rose and zoomed away in a cloud of dust.

Roz Forrester leant back on the stained plastic upholstery – stained with what, she hated to think – while the hovercab shouldered its way through Megacity's perpetual gridlock.

She felt tired and a little despairing. The unending hunt for the Ripper was wearing her down. Maybe she was getting old.

She became aware of the driver's grating voice.

'Hey, lady, you wanna ditch the big guy and come out on the town with me? I know everything that goes on in this town, all the bes' joints!'

Roz opened her mouth to blast him, then her cop instincts took over. A local source was a local source – even if it took the form of a giant rat with long yellow teeth and a lecherous disposition.

'What's the best joint in town? The absolute tops?'

'Gotta be Raggor's Cavern, classiest nightclub in Megacity. Hey, I can' take you there, lady.' The driver sounded alarmed. 'Thass only for the big boys. I'd haveta sell the cab, pay for the first drink.'

'Too bad, I don't go out with cheapskates!'

'Ah well . . . Still, maybe is no' such a good idea anyway.'

'Changed your mind about our date? What's the matter?'

'Word on the street is you and your big friend are dangerous company.'

'We are?'

'They say you're Pinks. Some people even say you goin' after the Project.'

'The how much?'

'Come on, don' pretend you don' know about the Project.' You could hear the awe-struck capital 'P' in his voice.

'I'm new in town, remember. What Project? What is it?'

'Somethin' big – real big. A scheme, a scam, a caper. Millions of credits, big people involved. The kinda people who don't like questions.'

Roz Forrester kept on asking questions nonetheless. Quite why, she wasn't sure; it was none of her business. Those old cop instincts again, probably. She soon realized there was just no hard information to be had, not from this source anyway. But there was plenty of gossip.

According to the rodent hovercabbie, Megacity was seething with stories that somewhere, somehow, some billion-credit big deal was being set up. What it was and who was operating it, no one seemed to know.

Some said it was being organized by one of a number of competing crime lords. Others thought it involved the corrupt city government, the big business corporations, or the complex banking and financial network – money-laundering was one of Megacity's major industries.

As for the Project itself – it was drugs, it was computer crime, it was some brilliant new con game. Everyone had a theory, no one really knew.

The hovercab stopped outside the hotel and Roz shoved a wad of credits at the driver.

He looked worried. 'Your boss said no more credits. I don' wan' him comin' after me.'

'He's not the boss. I am,' said Roz. 'And the money's not for the ride: it's for the information – about the Project. Maybe I'll look into it one day, if I get the time.'

The driver grabbed the money. 'Jus' remember, I din' tell you *nothin*'. One day my big mouth gonna get me in trouble.'

The cab zoomed away. Roz crossed the luxurious chandelier-hung foyer of Megotel One, and rode the lift to her room on the fiftieth floor.

She was heading for the shower when the comm unit buzzed.

'Yes?'

'Hotelcom here,' said a bored female voice. 'Got someone here wants to speak with one of the Pinks. I tried the big guy's room but he's out. You wanna take the call?'

'Why not?'

Reflecting that their cover story appeared to be public property in Megacity, Roz waited.

A nervous male voice said, 'Am I talking to one of the Pinkerton operatives?'

'You're talking to Roz Forrester.'

'Is it true that you're here to investigate the Project?'

'I'm not interested in discussing my private business with some stranger,' said Roz. 'You made the call, mister. If you've got something you want to tell me, I'll listen.'

There was a pause. Then the voice said, 'I'll have to take the chance. I've been involved in the Project from the beginning. In fact I started it.' The voice rose hysterically. 'I was obsessed with my work, but now I know I was

7

wrong. There are fatal flaws. It's got to be stopped. It's an abomination, a crime against humanity. They think they can control it, but they don't realize the danger. Once it gets away from them there'll be blood in the streets. The killing will begin again – and it'll spread from here to a hundred worlds.'

'So tell me about it.'

'Not over the comm. Meet me by the fountain in Mineral Plaza right away. It's in the business district, not far from your hotel. I'll bring evidence.'

The voice cut off.

'Hello?' said Roz. 'Hello?'

'Transmission ended,' said the Hotelcom operator's voice.

Roz looked longingly towards the shower. Then she sighed and headed for the door.

Once a cop . . .

In her windowless control room on the top of the hotel, the Hotelcom network operator touched a control.

A gravelly voice said, 'Yeah?'

'One of the Pinks just took a call might interest you. Word was to get in touch direct.'

'Go ahead.'

'Special rates?'

'Sure. If it's worth it.'

She touched a control.

A man's voice said, 'Am I talking to one of the Pinkerton operatives?'

'You're talking to Roz Forrester.'

When the recording finished the gravelly voice said urgently, 'Can you trace the call on the comm network?'

'It'll cost you.'

'Name your price.'

The Hotelcom operator set to work. She was vaguely aware that the required information might be someone's death warrant. But then, everything was for sale in Megacity.

* * *

The plump little man said, 'You're sure it was him?'

'Traced the call right to his office, Chief.'

'I thought those Pinks had been dealt with.'

'Minor hitch, Chief. I reckoned the prof was more urgent. What do I do about him?'

The little man's face twisted with rage. 'Get rid of him.'

'But Chief, the Project –'

'The Project's well under way now. We can do without him. I will not tolerate disloyalty. Get rid of him – now! And make an example of him – something spectacular to impress the Pinks!'

Roz Forrester found Mineral Plaza without difficulty. The result of one of Megacity's rare attempts at civic improvement, it was a scruffy little square with a nonfunctioning fountain, surrounded by towering office buildings.

It was also empty, and Roz settled to wait. She didn't really know why she was here at all, but, now that she was, she could give the guy a few minutes . . .

The white-haired old man in the office stuffed the last few computer disks in the briefcase and forced it to close.

A gravelly voice from the doorway said, 'Taking work home, Professor?'

The old man whirled round. A big hard-faced man had come into the room, followed by two others almost as large.

'Oh, it's you,' said the old man nervously. 'Yes, there's a great deal to do. We've had some problems on the Project and so I thought –'

'Now, Professor,' said the big man reprovingly. 'You know it's forbidden to take Project material out of the building. Suppose it got into the wrong hands?'

Gently he took the briefcase away from the trembling old man.

'Yes, of course,' babbled the old man. 'Why don't you look after it for me and I'll sort it out tomorrow? I really must go, now.'

He headed for the door but the two thugs barred his way.

'Late for your appointment, are you?' said the big man. He strolled to the window and looked out. Down below in the little square a small dark figure stood by the fountain.

'Don't worry, she's still waiting for you. But she'll be getting impatient by now. Tell you what, why not take the quick way down?'

The sound of shattering glass was so high overhead that Roz Forrester heard it only faintly. But it was enough to make her glance up.

Something was hurtling down towards her. As it came nearer and grew larger she got a quick glimpse of flailing limbs and white hair – and then the thing thudded into the stone fountain with hideous force. Something broken, bloody and shapeless lay sprawled across the jagged top of the shattered fountain, and blood, not water, began trickling down its side.

There was nothing to be done and Roz turned and walked quietly away. A gruesome rhyme from Old Earth, once recited to her by a scholarly friend started running through her head.

'Sammy met a tram –'

(What the hell was a tram? How did it go on?)

> Sammy met a tram and the tram met Sammy.
> The tram was jammy and the jam was Sammy.

It wasn't until she was nearly back at the hotel that she saw the splodge of blood and brains on her sleeve.

Showered and changed, Roz met Chris in front of the hotel. Her dark face was grim and tense. Chris looked worriedly at her.

'You OK?'

'Tell you later. Let's get on with it – call a hovercab.'

Chris stuck the call disc into the comm unit and a familiar voice crackled out.

10

'Hovercab seventy-nine, wha' you wan'?'

'Pick-up outside Megotel One to go to . . .'

He looked enquiringly at Roz.

'Tell him Raggor's Cavern,' she said.

'Hey tha' you again, boss?' said the voice. 'You an' the little dark lady? You have fine time at Raggor's Cavern! You stay right where you are, thass me you see comin' –'

There was the flat crack of an explosion and transmission broke up in a series of crackles.

After a few minutes a voice said, 'Hovercab Control, wha' you wan'?'

Chris said, 'I was talking to Hovercab seventy-nine –'

'Hovercab seventy-nine no' available, I sen' another cab. Where you at?'

Minutes later a slightly smarter hovercab appeared, driven by a rather sleeker rodent driver in a shiny red plasticloth jacket. After the usual exchange of threats, bribes and haggling, he agreed to take them to Raggor's Cavern.

'What happened to driver seventy-nine?' asked Chris, as the hovercab sped along the rutted streets towards Old Town.

'Din' you hear? Someone lef' a bomb in his cab. Helluva tip, hey?'

'Any idea who was behind it?' asked Chris.

'Coulda bin lotta people. Ol' seventy-nine, he like to talk. Maybe he talk too much, hey?'

'About the Project, for example?' asked Roz.

They heard the click as the rodent driver's jaws snapped shut.

'I said maybe he talked too much about the Project,' persisted Roz.

'Never heard of it.'

'I thought everyone in Megacity was talking about it.'

'No' any more,' said the driver grimly. 'Lissen lady, gimme a break. I just got this hovercab, she practically new. You think I wan' us both smeared all over Spaceport Boulevard?'

He drove the rest of the way in silence.

*   *   *

Later, much later, that night, Roz Forrester and Chris Cwej sat in a space shuttle, heading for Space Station Alpha.

The tip about Raggor's Cavern had paid off and they'd found their serial killer. Unfortunately, after killing and robbing Raggor himself and slaughtering a sizeable number of the nightclub's patrons, the Ripper had escaped, leaving Megerra on an earlier shuttle to Station Alpha.

Now Chris and Roz were once again in pursuit.

Roz whiled away part of the journey by telling Chris about her encounter with the Project – whatever it was.

Chris was interested, but not overconcerned. 'None of our business, really. And with the Ripper still on the loose . . .'

'The guy who called me said it was a crime against humanity,' said Roz. 'That's everyone's business.'

'Tell you what,' said Chris. 'When all this Ripper affair is cleared up, we'll come back to Megacity and sort out the Project.'

'Promise?'

'Promise.'

'Well, it's working, Chief,' said the big man with the gravelly voice. 'We blasted a few hovercabbies and barmen, beat up a few petty snitches and now you won't hear a whisper about the Project anywhere.'

'What about the two Pinks?'

'No problem. I sent round a few of the boys to see to them and they left the planet that same night.'

No need, thought the big man, to say that the attempted seeing-to had resulted in two thugs with minor concussion, a third with a severe groin strain and a fourth close to a nervous breakdown. Or to add that the two Pinks had left the planet on their own affairs and of their own accord.

The plump little man smiled. 'I told you the Pinks were nothing to worry about.'

Ah well, what you don't know won't hurt you, thought the big man. Or the Project either.

But he was wrong about that . . .

1

Vacation

Benny was bored.

On a fine summer afternoon, with the campus of St Oscar's bathed in Dellah's rare sunshine, Bernice Summerfield was sitting behind her huge desk in her impressively furnished Rector's office, wondering what the hell to do with her day.

She told herself she couldn't possibly be bored.

Look at who she was – Professor Bernice Summerfield, holder of the Edward Watkinson Chair of Archaeology, Rector of Garland College. She was a distinguished academic and she had far too many cultural and intellectual resources to suffer anything so mundane as boredom.

Professor Summerfield led a rich, full life. She was an important member of the faculty of St Oscar's University. She had committees to chair, essays to assess, courses to revise, pupils to nurture and advise, and overambitious academic colleagues to stab in the back.

She had her long-awaited master work of popular archaeology (currently entitled *So Vast a Pile*) to complete.

Well, more like start, actually.

Thanks to an atypical burst of energy and efficiency, she was up to date with all her academic tasks. Term was nearly over, the long vacation was looming up and her teaching work was winding down. Nevertheless, a number of important and worthwhile activities were available to her.

She could visit the Applied Arts Building and inspect progress on Menlove Stokes's latest project. Menlove had recently exhausted the artistic possibilities of his own bodily fluids and had moved on to explore the random aesthetic effects produced by the activities of the giant Dellahan dung beetle.

The results were fascinating but smelly.

She could go and see her head of department, Dr Follett, and lobby for the increased funds, extra staff and more elaborate teaching facilities which she undoubtedly deserved. She probably wouldn't get anywhere, but it would annoy Dr Follett – always a good thing.

However, since the good doctor was an aged reptilian who discouraged troublesome visitors with a permanent cloud of chlorine, this option was even less fragrant than visiting Menlove Stokes and his 'a hundred and one things you can do with beetle shit' project.

She really ought to do a bit of networking on the vidicom, to try to snag one of the interesting – and lucrative – off-planet archaeological digs that were floating around at this time of year. There were several interesting possibilities but she still hadn't fixed anything up. She told herself she was carefully considering her options. The truth was, she couldn't be bothered.

She could do some work on her book – no, she wasn't that desperate yet.

Or she could leave the office early, head for the Garland College bar, the Witch and Whirlwind, and spend the evening sorting out the universe with a few adoring students, over mugs of old ale.

The trouble was that none of these choices, not even the inevitable last one, really appealed to her.

Bernice looked up from her desk and caught her own reflection in an antique mirror. Impeccably made up and coiffured, wearing her newest power suit – Bernice had decided to clean up her act recently – there she sat. Professor Bernice Summerfield, glamorous, powerful and self-assured.

A successful career woman with an enviable life.

But inside there was still Benny – and Benny was bored.

Benny missed spending her days in boots, jeans and safari jacket with everything she owned in her pockets and the pack on her back.

She missed planet-hopping in battered space freighters, heading out into some hot and spicy alien night, stopping for a drink in the nearest bar and wondering if the life form with red eyes, scales and fangs in the corner really fancied her or was simply feeling a bit peckish.

A line from an Old Earth poet floated into her mind: 'Pull out, pull out on the Long Trail – the trail that is always new!'

There was nothing to stop her.

She had shillings in the bank and free time ahead. She could go to the spaceport and buy a ticket on the first ship to anywhere in the galaxy.

Only – it wasn't so much fun on your own any more, not when you'd been used to someone –

Blocking off that train of thought – what was Jason doing these days anyway? – she looked up and saw a black sphere hovering in front of her. This was Rodney, her secretary, who managed to be even more irritating than her porter, Joseph.

'There is an unscheduled visitor for you in the anteroom, Madame Rector. I informed him that an appointment was essential and that it would probably be several weeks before –'

'Name?' interrupted Bernice.

'I am Rodney, your secretary, Madame Rector.'

Bernice ground her teeth. '*Visitor's* name?'

A deep voice said, 'The name's Cwej. Christopher Cwej.'

A very large young man was filling the doorway. He had fair hair and blue eyes and he wore simple black travelling clothes.

'Chris!' squeaked Bernice delightedly. She jumped up and threw herself into his arms.

Chris lifted her high in the air, gave her a warm but essentially brotherly kiss and put her down again.

Rodney was looking shocked. (How does a plain black sphere register disapproval? thought Bernice. But it does.)

Remembering her academic dignity, Bernice waved him to a guest sofa and sat down beside him.

'This is wonderful, Chris! When did you get here? How long are you staying? What are you doing back at St Oscar's anyway?'

'Taking the questions in order, I've just arrived on the shuttle, just until tomorrow, and I came here to talk to you.'

Bernice jumped up again. 'And so you shall. But not here.' She turned to the still-hovering Rodney. 'The Rector's office is closed. I'll be in conference until tomorrow.'

'Certainly, Madame Rector. Shall I relay any urgent messages to the Witch and Whirlwind?'

'Not unless you want your circuits scrambled,' said Bernice coldly. 'Machines may or may not have developed sentience, but they've certainly developed insolence! Come on, Chris.'

'Nice to be back,' said Chris, as they strolled along brick walkways. 'The old place is looking good.' His gaze took in the vast redbrick building known as 'the Barrel' and the other, newer edifices around it. 'Quite a bit of new building since my last visit.'

'Oh, they've thrown up a few more hi-tech mud huts,' said Bernice. But Chris seemed genuinely impressed and she couldn't help feeling pleased.

They paused to admire the jet-black doors of the Advanced Research Department and came under the suspicious gaze of the Goll security guard.

She moved towards them, clearly intending to move them on, took another look at the size of Chris and decided not to bother.

Bernice beamed at the watching security camera, raised two fingers in salute and they moved on.

'What was all that about?' asked Chris.

'That's the Advanced Research Department – ARD for short. Place is full of paranoid mad scientists. I just enjoy winding them up.'

'That sign you made –'

'They asked me about that in the University Senate. I told them it was an Old Earth gesture signifying admiration and respect.'

'And is it?'

Bernice grinned. 'Not exactly. If they ever consult a cultural anthropologist, I'm in trouble!'

'What do they do in there?'

'Something sinister and nasty,' said Bernice darkly. 'Sounds from a horror holovid have been heard leaking out of the air vents. Mysterious misshapen figures emerge and lurch about the campus in the hours of darkness.'

Chris gave her a sceptical glance. 'I think you've been overdoing those horror holovids yourself.'

'Oh yeah? Listen! A few weeks ago a man in a hospital patient's gown appeared on the campus one night. He attacked a passing student coming home from the bar – for no reason at all. Luckily a gang of her friends came along. It took six brawny students to pull the man off her – he was chucking them about like ninepins.'

'What happened?'

'Suddenly the man collapsed and died. One of the students was a medic – he examined the man and said he showed signs of recent brain surgery. Reckoned he'd had an – an embolism or something. And here's the good bit. All of a sudden a gang of ARD security goons arrived and carted away the body.'

'Did they give any explanation?'

'You're joking! Total blackout, no statement, no nothing. The whole thing never happened.'

Always inclined to be charitable, Chris said, 'They could be doing legitimate medical research . . .'

'So what are they so secretive about? They've got all the money in the world and twenty-six-hour security. You know what they say – there's no completely honest way to make a million shillings.'

They made their way to the Witch and Whirlwind and settled themselves with mugs of ale at Bernice's favourite corner table, which was isolated enough to offer some privacy.

As they sat down Bernice noticed that the table had a new feature – a weirdly shaped lamp with a transparent columnar base inside which coloured bubbles rose and fell sluggishly.

She looked up at the student waiter, a haughty golden-skinned Lucidean working his way through college.

'What the hell's this atrocity?'

The Lucidean shuddered delicately. 'A new design feature, Professor. The bar got an unexpected grant. That thing is Old Earth retro, apparently. It's called a lava lamp. Don't you like it?'

'I hate it, take it away.'

'I'm afraid it's built into the table.'

'Oh well . . .'

Bernice ordered two tankards of old ale. When they finally arrived – Lucideans hated doing anything that seemed like service and compensated by doing it slowly and badly – she raised her tankard to Chris, took a restorative swig and glanced around the room.

It was still early, and there were only a handful of students at the scattered tables. Every single one of them registered Bernice's arrival, and took a good hard look at Chris. Rumours about the prof's after-work tryst with her new toy boy would soon be whizzing around the campus.

Utter nonsense, of course.

Chris was – well, he was just Chris. Ridiculously large, touchingly young and naive.

A skilled professional in police work, formidable in combat, an overgrown adolescent in everything else.

Or . . . Bernice studied him over the rim of her ale mug. There was something different about Chris. Of course, he wasn't quite so young any more – but then, who was? And Roz's death must have hit him hard.

But there was something else. A different look in the wide blue eyes, different lines on the handsome, open face.

A different aura.

Somehow he just *felt* different. Beneath the still-present puppyish charm was something solid, determined, focused.

Chris Cwej had grown up.

Suddenly Bernice realized that, while she was studying Chris, he was assessing her.

'Well, you made it,' he said softly.

'Made what?'

'It – everything you ever wanted. A top job, a big office, fame and fortune. Academic respectability . . .'

'Well, you know the old saying,' said Bernice. 'Be careful what you wish for – you might get it!'

'I looked you up in the St Oscar's Faculty Handbook. A string of impressive qualifications and publications. And you look . . . different. Powerful, impressive, sophisticated. Establishment!'

Bernice looked hard at him. It could have been a compliment, but it wasn't, not quite.

'It's all a front,' she said. 'I'm still Benny underneath.'

'That's what I was wondering about,' said Chris. 'I've got a weird sort of proposition for you. Professor Bernice Summerfield would probably turn it down flat, but Benny might be interested.'

'Go on.'

'It's about something that happened in a place called Megacity. Roz and I were hunting a serial killer. You were doing historical research on Sentarion, remember?'

'Shall I ever forget? On a teetotal campus where they served salad and fruit juice for dinner. I could cope with attacks by giant bloodsucking killer beetles, but all that healthy living nearly finished me off.'

Shuddering at the memory, Bernice ordered another round of drinks. 'So what's it all about?'

Chris drained the last of his tankard. 'Sometimes when you're investigating one crime you come across another, quite unconnected. You're chasing a mugger and you trip over a murderer. Or the other way round, of course.'

'And that's what happened in Megacity?'

'In a way. Roz ran into something called the Project . . .'

In a shadowy control room deep beneath the Advanced Research Department an alarm pinged gently.

The dozing octopod technician swivelled around to one of the surrounding control consoles, studying it with huge, glowing eyes. A light was blinking beside a touchpad, and the technician stretched out a tentacle.

A female voice said, 'And that's what happened in Megacity?'

Then a male voice: 'In a way. Roz ran into something called the Project.'

The female voice again: 'And which was it? A murderer or a mugger?'

'It was something big. According to Roz, even people who just talked about it got killed.'

Checking that recording was still proceeding, the octopod switched off the playback, swivelled round in its central command chair and touched another control.

A deep voice said, 'Yes?'

In its cool, dispassionate voice the octopod said, 'Two top-priority flag words showed up on the new surveillance system, Chief Kedrick. You asked to be informed when –'

'Words?'

' "Megacity" and "Project".'

'Surveillance site?'

'Witch and Whirlwind – it's a student hostelry –'

'I know what it is. Number of speakers?'

'Two, one humanoid female, one humanoid male.'

'Speaker identification?'

'One moment please . . .' Turning to another console, the octopod touched the controls. 'Female voice print identified as Professor Bernice Summerfield. Male voice unknown.'

'Prioritize. Continue audio surveillance. Make sure you

get a full recording, send me a copy.'

'Understood, Chief Kedrick. I shall send it –'

A faint click signified that the comlink was dead.

Unperturbed by his superior's rudeness, completely uninterested in the subject of his report, the octopod made a routine systems check. Bipeds had no manners anyway, and their affairs were of no interest.

Satisfied all was well, the octopod sank back into its doze.

Sometime later, in a comfortable office high up in the same building, Jarl Kedrick, Security Chief of the Advanced Research Department, sat listening to the end of the requested recording.

'And that's all?' asked Bernice Summerfield's voice, over a babble of conversation.

The male voice said, 'That's all.'

There was a moment's pause. Then Bernice Summerfield again: 'Let's get out of here. This place is getting crowded.'

The scrape of moving chairs, sounds of departure, and the recording ended.

Jarl Kedrick was thinking hard. The audio-surveillance experiment was his own particular pet project. It had proved a costly experiment to set up and it was nice to see it producing results so quickly.

He sat back in his big office chair, a cherubic smile on his lips. A tubby, red-faced man with a fringe of white hair and a neat white beard, Kedrick had the benign appearance of everyone's favourite uncle. He might have been planning a birthday surprise for a favourite child.

'Now then,' he said softly. 'What are we going to do about our dear Professor Summerfield?'

It would be best to move quickly, he thought. This sort of thing had to be stamped on – hard and fast. It would justify his audio-surveillance project, it would be an example to others – and it would impress the Director with his efficiency. He would handle the matter personally.

* * *

'Something called the Project, and a couple of corpses,' said Bernice. 'It's not a lot to go on.'

They had left the Witch and Whirlwind by now, and were strolling across the busy campus towards Bernice's living quarters.

The bar had filled up while they were talking, and although no one was obviously listening to their conversation, Bernice had been plagued by an odd feeling that they were being overheard.

'Roz felt sure it was something big, something important,' said Chris.

'But why? From your own account, Megacity must be full of criminal scams. What made Roz so sure this one was special?'

'Instinct,' said Chris. 'Roz Forrester was a good cop.'

And Roz Forrester's what this is all about, thought Bernice. Clearly Chris had never really got over his partner's death. No doubt he felt an irrational guilt because he hadn't been there to save her. This whole mad scheme was some kind of tribute to her memory. Somehow she had to talk Chris out of it.

'What can you possibly hope to do?' she asked gently.

'Go back to Megacity. Start poking around, ask a few questions, see what develops . . .'

'See who tries to kill you first?'

'Always a useful clue!'

Bernice shook her head despairingly. Another argument presented itself. 'Do you realize how much subjective time has passed in Megacity since you and Roz were there?'

She did a few rapid mental calculations, complicated by the fact that time travel was involved. 'It must be . . .'

She paused.

Chris smiled. 'I couldn't quite work it out either! But it's quite a while.'

'Exactly. By now this Project, whatever it is, will have run its course. Either that or it will be so well established it'll be untouchable. Either way . . .'

Chris sighed. 'I know. Everything you say makes absolute sense. But it's a kind of loose end in the fabric of my life. I thought perhaps you might like to come and help me tug it free – just for old times' sake.'

Forget it, thought Bernice. It was a totally lunatic plan and she wanted nothing to do with it. She glanced around the sunny crowded campus, thought of her luxurious living quarters, her imposing office, her adoring students and her important position at St Oscar's. Give it all up to go off and get killed on the Roz Forrester Memorial Crusade? No chance.

She glanced up and saw Chris looking anxiously down at her. For a moment she wavered, but she forced herself to be firm.

'I'm sorry, Chris, it's just not for me. I turned in the white horse and the suit of armour ages ago. I won't pretend I don't have moments of nostalgia – I was having one when you arrived as a matter of fact – but these days I've got a living to earn and a position to keep up.'

(Did I really say that last bit? she thought. 'A position to keep up'? Yuck!)

Still, she was sure it was the right decision and Chris seemed prepared to accept it.

'Yes, of course. I'm sorry, Bernice. I'd no real right to ask you. Look, let's have dinner tonight and a few more drinks . . .'

'A lot more drinks,' said Bernice. 'It's not every day you have a reunion with an old friend.'

(And turn him down flat when he asks for your help.)

'I'll get the first shuttle out of here in the morning,' said Chris cheerfully. 'Then you can forget all about this nonsense.'

'But will you?'

'Yes, very likely.'

The hell you will, thought Bernice. You'll go back to Megacity and get yourself killed for nothing. And there's nothing I can do to stop you.

She was trying to summon up more convincing arguments when a distant voice called, 'Professor! Hey, Professor!'

St Oscar's was a hilly campus, and they were standing at the top of a very long, very steep incline. In a little rotunda at the bottom a spindly young humanoid in a suit of red feathers stood waving and yelling. His other hand supported a wheeled machine.

'He's got my bike again, cheeky young devil,' said Bernice.

'Who has?'

'It's an Ootsoi kid called Jeran. I helped him pick up his books at the beginning of my first term and he's had a crush on me ever since.'

'What's that thing he's holding? Some kind of velocipede?'

'My bicycle,' said Bernice proudly. 'Souped-up Old Earth retro. I had it made specially when I got my bestseller royalties. Basket on the front, big brass bell, the lot . . .'

'Is the boy stealing it?'

'Call it borrowing,' said Bernice. 'Jeran adores it. Sometimes I think it's really the bike he's got a crush on!'

Jeran mounted the bicycle and rode towards them.

'I was just looking for you, Professor,' he yelled in his shrill, birdlike voice. 'I thought you might need your travel machine. I was bringing it to you!'

'Sure you were,' said Bernice indulgently.

As the hill grew steeper, Jeran began wobbling dangerously.

Chris grinned. 'I don't think he's going to make it.'

'Oh yes he will!' said Bernice. She cupped her hands and yelled, 'Use the motor, Jeran. There's a switch on the handlebars, on the right.'

Jeran waved, which caused an even bigger wobble, and began fumbling for the switch. Suddenly the bicycle began gliding smoothly up the hill towards them.

Chris gave her a quizzical look. 'An engine on a velocipede?'

'Just a simple gravitic motor on the back to help with all these hills. I'm not that fond of healthy exercise, you know.'

They stood at the top of the long hill, looking at young

Jeran as he sailed up the incline towards them. It was a sight Bernice was to remember always. Jeran's face radiant with delight, the red feathers fluttering on his suit . . .

With a dull boom the bicycle exploded into a fireball. Fragments of metal and flesh rained on to the path.

A few charred red feathers drifted down after them.

2

ESCAPE

Bernice started downhill, but Chris clamped a big hand on her arm. 'No. It's no use.'

'Jeran may still be alive.'

'Not a chance.'

'But we've got to go and see!'

'Benny, he was blown to bits,' said Chris. 'Very small bits.'

'We can't just leave him . . .'

'You want to say goodbye to a bloody smear on the ground? Remember him gliding up that hill. If ever anyone died happy . . . Now come on, we've got to get away from here.'

'I've got to report the accident.'

'Plenty of people to do that.'

Already an agitated crowd was gathering in the rotunda below. Retaining his grip on her arm, Chris led her away.

'What's the rush?'

'You're not thinking, Benny. You say there was a simple gravitic motor on that thing? Nothing nuclear?'

'Of course not. Just a rechargeable power pack.'

'Have you ever heard of a gravitic motor blowing up? The worst they ever do is grind to a halt. Someone planted a bomb on your bike. A bomb intended for you.'

'I told him to switch on the motor . . .'

* * *

They took a roundabout route back to Bernice's quarters, keeping well away from the scene of the explosion. She still couldn't take in what had happened, but Chris had taken charge. That focused quality she'd noticed earlier was working full blast.

'Now think hard, Benny. Are you mixed up in anything that could make someone want to kill you?'

'Currently, no.'

'No envious fellow professor nursing some grudge?'

'Some of my colleagues probably resent the publicity – and the profits – I got from my book. They'd be happy to steal my students or take over my budget. One or two probably have their eyes on my job. But academics fight with memos and meetings. That stab in the back you hear about is strictly metaphorical. And as for bombs . . .'

'You're sure?'

'Positive.'

'Then it's my fault,' said Chris. 'I'm sorry, Benny, but I've put you in danger – just by talking to you about the Project.'

Bernice stopped and looked up at him. 'Oh, come on now, that's crazy. We have a brief chat about this mysterious Project in a bar and ten minutes later my bike blows up?'

'It's what happened in Megacity. The people Roz talked to got killed, and after that everyone shut up.'

'That was years ago, and light years away. I still say it's ridiculous.'

'I'd call it frightening,' said Chris. 'To be prepared to kill so quickly – and to have the resources to do it.'

'Why me?' demanded Bernice as they walked on. 'Why not you as well?'

'Oh, they'll get round to me as well. But I'm still an unknown quantity to them. They need to study me for a while, discover my habits and my weaknesses. They already know yours.'

Bernice shuddered. 'There's a consoling thought.'

They made their way to Garland College Hall and up to Bernice's quarters. The small white sphere that was Joseph,

Bernice's porter, floated forward to greet them, and Bernice ordered wine and snacks. When the refreshments had been served Joseph purred, 'Will that be all, Madame Rector?'

It was always particularly obsequious in the presence of visitors.

'Just a little privacy, please,' said Bernice.

Joseph floated offendedly towards the porterhatch.

Chris gave her a warning look. 'That may be harder than you think.'

'What?'

'Privacy.' He made a sweeping gesture, indicating the room around them.

Bernice thought for a moment and then called Joseph back.

'Has anyone been in here recently, Joseph?'

'Many people, Rector. At your recent social gathering over fifty faculty members attended. The alcoholic liquor consumption was –'

'Never mind about my drunken friends,' said Bernice. 'Apart from me and my guests and my students, has anyone unusual been here?'

'Only the technicians, Rector.'

'What technicians?'

'A team from University Maintenance, checking the building's electronic systems. It's going on all over the campus.'

'I bet it is,' said Bernice. She waved Joseph away and looked helplessly at Chris. 'Now what? We can't even talk!'

Chris took a small black device from his pocket and began moving it around the room. The device gave out a low, soothing hum, then, suddenly, a loud, exultant ping.

Chris made an adjustment to the device, which emitted a high, intermittent pulsing.

'At least one in here. Bound to be more in the other rooms.' He tapped the device. 'This will jam them so we can talk.'

Bernice hated the idea of unseen listeners. 'Can't you find the bugs and take them out?'

28

'I could, but then they'd know we knew. This way it'll look like a temporary breakdown.'

'Who'd know we knew what?'

'The buggers – whoever they are – would know we knew we'd been bugged. We might want to use the bugs later for disinformation.'

'For how much?'

'If they don't know that we know they're listening,' said Chris patiently, 'we can feed them whatever we want them to hear.'

Bernice was starting to feel that she was trapped in an old-fashioned spy holovid. 'Of course. And we must make quite sure they don't find out that the secret microfilm is really hidden in the MacGuffin!'

Chris looked blank. 'I'm sorry?'

'Never mind.' Bernice shook her head helplessly. 'I'm an academic, not a spy, Chris. I just don't believe this is happening, not here, not at St Oscar's.'

'I know,' said Chris. 'I brought the danger here. I'd better go as soon as I can. Maybe I can draw their attention away from you.'

'Forget it,' said Bernice fiercely. 'We're going to get these buggers together.'

'But you said –'

'That was before they blew up my bike. Cost me a fortune, that bike did, I was . . . very fond of it.'

'Yes,' said Chris gently. 'Of course you were. Benny, are you sure?'

Bernice saw charred red feathers drifting down on to a redbrick path. 'Oh yes, I'm sure. But where do we start? We don't know what we're looking for or who we're fighting.'

'We know one thing we didn't when I arrived,' said Chris. 'There's a link between the Megacity Project and St Oscar's. A link someone's extremely sensitive about. The minute they pick up a mention of the Project they swing into action.'

'Yes, but how come they picked it up at all?' demanded Bernice. She broke off, realizing. 'Dammit, they must have bugged the Witch and Whirlwind as well. That's where we did all our talking. I bet it was in that bloody lava lamp!'

'So?'

'Don't you see? All the bugs must have been in place for some time – even before you ever came to see me.'

'I think that was just bad luck,' said Chris. 'The bugging wasn't particularly for your benefit. It was part of a broad-sweep intelligence-gathering operation. Someone's keeping tabs on the entire university.'

'That's insane.'

Chris shook his head. 'It's practically routine, at least for a big security organization with unlimited resources. It goes right back into history. Dictators were doing it on Earth way back in the twentieth century.'

'Why? Why bother?'

'Paranoia. Knowledge is power. You bug the homes of prominent people, friends *and* enemies, to see what they're really saying about you. But that's just the start. You bug top hotels, cafés, restaurants, anywhere where people may let something slip. I believe, er, "houses of ill fame" were particular favourites.'

Bernice grinned at his embarrassment. 'Houses of what? Oh, brothels! You mean they even bugged people's pillow talk?'

Chris nodded. 'The Nazis even set up a brothel of their own to bug visiting VIPs. Salon Kitty, it was called. And there was one American President who even bugged himself!'

'That's enough ancient history,' said Bernice impatiently. 'The important thing is, who's bugging us – here and now?'

Chris shrugged. 'It's your university, Benny. You tell me.'

Bernice wasn't in any doubt. 'If we're looking for a bunch of overpaid paranoids with a massive security setup, there's really only one candidate . . .'

Jarl Kedrick was afraid.

It was an emotion he was more used to causing than

feeling. Despite his jovial exterior, most people Kedrick met knew who he was, and what he did. Even those who didn't sensed something sinister beneath the surface jollity.

There was nothing obviously intimidating about the Director of the Advanced Research Department. A tall, thin, olive-skinned, silver-haired humanoid, beautifully dressed and impeccably mannered, he had the air of a high-level diplomat. Nevertheless, Kedrick never met him without feeling a thrill of fear. The sensation was so rare that he almost enjoyed it.

The Director rose as Kedrick entered his penthouse office.

'Chief Kedrick! How kind of you to spare me the time!'

'My pleasure, Director.'

The Director waved Kedrick to one of a pair of guest armchairs and took the other himself. 'Can I offer you some refreshment? Tea perhaps?'

'Thank you, no. I mustn't take up any more of your valuable time than is necessary.'

The Director settled back in his chair. 'I gather there was some kind of unfortunate incident on campus a short while ago.'

'Sadly, yes, Director. Bernice Summerfield, Professor of Archaeology, was killed when the engine on her antiquated travel machine exploded.'

'Not so, Chief,' said the Director softly. 'Professor Summerfield is quite unharmed. One of her students borrowed the machine and suffered the consequences.'

Kedrick jumped to his feet. 'I apologize, Director, for my ignorance, and for the error. It will be remedied at once.'

'Sit!' hissed the Director.

White-faced, Kedrick dropped back into his chair.

'Do not apologize for the error,' the Director went on. 'It may well have saved your life. What was your reason for this precipitate action?'

'A conversation recorded in the Witch and Whirlwind – a student hostelry, Director –'

'I know what it is. With whom and on what subject?'

'Professor Summerfield received an off-planet visitor today. They were discussing the Megacity Project.'

'Indeed.' The Director was silent for a moment. 'The visitor?'

'He is registered as Christopher Cwej, Director. It may be an alias. We are experiencing difficulties in tracing his background.'

The Director responded with another unnerving silence.

Nervously Kedrick asked, 'Do I gather, Director, that you do not wish sanctions imposed on Professor Summerfield?'

The Director sighed. 'There are sanctions and sanctions, Chief Kedrick. Our purpose on this primitive planet is to use this academic backwater to carry out a number of delicate assignments for some extremely important clients. The Megacity Project is one of the most important, and potentially one of the most lucrative. There has already been one unfortunate incident.'

'The escaped miner, Director? But the security blackout was absolute and we atomized the body that same night.'

The Director sat back, steepling his long, thin fingers. 'We chose St Oscar's University *because* it is new and obscure. Our influence here is consequently greater. But it must be discreet, behind-the-scenes influence. The precipitate detonation of popular female faculty members is liable to attract unwelcome interest.'

'My apologies, Director.'

The Director waved them aside. 'The death of an obscure student can be glossed over far more easily. He was an Ootsoi, I gather. They are a backward people, and fortunately his family are persons of no importance.'

'And the stranger, Director? Arrangements concerning him are already in place. If you wish me to cancel them, I must act quickly.'

The Director considered. 'Let your arrangements stand. The death of a stranger – some criminal, no doubt – is of little concern. Moreover, his fate may serve as a warning to Professor Summerfield.'

'Is it your view that such a warning will be sufficient, Director? Do you wish me to take any further action in that quarter?'

'You may leave Professor Summerfield to me, Chief. She is an academic – and there are ways of dealing with academics.'

Bernice studied the almost empty flask of Eridanean brandy, decided she really shouldn't drink any more, decided that the remnant wasn't worth saving, and poured a final slug into the heavy crystal glass.

'Just a nightcap,' she muttered to herself. It was late, and she really must go to bed. She and Chris had discussed the situation for ages without getting much further, and eventually Chris had insisted on returning to his bed in the visitors' hostel. She'd offered him the spare bedroom but Chris had insisted on going back, and Bernice knew why. He'd noticed the interested looks in the Witch and Whirlwind and was afraid of compromising her.

Bernice had insisted that she didn't give a damn about her reputation, and that anyway she didn't really have one to lose, but Chris wouldn't listen.

He'd stridden off nobly into the night, promising to call her when he was safely installed. Come to think of it, the hostel wasn't that far – he should have called by now . . .

The vidicom chimed discreetly and Bernice felt a surge of relief. 'Chris?'

But the face on the screen wasn't Chris at all. It was a cross-looking Irving Braxiatel.

'What have you been up to?' he demanded.

'Moi?' said Bernice defensively. 'Why?'

'They're planning to haul you up before the Faculty Ethics Committee.'

'On what grounds?'

'You name it, there's quite a list. It starts with insufficient attention to student welfare . . .'

'Rubbish. I spend more time with my students than anyone else on this Faculty.'

'Apparently there are those who feel more of that time should be spent in the lecture room and study halls and less in the Witch and Whirlwind.'

'What else am I supposed to have done?'

'Unorthodox and inadequate teaching methods, failure to publish projected work, inappropriate dress and demeanour, overindulgence in alcoholic beverages . . .'

'Nonshense – I mean nonsense,' said Bernice indignantly. She drained her Eridanean brandy, attempted to pour another and remembered the flask was empty.

'Oh, and causing the death of one of your students by importing an antiquated and dangerous travel machine.'

'That explosion was the result of an attempt to kill *me*! This is all a calculated smear campaign. It isn't fair!'

'Of course it isn't fair,' said Irving Braxiatel impatiently. 'This is academic politics, Bernice. It isn't a matter of fairness, or justice, or anything like that. You seem to have offended some very powerful people. Now it's a matter of whether those of us who want to keep you have got more clout than those who want to chuck you out.'

'And have you?'

'It's running about fifty-fifty,' said Irving Braxiatel with ruthless frankness. 'But I'm working on it, calling in a few favours. We may tip the balance.'

'So what do I do?'

'Nothing. You'll probably be called up before your head of department tomorrow. Just accept whatever he says and lie low till we get this sorted out. And stop drinking. A hangover won't help you.'

The screen went blank.

'Thanks a million,' muttered Bernice. 'With friends like you . . .' But she knew Braxiatel would do his best to save her.

Then she remembered that Chris still hadn't called.

Hands plunged deep into his tunic pockets, Chris Cwej strode through the warm dark Dellahan night. The campus

34

seemed very quiet. The brick paths were lit only by the occasional glo-globe, and most of the buildings were in darkness. Bernice had assured him that there were late-night places to go, but you had to know where they were. By and large Dellah was an old-fashioned, provincial, early-to-bed sort of planet. Chris rather liked it.

The massive black doors of the Advanced Research Department loomed up ahead, guarded by the ever-present sentry. Chris wondered if Bernice's theory was right, that the Advanced Research Department was responsible for the campus bugging and the bomb attack.

It seemed highly likely. Who else was there? Most of the other faculty disciplines were concerned with abstract academic theory. Many, like Bernice's archaeology, were firmly focused on the past.

Advanced scientific research was, by definition, on the sharp edge of galactic affairs, the frontiers of weaponry, medicine, bioengineering. It meant wealth and power.

It meant danger.

As he came abreast of the black gate the sentry stepped out to bar his way. Suddenly Chris realized that this sentry didn't have the bulky shape of the guard he'd seen earlier.

The cloaked figure was tall and elongated with a tufted head, black glittering eyes, a sharp beak and long sinewy limbs ending in clawed feet.

It was a Dethak.

Chris had heard of the species – everyone had – but he'd never actually encountered one before.

An avian-evolved life form which had long ago lost the power of flight, the fierce Dethaki had been driven into the mountains when their remote planet had been taken over by the big mining corporations.

Too few to regain their planet, too proud to adapt, the surviving Dethaki became mercenaries.

What was a Dethak doing on sentry duty? wondered Chris. They were too temperamental for routine military duties, but they were incomparable guerrilla fighters – and assassins.

It was said that no Dethak returned unsuccessful from a mission. They made their kill, or they died.

The Dethak spoke in a harsh, screeching voice. 'You are the one called Christopher Cwej?'

'That is my name.'

'I offer you challenge.'

'I have no quarrel with you.'

'Nor I with you. The quarrel belongs to those I serve. I offer you fair contest.'

The Dethak swept back its cloak to reveal sinewy feathered arms ending in clawlike hands. Each hand held a sword.

The swords whirled and spun and then became still. It was a dazzling, deliberately intimidating display.

'I offer fair challenge,' said the Dethak.

Chris stood silent for a moment. Then he said mildly, 'How can the challenge be fair? I have no sword.'

The Dethak tossed him one of the swords. Chris caught it by the hilt and studied it curiously. It was beautifully balanced, relatively short, slightly curved, and razor-sharp.

The Dethak bowed, and stepped back a few paces, its remaining sword held high. 'Fight!'

'Sorry,' said Chris. He tossed the sword to the ground, plunging his hand back into his pocket.

'Then die!' The Dethak sprang, curved blade held high.

Chris took a stubby black blaster from his pocket and shot the Dethak in the heart at point-blank range.

It staggered back, dropping its sword, and toppled to the ground.

Kicking the swords out of reach, Chris knelt beside it.

The glittering black eyes opened and looked reproachfully at him. 'You have no honour. You have slain me by treachery!'

'Sorry, I'm not into ritual combat,' said Chris. 'If I have to fight I like to get it over with quickly, before I get hurt. Besides, I haven't actually slain you at all.'

'I feel the coldness of death . . .'

'You feel the effect of a neuron blaster set to stun.'

Chris flicked a lever on the side of the blaster. 'Now it's on maximum. If I see you again, I'll kill you.'

The Dethak said harshly, 'You will not see me again.'

'Good!' said Chris. He rose and marched away into the night.

For a time the Dethak lay still. Then, slowly and painfully, it got to its feet, picked up both swords, and staggered towards the black gate.

Chris went back to the hostel and called Benny on the vidicom, telling her he'd arrived safely. He didn't mention the Dethak.

He noticed that Bernice looked pale and shaken.

'Benny, what's the matter? Are you all right?'

'Not really. They're trying to get me flung off the faculty.'

She told him about her conversation with Irving Braxiatel.

'Oh well,' she concluded, 'easy come, easy go!'

'Cheer up,' said Chris. 'At least they've stopped trying to kill you. Get some sleep, Benny. I'll come and see you tomorrow.'

Jarl Kedrick was still at his desk, working late. It had not, he felt, been one of his best days. He was waiting for the Dethak assassin to report that its task had been carried out.

The voice of a security guard came over his comm unit.

'The Dethak is at the main gate.'

'Admit it, and escort it here immediately.'

Jarl Kedrick looked up eagerly as the Dethak entered the room. It stood before the desk, towering over his seated form.

'Is it finished?' asked Kedrick eagerly.

In a harsh grating voice the Dethak said, 'Not yet.' It whipped the glittering swords from beneath its cloak.

Jarl Kedrick cowered back. 'He bribed you to kill me! You've changed sides! What about your famous Dethak honour?'

The Dethak said, 'I have no honour.'

37

Both swords swept down, slicing open its own abdomen, depositing its entrails in a neat steaming pile on Kedrick's desk.

The Dethak stood upright for a moment longer, and then fell stiffly, like a tree.

With a yell of rage and repulsion Jarl Kedrick leapt to his feet, stabbing at an alarm.

Security guards ran into the room and froze at the gory sight before them.

'Don't just stand there, you fools,' screamed Kedrick. 'Get that useless bloody turkey out of here!'

'What shall we do with it, sir?' stammered a guard.

'You can roast it for your supper for all I care!' Kedrick pointed a shaking finger at his desk, and laughed hysterically. 'Look! The giblets are out already!'

Next morning Bernice Summerfield had a brief and unpleasant interview with Dr Follett, her head of department. He informed her that she was suspended from the faculty of St Oscar's University, pending the investigation of 'certain allegations'. He advised her to go away for a while, lie low, and avoid all controversy. He intimated vaguely that, if she followed this course, the whole matter might well blow over.

Holding her breath against the chlorine fumes, Bernice nodded silently and left without protest.

Chris was waiting for her in her quarters with his travel pack. He helped her to pack and after a brief conversation they left for the spaceport together.

It was some time before Jarl Kedrick recovered his composure, but he managed it at last. Later that same day he went back to see the Director.

'I know things didn't work out *exactly* as planned, Director,' he said smoothly. 'But I think you'll agree that the end result is satisfactory. This is the relevant part of their conversation before they left for the spaceport. With your permission, Director?'

Chris's voice came first: 'So what'll you do?'

Then Bernice Summerfield: 'Take a bit of a holiday. I've got a few shillings piled up. I'll probably book a cruise on one of those spaceliners. Old Follett reckons all this fuss will soon be forgotten if I keep my nose clean. What about you? Are you going on looking into this Megacity Project business?'

'No, I've decided you were right. Too far away, too long ago – and much too dangerous. No, there's nothing to be done now, not without treading on some very powerful and sensitive toes. And I don't want to meet any more Dethaki. I might not be so lucky next time . . .'

The recording clicked off, and Kedrick looked triumphantly at the Director.

After another of his unnerving silences the Director said, 'Now isn't that convenient?'

Suddenly Kedrick felt his recovered confidence ebbing away.

'What's that, Director?'

'They're saying exactly what we want to hear . . .'

Many days and light years later, Bernice Summerfield turned to her travelling companion and said, perhaps for the hundredth time, 'Do you think they bought it?'

He glanced out of the thick plastiglass window of the space shuttle. At first there was little to be seen, just a thick blanket of smog, broken by occasional flares. Then, as they descended further into the choking smog, a sea of flickering neon appeared through the grimy clouds.

'We'll soon know,' said Chris Cwej. 'That's Megacity.'

3

CRIME SHEET

MEGACITY:

Megacity is the only town of any size on all Megerra.

The city, and indeed the planet, have a strange history and an oddly mixed economy.

A bleak and isolated planet on the fringe of the galaxy, incredibly rich in valuable minerals, Megerra was grabbed and carved up by the big mining corporations in their early expansionist days.

At first it was purely an industrial planet. But mining corporations employ vast numbers of personnel. There are highly paid executives and engineers. To back them up there is a whole network of administrative staff – who have to be paid high salaries to lure them to unpleasant planets with few amenities.

Miners make good money too, though only by working brutally long shifts all round the clock.

For a time Megerra was full of hard-working people with money in their pockets and nothing to spend it on. It was a situation that couldn't last. Soon entrepreneurs flooded in from all over the galaxy to supply the lack. They included hoteliers, restaurateurs, bar owners and show-business people of every kind. They also included gamblers, whores, drug dealers, killers and thieves.

Megacity mushroomed, spreading until it coverèd much of one of the planet's smaller continents. Soon there were hotels, bars, restaurants, casinos, nightclubs, establishments to cater for every pocket and every taste. Everything from expensive high-class casinos, where you could lose a fortune under glittering chandeliers, to cellar gambling dives where you would be robbed much more cheaply by a roll of the loaded dice.

Then a strange thing happened. Megacity became so well known as a wide-open pleasure city that it started attracting tourists from other planets. Word spread that for a wild time with no questions asked Megacity was the place to go. An ugly, sprawling, incredibly large metropolis on an industrial planet with no natural amenities of any kind has become an intergalactic tourist attraction.

Tourism and entertainment – in the widest possible sense of the words – have grown into an industry that rivals the big mining corporations themselves. The new industry now has representation on the Planetary Council, and mining magnates and show-business tycoons jostle for civic power.

With so much money being made, much of it in fairly dubious ways, there is also crime. It's no secret that many of the clubs and casinos are owned and run by criminals of one kind or another. In the early days there were savage territory wars, but in time things settled down. Just as the mining corporations have carved up Megerra, the gang lords have divided Megacity among them.

Today the crime situation in Megacity is of a rather strange and specialized nature. Booze, gambling, most drugs, prostitution and money-laundering are treated as everyday businesses in Megacity – a fact some off-planet criminals find distinctly unnerving.

(The celebrated gangster Big Rocco from Formalhoute Four was once heard to say, 'Here in Megacity I'm practically legit. I can't hardly find no crimes to commit!')

All the same, there are limits. It's perfectly all right to rob the off-duty miner or the visiting tourist with rigged cards, a *crooked wheel, or loaded dice. If drinks with a friendly local life form, encountered in a dimly lit bar, lead to the visitor waking up in some alleyway with a thick head and an empty wallet – well, that's only to be expected.*

It's severely frowned upon, however, to follow the visitor into that same dark alley and relieve him of his credits by more direct means, such as a blow on the head or a knife in the back.

This sort of thing harms the tourist trade, which means it's bad for business. In Megacity, anything that's bad for business is a crime.

Some entertainments are forbidden as well. Brutal bare-knuckle prizefights are extremely popular, but the arenas, where gladiators fight savage beasts, and each other, to the death, are technically illegal – though widely available if you know where to go.

Paradoxically, Megacity is not too unsafe a destination for the ordinary tourist. City Council and criminals alike frown on any harm being done to those who bring them the money. You can more or less bank on being swindled, but on the whole you're rather less likely to be robbed or killed – though it still happens from time to time. And there's always the danger of being caught by a stray blaster bolt in one of the occasional gang wars – in which case the Megacity Council will ship your body home free of charge.

Even the legendary Megacity cops are less fearsome than they used to be. In the bad old days law and order was maintained by Chief of Police Garshak and a squad of head-cracking Ogrons.

But as time went by his methods were felt to be a touch too flamboyant, and he has been replaced by a succession of police chiefs who maintain a lower profile.

There are, however, disturbing rumours lately of an upswing in violent crime. The Tourist Board says these rumours are greatly exaggerated, and the police force have the situation well in hand – but then, they would, wouldn't they?

Quite frankly, we still advise against making Megacity a

That's how it was, at least for a very long while. Finely poised between mining business, show business and crime, Megacity found a kind of uneasy equilibrium.

But strange forces were seething below the surface, and they started to erupt . . .

His Honour Markos Ramarr, Mayor of Megacity, studied the computer printout.

'Up!' he said bitterly. 'The goddam figures are up again.'

His Honour was a big, imposing figure with a politician's ready smile. At the moment his handsome features wore a look of gloomy resignation.

He swung round on the other occupant of the penthouse office, a stocky, ornately uniformed figure with a low forehead, beetling brows and a heavy jaw. Chief Harkon's subordinates called him 'the Chimp' – but not where he might hear them.

'The figures aren't all up, Your Honour,' said Harkon stubbornly. 'Fraud's down, burglary's down . . .'

'Yeah, but crimes of violence are up!' said Ramarr. 'And that's what people care about. Murder, muggings, assaults, criminal damage . . .'

'I know it looks bad,' said Harkon defensively. 'But a lot of that stuff's really pretty small-time. Every time some drunk miner picks a fight and wrecks a bar, or some fool of a tourist gets himself mugged, it shows up in the violent-crime statistics.'

'Those fools of tourists pay most of our salaries, Chief,' said Ramarr. 'If they stop coming times will be hard around here. The Tourist Board says bookings are starting to fall off – not by much yet, but it's a trend. The mining corporations are complaining as well. When their miners go out for a night on the town, the bosses like them to report back for duty in one piece. They say profits are down and investment's slowing up.' He scowled down at Harkon. 'You'd better do something about these violent crime stats, Chief. People are starting to say we ought to get the Ogrons back!'

'Things aren't that bad, Your Honour.'

'They're getting that way,' said the Mayor gloomily. He looked thoughtfully at Harkon. 'I hear Garshak's still around . . .'

'Garshak? I thought he died years ago,' said Harkon, well aware that Garshak was still very much alive.

Ramarr shook his head. 'Garshak's too mean to die. He'll probably live for ever. One or two of his boys are still around, working as bouncers and bodyguards. Maybe I should ask Garshak if he wants his old job back.'

Harkon scowled, hoping His Honour was joking. The trouble was, he wasn't really sure.

'I'll crack down harder, Your Honour,' he promised. 'The problem is, these things flare up so suddenly – and in such unexpected places.' He picked up a computer printout at random.

'Look at this crime sheet here. Little Louie's Hotel and Piano Bar Lounge, a perfectly respectable criminal hang-out, never any trouble. Late last night a fight starts, somebody hits the bouncer with the piano and a riot breaks out.'

The Mayor snatched the printout. 'You picked a very good example, Chief. You realize the consequences of what happened here? The place gets wrecked so the owner is complaining. Three Alpha Centaurian tourists are hospitalized, so the Consul from their home planet is complaining, and so is the Tourist Board.

'Elections are coming up soon and this is just the sort of incident that's hurting the administration. And what are our wonderful Megacity Police doing about it? Nothing!'

'There's nothing to go on,' growled Harkon. 'By the time my boys got there, the fight was over, the place was wrecked and the guy who started the trouble had vanished. If I know Louie he's looking for him harder than we are – and if Louie finds him before us, believe me, he really will disappear . . .'

'I should never have employed an Ogron for a bouncer,' said Little Louie. Louie was a round, troll-like figure from the high-gravity planet Vathek II, and his usually cheerful face was contorted in a scowl. Since Louie had the bald head, wide mouth, hooked nose and flapping ears typical of his species, his scowl was really something to see.

He looked around the wreckage of his bar, and glared reproachfully at the massive figure towering above him. 'You're paid to stop fights, not start them.'

'Not start fight,' said the Ogron patiently. His name was Murkar, and once, a long time ago, he had been a policeman, one of Chief Garshak's principal assistants. Now, like the other survivors of Garshak's special squad, like Garshak himself, Murkar earned his living as well as he could: as bodyguard, bouncer, whatever came along.

Murkar had enjoyed working at Louie's Lounge. He liked the easy-listening music and the fact that there were few fights. He even liked Louie himself. This latest job had been a good one. He would be sorry to lose it.

'OK,' said Louie. 'Tell me one more time.'

'Man come in,' said Murkar. 'Big man, quiet, well dressed. Maybe miner in best clothes. Not drunk, not angry. Sad. Sits at bar, listens to music, drinks. Bar gets crowded. Man orders another drink.'

'Was he drunk by now?' interrupted Louie. 'Had he been tossing them down?'

'Barman say no,' said Murkar. 'Man still sober. Orders

drink, barman busy, say just a moment, serves someone else. Man grabs barman, pulls him over bar.'

Little Louie looked sadly around the shattered bar.

'He caused all this because he had to wait for his drink?'

Murkar went on with his tale. 'I hear noise from door, come in, tell man to let barman go. He throws barman through mirror behind bar. Then he hits me.' Murkar frowned. 'Not usual, hit Ogron.'

The whole point of employing Ogrons was that their very presence usually prevented trouble. Nobody in their right mind would attack an Ogron.

'I surprised, stagger back,' Murkar went on. 'Man picks up piano, hits me with that, I fall.'

'He picked up the piano?' said Louie incredulously.

Murkar nodded. 'Small piano,' he pointed out. He hesitated. 'Something else.'

'What?'

'In his eyes, when he first turn round to hit me,' said Murkar. 'Something like red flame. Something . . . not human.'

'Guy must have been wired,' muttered Louie.

'Wired?'

'High, flying, on something. There are drugs that do that – abnormal rage, abnormal strength. Skoob, for instance. Go on.'

Murkar shrugged. 'Someone grabs man's arm, he knocks them down, big fight starts. Time I get up, stop fighting, man gone.'

Louie wondered briefly if one of his competitors could be behind the attack. It wouldn't be the first time that a wrecked bar was the first move in an intended takeover.

He rejected the idea almost at once. As far as he knew the latest territorial treaty still held, and this didn't feel professional – it was too weird, too irrational.

'Guy was definitely wired,' said Louie decisively. 'Someone's putting some bad stuff on the street. I better check it out.'

There was no other explanation, he thought. The man's behaviour was simply insane. Louie was connected, everyone

46

knew that, and to start trouble in a mob-connected joint was suicide.

But then, so was hitting an Ogron with a piano . . .

Louie turned to the huge patient figure beside him.

'I'm afraid I'm going to have to let you go, Murkar, at least for a while.'

Murkar nodded sadly. 'I understand, Louie. I let you down.'

Louie shook his head. 'No, it wasn't your fault.'

'I should have seen fight coming, stopped it.'

'No way you could know. Anyway, apart from anything else we'll have to close down for a while, get this mess sorted out.' He reached in his pocket, produced a massive roll of credits and peeled off a few notes. 'Here, little something to tide you over.'

Murkar waved the offered credits away. 'No. You already pay me up to date, Louie.'

He turned away and trudged across the rubble-littered floor.

'Come and see me when we reopen,' yelled Louie. 'We'll work something out.'

Murkar raised a huge hand in farewell, and disappeared into Megerra's perpetual murk.

Suddenly Louie realized he was going to miss him. Murkar was a nice guy – for an Ogron.

He began to calculate how many credits it was going to cost him to get the bar up and running again. And what was he going to do about this new drug that was turning miners into madmen?

The big man waited patiently at the queue in the little money-changing booth on Spaceport Boulevard. When he got to the head of the line he produced not a bundle of off-planet currency but a heavy-duty military blaster. He aimed it at the spindly grey-haired clerk on the other side of the plastiglass screen.

'Just shovel out all the Megacity credits you can reach.'

The clerk's foot touched the alarm button set into the floor.

'Get lost, chump. That screen is blasterproof.'

'You sure?' The man raised the blaster and fired and the screen exploded into thousands of shining fragments.

There were shouts of alarm from the other clerks and customers. 'Nobody move!' yelled the man. He grinned at the terrified change clerk. 'Don't believe all your employers tell you. Good armour glass costs credits, and they're too tight to pay out just to save your miserable skin. Now, get the money!'

Hurriedly the clerk shoved credit notes over the counter and the man stowed them away with his free hand.

When he finished he turned to force his way out of the shop. But the narrow booth was crammed and the terrified customers were still obeying his original command not to move.

The man started shoving his way through the tightly packed crowd. 'Out of my way!' he screamed. 'Get the hell out of my way!'

The electronic howl of a police hovercar came from outside the shop. The man whirled round on the clerk he'd just robbed.

'You bastard, you pressed an alarm!'

A red flame flickered deep within his eyes.

The world narrowed, focused, seemed to slow down. He saw everything through a burning red haze. His mind, his body, his whole being pulsed with one fierce perception. Enemy, enemy, enemy. Danger. Kill! Kill! Kill!

He raised the blaster and fired. The impact of the blast slammed the clerk's body across the inner room.

There were more screams from the crowd, and the man with the blaster went berserk. He fired blast after blast into the crowd ahead of him, searing a path through packed bodies, trampling over the dead and dying as he escaped.

Once clear of the booth he turned and raked the crowd with blaster fire until the charge was exhausted. Throwing the

48

weapon down, he turned and ran, disappearing into the fast-gathering crowd. Nobody tried to stop him.

When the police hovercar swung round the corner it found a scene of panic and carnage. There were bodies everywhere, some dead, some dying, some with blaster burns of varying severity. The two hovercops called for immediate backup and a medical team and soon the street was filled with ambulances and more police hovercars.

While the medics carted away the dead and wounded, the cops secured the crime scene, questioned witnesses and chased away the merely morbidly curious.

By the time Chief Harkon arrived they'd got things pretty well sorted out.

'Basically just a simple stick-up, Chief,' said a hovercop sergeant who'd been one of the first on the scene. 'Guy sticks a blaster in the clerk's face, shoots out the screen, grabs the money and takes off.'

'Pausing only to kill – how many people?' The Chief grabbed a passing medic by the arm. 'What's the score so far?'

The medic checked a list. 'Seven stiffs, three more probably won't make it, about a dozen blaster burns, ranging from severe to minor.' The medic pulled free. 'Do you mind, Chief? There's still a lot to do.'

'Ten people killed and twelve wounded,' said the Chief bitterly. 'All for a lousy handful of credits. Just a simple stick-up.'

'That's what's so weird, Chief,' said the hovercop. 'He already had the credits. He didn't have to blast anybody. From what the witnesses say he just snapped when he heard our siren.'

'Must have been on something,' muttered Harkon. 'A vrax-head.'

The sergeant shook his head. 'Vrax-heads go all to pieces, shaking all over. Wouldn't have the strength or the concentration.'

'Maybe something new,' said Harkon. 'I'll check it out. What about the weapon?'

The sergeant produced a sealed transparent evidence bag.

'We found this just outside. It fits the description of what he used.'

Chief Harkon examined the squat heavy weapon. He sighed.

'What we got here, Sergeant, is your standard military heavy-duty hand blaster. Millions of 'em all over this sector of the galaxy. Untraceable.'

The sergeant nodded. 'Some busted mercenary probably traded it in for a few free drinks.'

Chief Harkon handed back the bag. 'Get it to the lab, see if they can pick up some DNA traces. Maybe just once we've got a killer who didn't wear gloves. Have we got any kind of description?'

'Just a guy, Chief. Not old, not young, not big, not small, not spiffy, not shabby. Just a guy.'

'That's all?'

'Very nearly. Human, or at least humanoid, somewhere between young and middle-aged, average height, strongly built. Someone said he could have been a miner. Not the way he was dressed, just something about the way he looked.'

'Miners don't do stick-ups,' said Harkon. 'They don't need to. All they do is get drunk and bust up bars occasionally –' He broke off. 'Hey, just a minute! Some miner type busted up a piano bar late last night.'

'You think it was the same guy, Chief?'

'As far as I remember the description fits. And it had the same screwy feel to it. This guy went berserk for no real reason at all.'

'Well, if the same guy pulled this stick-up and he did it for booze money, he'll spend the money and do it again,' said the sergeant philosophically. 'Maybe we'll get him next time.'

Chief Harkon nodded. 'Let's try to do it before he kills another ten people – just to keep the Mayor happy.'

* * *

In a rundown back street not far from Spaceport Boulevard was an old-fashioned pledge shop. You could raise money on almost any article of value – not much, but the price of a few drinks.

You could sell – for a fraction of its value, but with no awkward questions – a vidiphone, a comm unit, any odd portable item that might come into your hands. You could pick up a bargain, if you too asked no questions, and were prepared to keep your new purchase out of sight for a while.

The shop was run by a Pakhar called Zarnek, who was so old that his fur had turned entirely white. He was never seen outside his shop, where he lived surrounded by a clutter of miscellaneous objects – clothes, jewels, weapons, ornaments and antiques.

There were those who said that all this clutter was just protective coloration. They said that old Zarnek dealt in goods of considerably more value – often buying and selling valuable property while it was still in the possession of unsuspecting owners, arranging for collection and delivery by freelance entrepreneurs.

On this, his last morning, old Zarnek sat hunched over a vision screen watching the mid-morning newscast with an expression of frozen horror on his hamster-like features.

'Massacre on Spaceport Boulevard,' intoned the commentator. 'We bring you up-to-date pictures of the shocking crime, just one of the latest horrors that have shocked and shaken Megacity . . .'

Zarnek sat motionless as the scene outside the change booths flowed across the screen – the police hovercars and ambulances, the grim-faced hovercops, the terrified witnesses.

'He just went on blasting and blasting,' sobbed a frightened woman, the camera closing in voyeuristically on her ravaged face. 'There was no reason, he had the credits . . .'

Zarnek reached out and switched off the screen with a trembling paw. A shadow fell across him and he looked up. A man stood on the other side of the counter. An average-looking man in everyday clothes, not old, not young.

Zarnek shrank back in horror. 'What have you done?' he whispered. 'What have you done?'

'What you sent me to do,' said the man. 'It went very well.' He fished out a bundle of credits and tossed them on the counter. 'Here's your percentage.'

Zarnek made no move to touch the notes. 'I sent you to steal, not to kill. You come to me penniless and beg for work. I happen to know that a certain change booth has installed substandard armour glass, that a determined man with the right weapon could clean the place out. I tell you of the place, I even give you the weapon, and you bring me this!' He jabbed a stubby paw at the credit notes. 'A miserable handful of credits – in exchange for ten lives!'

'There was some trouble,' said the man vaguely. 'People got in my way. Why did you give me the blaster if you didn't want me to use it?'

Old Zarnek was genuinely shocked. 'To smash the screen – and then to get the money. You shout, you yell, you even fire a blast into the ceiling. You frighten people – but you don't hurt them. And you certainly don't kill them.'

The man shrugged. 'Oh well, these things happen. Do you want your credits or don't you? And what about another job?'

'No, I don't want the credits,' snarled Zarnek. 'As for giving you another job – you're a savage, a wild beast. Do you realize how hard the police will be looking for you now?'

'Then you must help me, find me a place to hide.'

'Help you? I don't know you, I've never seen you. Hide you? There's nowhere in Megacity for you to hide, nowhere on the planet. Now get out of here. Get lost!'

Yet again the slowing down, the focusing, the burning red haze. The urgent demand pulsing through his entire being. Danger! Enemy! Kill!

Suddenly the man sprang. He stretched an arm over the

counter, grabbed Zarnek by the throat and lifted him high in the air.

Old Zarnek choked and kicked and writhed, but his struggles became weaker and weaker.

The man held him in the air, one-handed, watching him die, a red flame burning deep in his eyes . . .

4

WELCOME TO MEGACITY

Travel packs at their feet, Chris and Bernice stood in the centre of Megacity Spaceport.

'They've done it up,' said Chris approvingly.

Bernice stared grumpily round the crowded concourse.

'Well, I'd hate to have seen it before!'

They were inside an enormous metal dome, the walls broken up by the arched entrances to the various landing and departure bays. Periodically the whole place shook with the roar of retrorockets as another space shuttle landed or blasted off.

The atmosphere was muggy and the air was heavy with strange odours from the fast-food and drink stalls that dotted the concourse.

The place was swarming with newly arrived tourists, eager to sample the delights of Megacity. There were banks of gambling machines everywhere, so they could start parting with their credits right away. Heading in the other direction were departing tourists, haggard and hung-over, who'd obviously enjoyed all that Megacity had to offer and were heading home, sadder, possibly wiser, definitely poorer.

Mingling with them were serious-looking men in formal clothes clutching document cases, mining executives going off on leave, or returning for another tour of duty.

There were also quite a few less prosperous-looking types,

stocky, broad-shouldered men with beetling brows, jutting jaws and pitted skins. Some wore black coveralls with a shoulder patch bearing a red letter D.

Bernice guessed that they must all be miners. Curious, she thought, how alike they all looked. Did mining attract a particular physical type? Or did you somehow grow like that just through working in the mines?

Most of the miners seemed to be human or humanoid. The tourist crowd was more varied, and Bernice recognized Falardi, Foamasi and Arcturans, among others. There were even a few nervous-looking Alpha Centaurians hurrying, head down, through the crowd.

A few of the nonhumans were bearlike in appearance, barrel-chested creatures covered in thick black or brown fur. Bernice tugged Chris's arm as a couple of them moved past, shouldering their way roughly through the crowd.

'Look, teddy bears!'

'Don't stare at them,' warned Chris. 'Those are Ursines. They may look cute but they've got a very unpleasant attitude. When Roz and I were here a couple of them tried to mug us.'

Bernice turned hurriedly away – and found herself staring into the face of yet another nonhuman. This face was furry too but thin and sharp with long yellow teeth. It belonged to a thin sinuous creature wrapped in a tattered cloak.

'Porrer, lay?' it snarled.

'I'm sorry?'

'Porrer, lay!' growled the alien again, and pointed to her travel pack.

Bernice realized that it was saying 'Porter, lady?'

She nodded. 'Sure, why not?'

The creature's claw grabbed the travel pack – and Chris's big hand swept down and chopped it away.

'No thanks. We can manage,' said Chris. His voice was deep and menacing.

The alien sprang back with a snarl, its hand disappearing under its cloak.

Chris slipped his hand inside his tunic.

For a moment they confronted each other. Then, with a final snarl, the alien turned and slipped away into the crowd.

Bernice frowned. 'What's wrong with hiring a porter? I'm tired of lugging that thing around anyway.'

Chris took his hand out of his tunic. 'That porter was a Wolverine. They run the local street gangs, and they don't go in for honest toil.'

'Maybe that one was trying to go straight.'

Chris grinned. 'Straight to the nearest hock shop with all your luggage. You'd never have seen that travel pack again. Welcome to Megacity, Benny!'

'Terrific!' said Bernice. Wearily she shouldered her travel pack. Chris did the same and they began walking across the concourse towards the main exit.

'What now?' she asked.

'We need a base of some kind – a hotel.'

'Where did you and – Where did you stay last time?'

Chris smiled reminiscently. 'Megotel One, the biggest and most expensive place in town. There was this topless waitress, I remember –' He caught Bernice's eye and broke off hurriedly. 'But then, last time we were working for someone with unlimited financial resources.'

'This time it's different,' said Bernice. 'This time we're spending our own money.'

They'd agreed to share expenses for the expedition. Chris had funds from some undisclosed source, and Bernice had just received another chunk of her bestseller royalties. They'd be all right for a time – but not if they threw their credits around.

'We'd better try to find somewhere cheap,' Bernice went on.

'Not too cheap,' warned Chris. 'Not in Megacity.'

'If we go somewhere too high-class we can't afford to stay on here.'

'If we go somewhere too low-down, Benny, we probably won't live through the night.'

'Terrific,' said Benny again. 'There must be some happy

56

medium between being robbed and being murdered. Maybe there's somewhere we can ask. Let's try over here.'

They were approaching a row of ticket booths when the row broke out. A big, broad-shouldered man was shouting at a clerk.

'I want a ticket on the next shuttle out and I want it now.'

They heard the woman's voice, sharp with anger.

'I'm trying to tell you, sir, the next three shuttles are fully booked. It's our busiest time. I can get you on the midnight shuttle to Space Station Alpha. You can pick up a connection to anywhere in the galaxy from there.'

'I can't wait that long. I've got to get away now. If it's the credits you're worried about . . .' The big man started pulling credit notes out of his pockets and slamming them on the counter.

'It's not the money, sir, there simply are no seats.'

Bernice wasn't surprised to see Chris stop and observe the situation. He'd been an Adjudicator for so long that it was hard for him to realize that any public disturbance was no longer automatically his business.

She tugged at his arm. 'Come on, Chris, let's not get involved. We've got more important things to do.'

'I suppose so.' Reluctantly Chris started to move away.

The big man shouted, 'Give me that ticket, you bitch!'

He grabbed the clerk, a stout middle-aged woman with a purple bouffant, dragged her over the counter and held her high above his head.

'Give me that ticket before I break your fat neck!'

He shook her so violently that the threat seemed likely to be fulfilled at any moment. Angry shouts and screams of fear came from the nearby crowd, but nobody moved to help.

Nobody but Chris.

He ran towards the ticket booth and grabbed the big man by the shoulder, feeling iron-hard muscles beneath his fingers.

'All right, that's enough. Let her go.'

The man tossed the clerk almost carelessly back over the

counter and she crashed screaming to the ground amid a litter of exploding computer terminals.

Then he grabbed Chris and threw him across the concourse. Considering Chris's size it was an extraordinary feat of strength.

Astonished as he was, Chris hit the ground in a smooth, controlled roll, sprang to his feet and ran back in for the attack. His hand lashed out in a savage chop, aimed at the big man's jugular.

The big man brushed the blow aside and clamped his hands around Chris's throat. Chris swung up linked hands to break the stranglehold and found he couldn't do it. All he could do was try to force the hands apart to relieve the pressure, enough to stop the big man from killing him – at least for the moment. But the man was incredibly strong.

Bernice ran up and punched Chris's attacker in the face as hard as she could. It was like hitting a rock.

Forcing Chris down, the man raised his head and glared at her over Chris's body.

Bernice saw red flames burning deep in his eyes.

For a moment she felt almost hypnotized. Then she cupped her hands and brought them down both at once over the man's ears.

The head jerked back and the man gave a roar of pain – just as Chris, with a last convulsive effort, broke the stranglehold and broke free, jumping to his feet.

The big man sprang up too. For a moment he stood hunched, swinging between Chris and Bernice as if wondering which to kill first.

A magnified voice boomed, 'Armed police – down!'

Chris reacted instantly, dropping to the ground and sweeping his legs round in a scything motion that knocked Bernice off her feet. Blaster bolts crackled over their prone bodies and then Chris rolled protectively on top of her.

Bernice struggled wildly. 'Gerroff, you're smothering me!'

Wriggling from underneath him, she raised her head and saw the big man running *towards* three armed policemen.

They fired again and he staggered to a halt, caught in the crossfire from three blasters. Incredibly he lurched forward for a few more paces.

The police fired again and the charred smoking body crashed to the ground.

Chris helped Bernice to her feet and began clumsily brushing her down.

Crossly she pushed him away. 'Keep your hands off me you big ape or I'll have you arrested for assault.'

Chris looked hurt. 'Are you all right, Benny?'

'No thanks to you if I am. You knocked me down and squashed me flat.'

'I thought maybe you'd sooner be squashed than blasted.'

'You'd no business interfering . . .'

Her opinion seemed to be shared by the grizzled, heavily moustached police sergeant who came to take their statement.

'Very rash of you to interfere in police business, sir,' he said severely, when Chris had finished telling him what had happened. 'Much safer to leave it all to us.'

Perversely, Bernice leapt to Chris's defence.

'If you'd managed to arrive a bit earlier, you'd have seen that lunatic waving some unfortunate fat lady like a flag. She'd probably be dead by now if my friend here hadn't interfered in police business.'

Hurriedly Chris said, 'I'm sorry, Sergeant, my companion is still a bit upset. And I'm sorry about interfering, but I acted on instinct. I used to be in the job myself — Adjudicator.'

The sergeant's manner changed at once. The Adjudicators were recognized as an elite police force all over the galaxy.

'Quite all right, sir, and the lady's right too. You probably saved that poor woman's life.'

'What's it all about, Sergeant?' asked Chris.

The sergeant looked down at the big man's body.

'Nasty piece of work, this one, sir. We've been on his tracks for quite a while.'

'Who is he?' asked Bernice.

'We're still not sure. Ex-miner, by the look of him. What

we do know is he went off on a killing spree. He smashed up a bar, killed ten people while he was robbing a change booth, then murdered the old crook who set the job up for him. He was spotted leaving the murder scene and heading here.'

Bernice was horrified. 'He killed ten people – in a robbery?'

The sergeant nodded. 'No reason for it, either. Just went berserk, same as here.'

Chris's professional interest was stirred. 'Do you get much of this sort of thing?'

'Seems to be on the increase, sir. To be honest, Megacity's never been famous for law and order, but the amount of violence these days – well it's pointless. Unprofessional. Even the old crooks don't like it.' He lowered his voice. 'Between you and me, Chief Harkon is dead worried. He'll be lucky if he holds down the job much longer.'

A team of medics arrived to take away the dead body. The sergeant took a mini-comp recorder from his pocket.

'If I could just have your names, please, for my report.'

He held the mini-comp out to them.

'Christopher Cwej,' said Chris.

Bernice said, 'Professor Bernice Summerfield.'

As they spoke, their names appeared on the tiny screen.

The lettering faded and more data appeared.

The sergeant studied it and then said, 'Mr Christopher Cwej and Professor Bernice Summerfield? That is correct?'

'That's right,' said Bernice impatiently. 'Can we go now?'

The sergeant looked embarrassed. 'I'm afraid not. I must ask you to come with me.'

'Whatever for?'

'Warrants have been issued for your arrest.'

'By whom?' asked Bernice indignantly.

'And on what charges?' demanded Chris.

The sergeant studied his screen. 'The warrants originated on the planet Dellah, on behalf of St Oscar's University. The charges are: Professor Bernice Summerfield, embezzlement of university funds. Mr Christopher Cwej – murder.'

* * *

'I think this must be a record,' said Bernice bitterly, as the police hovercar, siren blaring, bulldozed its way through Megacity's permanent traffic jam. 'I mean, I've been in trouble before as soon as I arrived on some strange planet – but this is the first time I've ever actually been arrested in the spaceport!'

'It took Roz and me several days to get arrested,' said Chris. 'We were investigating one of the Ripper murders when the Ogron police turned up and chucked us in a paddy wagon with two drunk miners and a very unhappy Alpha Centaurian.' He chuckled. 'Roz was furious. That was the first time we met Garshak.' He leant forward and spoke to the sergeant in the front passenger seat.

'I take it Garshak's not still Chief of Police?'

'Not for years. It's the Chimp – er, Chief Harkon now. You knew Garshak?'

'Best of friends,' said Chris.

'I'm not sure that's much of a recommendation these days.'

'Is he still around?'

'Oh yes, he's still around.'

Chris turned to Bernice and said quietly, 'It looks as if we didn't fool the good folks at St Oscar's after all then.'

'What's the point?' demanded Bernice. 'They must know none of those charges will stand investigation.'

'I don't think they're worrying about that. They just want to nail us down till they can get their hands on us.'

'How will they do that if we're in jail?'

'Very easily, I imagine,' said Chris grimly. 'If we end up in Megacity Prison, there's a very good chance we'll never get out alive.'

The police hovercar came to a halt, and Chris looked out of the window. As before, he saw a cobbled yard behind a high stone wall. As before, he and his complaining companion were marched up a grimy stone staircase and along a stone corridor.

This time, however, they weren't thrown into a holding

cell to stew for a while but taken straight to the office of the Chief of Police. Maybe, thought Chris, it was a reflection of their double status as have-a-go heroes and suspected criminals.

They were left outside under guard while the sergeant went in and made his report. About ten minutes later, he came out and beckoned them inside.

'Chief Harkon wants to see you. Listen, he's not a bad guy, for a chief – he's as honest and fair as they let him be. I tried to put in a good word for you. But he's under a lot of pressure, so handle him carefully.'

'Thanks,' said Chris.

The sergeant ushered them inside.

With a weird feeling of *déjà vu* Chris looked around the enormous office. Nothing seemed to have changed since Garshak's day. The same lavish carpeting, the same gorgeous hangings and colourful holographs, the same chairs and tables, the same pictures and pieces of sculpture. They all had a dusty neglected air, as if nobody really cared about them any more.

There was even the same massive desk, although the computer terminal on it looked considerably more up to date.

The figure behind the desk had changed as well. Instead of the massive, incongruously elegant figure of Garshak, Chris saw a squat, beetle-browed figure in an elaborate uniform. A chimp in uniform instead of a gorilla in a silk shirt, thought Chris, and wondered guiltily if he was being speciesist.

Chief Harkon noticed Bernice staring around in amazement.

'Pretty fancy for a cop's office, ain't it?' he said gruffly. 'One of the chiefs before me had it done. I keep meaning to clear all this junk out, but I never had the time.'

'Don't change a thing,' said Bernice. 'I love it!'

Harkon waved them to a couple of seats before the desk. 'Siddown!'

They sat. There'd be no herbal tea and spiced cakes with this Police Chief, thought Chris. Harkon was all business.

62

He punched keys on the computer terminal for a few moments and stared at the readout. He punched a few more keys, frowned and stared some more.

Then he looked up, giving them both a cop's hard stare.

'Mr Christopher Cwej and Professor Ber-nice Summerfield.' He looked from one to the other. 'I don't know what to make of you two.' He pointed a stubby finger at Chris. 'My sergeant seems to think you're a pretty good guy. Ex-Adjudicator. Says you tackled a mad killer at the spaceport, saved some woman's life. Says you joined in pretty good too, lady – sorry, Professor.'

'I did my best,' said Bernice. 'I don't think I achieved much.'

'You stopped him from strangling me,' said Chris. 'It seemed like a lot to me.'

'Point is, you both tried,' said Harkon. 'Lotta people don't do that. That puts you with the good guys in my book.' He nodded towards the computer screen. 'But according to this, one of you's a swindler and the other's a murderer.'

'Just out of interest, who am I supposed to have murdered?' asked Chris.

Harkon peered at the screen. 'Someone called Arego – a Dethaki.' He looked up at Chris. 'Ring any bells?'

'A Dethaki assassin attacked me when I was on Dellah.'

'So you killed him? In self-defence of course!'

'Not even that, Chief. I stunned him at close range.'

'Maybe he died of it later.'

Chris shook his head. 'No way. The Dethaki are tough. If he is dead, he was probably killed by his own employers to shut him up. Or he may have committed suicide.'

'What the hell for?'

'He was sent to kill me and he failed. He would have felt dishonoured. The Dethaki are very sensitive about their honour.'

Harkon shook his head. 'Lotta weird shit going on out there,' he muttered. He turned to Bernice. 'And you, Prof? Did you take off with the university piggy bank?'

Bernice shook her head. 'Those charges are false, Chief. All of them. They're designed to put us in the hands of our enemies so they can murder us.'

'What enemies?' asked Harkon. 'Why do they want to kill you?'

Bernice hesitated. Chris suspected she was wondering how much to reveal. She gave him an enquiring look.

Chris, meanwhile, had been thinking hard. Long experience of difficult and dangerous situations had made him cautious. At times like this, the smart thing to do was either to say nothing or to lie, to come up with a good cover story.

For some reason he found himself remembering something an old friend had once told him: 'I know it seems safest to keep your own counsel, trust no one. A lot of the time it is. But there's a danger. One day you might meet someone you can trust, and you won't know how to deal with them.'

Chris came to a decision.

'We're investigating something,' he said. 'Privately, on our own behalf. Something big, right here in Megacity – with links to the Advanced Research Department at St Oscar's University on Dellah. Some very powerful people want us to stop looking.'

'Looking for what?'

'The hell of it is, Chief, we don't really know. It all started here in Megacity, a long time ago . . .'

Briefly and simply he told of his earlier visit to Megacity, of Roz's stumbling upon the Project, and of what had happened afterwards, in Megacity and later on Dellah.

Harkon heard him out in silence. When Chris finished his story Harkon said, 'So all this comes second-hand from this partner of yours? She around to back up your story?'

'Not any more. She died.'

'And all she knew about this Project, all she told you, is what this guy who conveniently jumped out of a window told her?'

' "It's got to be stopped," ' quoted Chris. ' "It's an abomination, a crime against humanity. They think they can control it,

64

but they don't realize the danger. Once it gets away from them there'll be blood in the streets. The killing will begin again – and it'll spread from here to a hundred worlds . . ." '

Chief Harkon shook his head. 'It's a helluva story. I'm not sure I want to get mixed up in it. Maybe I should just lock you up and let them sort it out on Dellah.'

Bernice echoed Chris's sentiments from the hovercar: 'If you do that you'll just be setting us up for our enemies to murder us.'

Harkon shrugged. 'So?'

'So you're a cop,' said Chris. 'That's not the kind of thing cops are supposed to do.'

'Don't you preach at me!' snarled Harkon. 'I'm a cop in Megacity. That means I've got problems of my own.'

Bernice seemed to have a sudden inspiration. 'Does it occur to you, Chief, that your trouble and ours might be connected?'

'How's that, Prof?'

'We've only been in Megacity for a few hours,' said Bernice urgently. 'All we've seen is the spaceport and this police station. But we've already learnt that things are going badly wrong here.'

'Like what things?'

'Like an upsurge in violent crime that you can't explain and can't handle,' said Chris. 'Like the fact that your job is on the line if you don't produce results – and you're not getting results.'

'I'm doing all I can,' said Harkon angrily. 'All anyone could do. Megacity's a tough town. Always has been, always will be.'

'It used to be a tough town back in the old days,' said Chris. 'I know, I was here. But the way I heard, it got organized. There was still crime, sure, but there was no violence – because violence is bad for business. Now it's out of control again. There's blood in the streets – *just as Roz Forrester's informant prophesied before they killed him*!'

Chief Harkon looked from Chris to Bernice, then back to Chris.

'Lemme get this straight. You're saying that what's happening here and now, stuff like that business at the spaceport, is caused by this Project that was set up way back then?'

'We're saying it's possible,' said Chris. 'Have you got a better explanation right now?'

Chief Harkon scowled, swinging his head to and fro. He looked, thought Chris, like an old bull-ape tormented by flies.

'That's crazy,' he growled.

'Maybe it is,' said Bernice. 'But maybe it's true all the same. Why don't you let us find out for you?' She gave him her most winning smile. 'After all, Chief, what have you got to lose?'

A hovercab stood waiting outside the police station.

The driver watched curiously as two prisoners, a big humanoid male and a smaller humanoid female, were escorted to the front steps of the police station by Chief Harkon and a squad of his men. At a nod from Harkon one of the cops opened the passenger door.

The male stood back deferentially, the female got in, the male followed. The driver's long furry ears twitched as Harkon leant through the still open door.

'Now listen, you two creeps, and listen good. I don't care how big you are back on your home planets, how connected you are to the Combine, here you're nothing – and there's nothing here for you. We don't need imported scumbags here, we got plenty of our own. So get out of Megacity – and I mean today. Because if you're not both on the next shuttle, I'll find some reason to slam your asses in jail.'

The big male stared impassively ahead, as if he'd heard many such speeches before.

The female leant across him and said, 'Thanks for the civic welcome, Chief.'

Harkon slammed the door in her face and roared, 'Get moving, cabbie. Get these two sleaze balls out of my sight!'

The hovercab zoomed away.

Chief Harkon glared after it for a moment. Then he grinned to himself and stomped back inside.

As the hovercab sped downtown the driver heard the big man mutter, 'Can he make it stick?'

The female shook her head. 'Hick-planet police chiefs!' she snarled, equally loudly. 'He was just blowing smoke. There are no charges against us here, and Megerra doesn't have an extradition treaty – with anybody! It's the perfect planet to take over a big operation.'

'The local talent may object.'

'Then teach 'em different, Chris. That's why you're here.'

'Anything you say, Dragon Lady. You set 'em up, I'll blast 'em down.'

In the front seat of the cab the driver's sharp furry ears pricked up, and his ratlike muzzle twitched.

He spoke over his shoulder. 'Spaceport, lady?'

'Spaceport hell,' said the big man. 'Take us to a hotel.'

'Sure, boss. I take you to Megotel One, best in Megacity.'

The big man glanced at the female, who shook her head again.

'Too conspicuous.'

The big man leant forward and clamped a massive hand on the driver's shoulder. 'Listen, we want a nice quiet hotel, somewhere comfortable but discreet. Somewhere they don't ask questions – or answer them either.' He reached into his pocket with his other hand, pulled out a handful of credit notes and stuffed them inside the hovercabbie's leather jacket. 'You know the kind of place I mean?'

'I know exactly the kind of place you mean, boss. Jus' you leave it to me.'

Sometime later, the hovercab, now empty, was cruising Spaceport Boulevard. The driver was talking into his comm unit, so intent on his conversation that he drove past several frantically waving tourists.

'I tell you, boss, they're a couple of heavy hitters. Chief

Harkon ordered them out of town and they just laughed at him. They're connected to the Combine, and they're here to take over some big operation . . . Yeah, two of 'em. A dame and a big fair guy called Chris. The dame's the boss, though. He's just the muscle. He called her Dragon Lady . . . I took 'em to Little Louie's joint. They wanted somewhere discreet, know what I mean?'

The hovercabbie network was the fastest information system in Megacity.

Very soon the word was out all over town.

5

MEGACITY EYE

My office that year was on the first floor of a rundown office block just off Spaceport Boulevard. It wasn't much, just a desk, a chair, a beat-up comm unit and an antique filing cabinet, empty except for Megacity smog.

The only other features were a pair of large glass doors, giving on to a ridiculously small balcony. The balcony looked out over a sleazy side street filled with bars, hotels and hock shops.

Things were quiet that particular morning. It was a dull muggy day and I had the windows wide open, letting in the choking fumes that Megacity calls air. Cat, a werecat who sometimes drops in, was nowhere in sight. I bought myself a drink from the office bottle, put my feet up on my desk, and started thinking about how and why I'd ended up in this dump.

I'd had a much bigger office once, an elegant place, full of paintings, holograms, precious hangings and priceless antiques. I'd had power, authority, squads of men under my command.

That was when I was Chief of Police. Now all I had was this shabby office, a hat, a trenchcoat and a blaster.

The name's Garshak. I'm an Ogron – and a private eye.

I came to Megacity with a handful of my people a long time ago. We were the remnants of a botched experiment in brain enhancement. Most of the subjects of the experiment died, others went mad. A few survived, with varying degrees of increased intelligence.

There was just one spectacular success. One Ogron whose brain power got boosted to genius level – me!

The mad professor who was running the experiments was delighted, until I put an end to the experimental programme by breaking his neck. I killed the Ogron chief who'd sold us to him too. Then I stole the professor's spaceship and blasted off with my fellow survivors. For some reason I felt responsible for them.

We planet-hopped for a while, earning a living as mercenaries, bodyguards, the usual thing. Then we arrived in Megacity, back in the days when it was a boom town, when anything went. They needed a police chief and I applied for the job. There was one other strong contender, an Ice Warrior, but he had an unlucky accident.

(Somehow he ended up in a vat of boiling metal in a smelting works. Nobody ever figured out what he was doing there – Ice Warriors hate high temperatures. Still, like I always say, if you can't stand the heat, stay out of the foundry.)

I became Chief of Police, with my fellow Ogrons as a special flying squad. I did pretty well at it. I cleaned the muggers and the petty thieves off the streets and made Megacity safe for the tourists – and for the bigger thieves who were running the town.

There was no salary as such, but fines and bribes more than made up for it. It was a pretty good life for a while. But times change and Megacity changed with them. Everything became more organized, including the crime. The tourist trade grew until it rivalled the mining business, and it was felt that Megacity needed a more low-profile form of policing. It's hard to be low-profile when you're an Ogron.

Eventually the City Council made it clear it was time for me to go. They also made it clear that I had a choice. I could go gracefully, or be shipped back home in a body bag.

70

I decided to take the retirement option. No pension, but a handsome sum in severance pay – a bribe for going quietly – plus all the credits I'd stashed away in a long and corrupt career in Megacity law enforcement.

My Ogron Flying Squad wasn't wanted, either, and I made sure they all got good leaving bonuses as well. Ogrons being Ogrons, they soon boozed and gambled it away. Some got themselves killed, some drifted off-planet, until only Murkar, my old number two, was still around.

I stayed around as well – quite why I didn't really know. I'd been in Megacity so long it was the only home I had. There was nothing for me on the home planet any more, with fellow Ogrons still communicating, no doubt, in grunts and blows.

Anyway, I stayed. I moved into a penthouse suite in Megotel One and started living the high life: fine food, fine wines, and everything in the way of entertainment Megacity had to offer – which covers a hell of a lot of ground.

For a while everything was fine. I had plenty of credits, lots of highly placed friends. I became quite a figure in what passed for society in Megacity.

When the credits started to run out, so did the friends. I soon realized I'd only been a sort of interesting freak anyway.

I left Megotel One and booked into a sleazy downtown hotel while I still had enough credits left to get by. I lay on the bed boozing and watching old holovids all day and all night.

In a weird kind of way those old holovids were to be my salvation. A lot of them were historical cop shows set on Old Earth. Seems there was once a town called Chicago that was almost as corrupt as Megacity . . .

Some of them were about a special kind of detective, private not police. Tough lonely men who took on crooks and gangsters and sometimes the law itself, with nothing but guts and a gun.

They were called shamuses, gumshoes, private eyes . . .

I did some research and found that this kind of story had started on early-twentieth-century Earth. Some of them were still available in vidbooks, and I read as many as I could find.

Some words from one of these old writers seemed to stick in my head. Something about a man going down the mean streets who wasn't mean, wasn't tarnished or afraid. 'The best man in his world, and a good enough man for any world . . .' How did the rest of it go?

There was something about taking no man's money dishonestly, and no man's insolence without a due and dispassionate revenge.

'He is a lonely man and his pride is that you will treat him as a proud man or be very sorry you ever saw him.'

Over the years I'd been about as tarnished as they come. As for honour, it wasn't a word for Ogrons – any more than intelligence. But I suppose you could say I was unafraid. And poor and proud and lonely – I was all of that. I'd been a corrupt cop for a hell of a long time. Being a fairly honest private eye was something to aim for. Something to give some point to a life that had gone on too long.

So I opened the office and waited for business. It was a long time coming, but eventually a few cases started drifting my way.

The first was a wandering-daughter job. I found the missing daughter of a wealthy off-world businessman. She'd fallen in love with a gambler from Rigel II and run away with him to Megacity.

By the time I caught up with her, she was glad to go home. The gambler wasn't so keen on the idea but I reasoned with him. I even went to see him in hospital afterwards.

I discovered why one of the smaller mining operations was losing money. The guy who hired me, their chief accountant, was siphoning it off to spend on drugs and dancing girls. He'd hired me to make it look like he had nothing to hide – and because he thought an Ogron detective would be too dumb to catch him.

I even caught a murderess — a mining president's pretty young wife. She'd been poisoning her husband's favourite dish — fugora-fish stew — on a regular basis, using arsenic she'd stolen from the mine's laboratory.

She nearly got away with it. She'd kept the doses small and fugora-fish stew is pretty poisonous in its normal state. But she forgot that arsenic grows out into the hair and nails of the victim. She had the body cremated — but before she managed it I gave the corpse a quick haircut and manicure. I got the lab to check — the old boy's hair and nails were loaded with arsenic.

Gradually I started to make a living.

Sometimes I had more cases than I could handle and had to take on Murkar as an assistant. At other times, like now, business was slack. I had time to sit back in my office chair, smoke my nicotine-free cigarettes — 'I'd walk a mile for a Drashig' — and catch up on my drinking.

The drinking was fine — I'd got hold of some *vragg* strong enough to burn a hole in the filing cabinet — but I didn't really enjoy the smoking. Still, it was all part of the image. I practised blowing smoke rings at the ceiling and brooded about the state of things in Megacity.

I knew Megacity better than anyone else alive. I'd been here in the wild and wicked early days. I'd seen the city settle down into a highly efficient, tightly regulated machine for extracting minerals from solid rock and credits from visiting tourists.

But now something was going on. Maybe they'd just been sitting on the lid for too long. Like a half-tamed wild beast, Megacity was reverting to type. Sudden gang wars were breaking out, meaningless eruptions of savage violence between mobs that had always gotten along pretty well.

The murder count was up for the first time in years.

I knew Chief Harkon pretty well — it shows how far Megacity had come that they actually had an honest Police Chief. 'Chimp' Harkon and I weren't exactly friends — I think he tolerated me as a necessary evil — but I knew him well enough to know he was badly worried.

At this point in my reflections the two Ursines came in. Ursines are a large, furry, not very intelligent life form who resemble, as their name implies, an Old Earth species called bears. Like their namesakes they are truculent and bad-tempered.

At one time most Ursines used to work in the mines. But when the machinery got more sophisticated the Ursines couldn't cope. Many left Megacity, and those that stayed drifted into low-level crime. They weren't bright enough for anything too complicated, but they were OK as enforcers and general hired muscle. They didn't usually bother to carry weapons. The big paws could stun you, the sharp claws rip you to bloody shreds.

So when these two shouldered their way into my office, getting jammed in the doorway in the process, I knew they weren't collecting for charity.

When they'd sorted themselves out I gave them a friendly nod.

'Morning, boys. What can I do for you?'

There were two of them, one black and one brown. I'd heard somewhere that the black ones were supposed to be brighter – which wasn't saying much. The black one seemed to be in charge.

'OK, Garshak, move it!'

I blew a smoke ring. 'Move what, where?'

'Move your Ogron ass downstairs. The boss wants to see you.'

'The boss being?'

The brown one said proudly, 'We work for Nastur.'

The black one said, 'He's outside, in the Caddy.'

They both looked at me, waiting for me to shake with fear.

Nastur was bad news all right. He ran the drugs and liquor on the South Side, which made him one of the most powerful of Megacity's merchants. He was an immensely fat toadlike reptilian who seldom left the fortified warehouse that formed his South Side HQ. If Nastur had ventured out it was something big. Which meant mega-credits. Nastur could afford to pay well – and my bank account was getting low enough to crawl under a Dalek.

All the same, I wasn't about to come running when Nastur croaked. Bad for my image.

'If Nastur wants to see me he can call for an appointment.'

The black one growled, 'You deaf as well as stupid, Garshak? The boss wants to see you, downstairs – now!'

I yawned and stretched. 'Tell you what, I happen to have a gap in my busy schedule. If your boss likes to come up I'll see him right away.'

'There's no elevator in this crummy joint,' said the brown Ursine. 'The boss don't like to climb stairs.'

'So carry him up.'

'Easier to kick you downstairs,' said the black one. 'Come on, Garshak, quit jerking us around. You're coming down to see the boss, right now. Hard or easy, your choice.'

'If you insist, boys,' I said. I stood up, ducking my head to avoid hitting the ceiling. I headed for the door and they fell in beside me. I stopped so they came level and draped a friendly arm across each of their furry shoulders.

'Hey!' protested the black one.

'It's all right, boys,' I said. 'We're all friends, right?'

Then I grabbed each one by the loose fur at the scruffs of their necks and lifted them off the ground, holding them out at arms' length. Sometimes there are advantages to being an Ogron.

The Ursines were so amazed that they didn't even struggle. They just hung limp, like oversized furry kittens.

I wheeled round, headed for the balcony, and peered out. Sure enough there was a big, black Cadillac hoverlimo down below, making my own cheap hovercar and the rest of the street look shabby.

'Tell your boss I don't do business on the street,' I said. 'Or in hovercars either, not even Caddys.'

Then I tossed them out of the window, first the black one, then the brown. The black one hit the roof of the Caddy and the brown one hit the black one.

An angry roar came from inside the limo.

I went back to my desk, poured another drink, set fire to another Drashig and awaited developments.

I was on my sixth smoke ring when I heard huffing and puffing and grunting coming from the bare wooden stairs. Then the two Ursines carried Nastur up to my office. He sat between them on a massive round seat specially built to carry his enormous bulk.

The Ursines manoeuvred him into my office and put him down in front of my desk. He waved them away with a vast flipper-like hand and they took up positions by the door.

They looked a bit ruffled, but they didn't seem to be damaged. Ursines are tough all right. They're just not as tough as Ogrons.

Nastur glared at me with huge orange eyes.

'Those clowns made a dent in the roof of my brand-new Caddy. I oughta have you wasted, Garshak.'

'Then I wouldn't be able to do whatever you want me to do,' I said reasonably. 'It must be something important or you wouldn't have come. Have a drink, Mr Nastur. Tell me how I can help you.' I took a glass from the desk drawer, poured a belt of *vragg* and held it out to him.

He wrapped a flipper round the glass, sniffed the liquor suspiciously, opened a wide lipless mouth and tossed it down. He grunted as the fiery liquor hit him, gasping frantically for air.

I knocked back my own drink and sighed with content.

'Good health, Mr Nastur.'

Nastur belched, and gasped some more. 'Can't you afford to drink something decent, Garshak? Remind me to send you a case of Algolian champagne.'

Relieved that wasting me seemed to be off the agenda, I gave him my serious professional look. 'Now, what's the problem, sir?'

Nastur turned to his two furry henchmen. 'You two – get downstairs and see no local scumbag steals my Caddy.'

Black Fur looked worried. 'You sure you want us to leave

you alone with him, Mr Nastur?'

'He was gonna waste me, he'd a done it by now. Damn little you two pussies coulda done to stop him.'

Looking hurt, the two Ursines lumbered off downstairs.

Nastur belched again, and studied me through big orange eyes.

'I hear you find things, Garshak. Things and people. I even hear you're reasonably honest – which is a very strange thing to hear about a Megacity cop.'

'Ex-cop, Mr Nastur. I'm trying to live down my sordid past. Who or what do you want found?'

'Who *and* what,' corrected Nastur. 'The who is a guy called Razek, works for me, or used to. The what is a hovertruck full of booze and drugs and a bundle of credits, money Razek was supposed to be paying out for me.'

'So what happened?'

It appeared that Nastur's shipments of booze and drugs had to pass through the territory of Lucifer, another crime lord, on their journey from the spaceport to his various joints way out on the South Side. The shipments were sent under escort and they paid an agreed toll. Razek had been in charge of the latest shipment – and the passage money.

'So what went wrong?' I asked.

'Who the hell knows?' wheezed Nastur. 'All I heard is there was some kind of beef when the hovertruck reached Lucifer's territory. Razek blasted several of Lucifer's guys – and *my* guys when they tried to stop him. Then he took off with the hovertruck and the rest of the toll money.'

'Any idea where he is?'

'I heard a rumour he was heading for the Lair.'

The Lair was a ruined area of Megacity, blown up in the last of the big gang wars. It had been taken over by the Wolverines, the biggest and most vicious of the Megacity street gangs, and was pretty much a no-go area for cops and other crooks alike.

I shook my head. 'I'm not sure if I can help you, Mr Nastur.'

'You gotta help me, Garshak,' said Nastur. The throaty voice was almost pleading. 'I've lost a whole shipment – I've just gotta get that hovertruck back!'

He seemed absolutely frantic – so frantic I was suspicious. 'I wouldn't have thought losing just one booze shipment would mean so much to a big-time operator like you.'

'It's the next one I'm worried about and all the ones after that. At the moment, Lucifer's threatening to blast any of my boys on sight. I've got to get things running smoothly again, and to do that I gotta know what happened.'

'It's one hell of a job,' I said. 'It'll cost you.'

'It's costing me now,' howled Nastur. 'Every day those hovertrucks don't get through.'

'Have you tried talking to Lucifer?'

'Sure, I tried. I sent him one of my top men as a messenger. Told him to find out what was going on and get it sorted out. Lucifer sent him back – or part of him.'

'Which part?'

'He sent me his head.'

'Now you want to send him mine?'

'You're not one of my boys – you're a neutral. Maybe he'll listen to you. Come on, Garshak, whaddya say?'

What I ought to have said was no, but I needed the job.

My mission, should I choose to accept it, was two-fold. First, to recover the stolen hovertruck and contents, the missing credits, and if possible the missing Razek, dead or alive – it didn't seem to matter much to Nastur. It was the hovertruck he wanted.

That was the easy part.

Equally important was to find out what had happened and convince Lucifer it wouldn't happen again, so shipments could be resumed. Nastur gave me authority to negotiate a settlement for him. We started haggling about terms.

Eventually we settled on a kind of sliding scale. If I accepted the job, there would be an immediate, nonreturnable advance. Nastur would pay me my usual daily rate and cover all expenses. In addition there would be a handsome bonus for success in each part of the job.

When agreement was reached, Nastur handed me a bundle of credits and I went to the window and looked down. The two Ursines were leaning against the Caddy, looking tough for the benefit of the local street urchins – who didn't seem all that impressed.

I whistled and jerked a thumb and they pounded up the stairs.

As they lifted Nastur's chair I said, 'You'll be hearing from me, Mr Nastur.'

'Make it soon,' wheezed Nastur. 'Or *you'll* be hearing from *me*!'

The Ursines gave me their tough looks and I blew them a kiss.

'Take care, girls. Don't drop Mr Nastur down the stairs. He's worth a lot of money to me.'

The trio made their way out and I heard grunts from the two Ursines and curses from Nastur as they staggered downstairs.

A few minutes later I heard the big hoverlimo roaring away.

I riffled through the bundle of credits, stuck it inside my jerkin and poured myself the last of the *vragg*. I fired up another Drashig and blew a few more smoke rings as I considered the job I'd just taken on.

Did it infringe my private-eye code?

Nastur was a sleaze ball, true enough. But then, all he was asking me to do was recover stolen property, catch the thief, and negotiate the resumption of normal business. The last bit could even be seen as a peacemaking mission. A lot of blood would be spilt if Nastur and Lucifer got into a turf war.

No, I decided, it was an honest enough job. As honest as I was likely to find in Megacity anyway.

Full of virtue and *vragg* in roughly equal amounts, I closed up the office and hit the mean streets of Megacity.

6

THE BIG SHOP

'*Dragon Lady*?' said Bernice Summerfield.

Chris looked awkward. 'It just popped into my head – out of some old holovid, I think. Anyway, the underworld likes that sort of thing – criminals have lurid imaginations. I was just trying to help your scheme along.'

They were breakfasting in the little sitting room that came with their suite in a discreet downtown hotel. The place was shabby on the outside, luxurious inside. It wasn't particularly cheap, but the hovercabbie's whispered recommendation and a bundle of credit notes had procured them a suite of surprisingly comfortable rooms without the tiresome formality of registration.

They'd had an excellent dinner in the little restaurant, and breakfast had been just as good. Service was quick and efficient, but everything had to be paid for in cash and at once.

Chris reckoned they were used to guests making hurried departures, voluntarily or otherwise.

Bernice finished her herbal tea and sat back. 'Now what?'

'You tell me,' said Chris. 'It's your plan!' Once convinced that their investigation just might be connected with his problems, Chief Harkon had offered to take them on as special investigators. Chris had been ready to accept, but

Bernice had had a sudden inspiration.

'Our enemies have gone to some trouble to make us look like criminals. Let's take advantage of it.' She had turned to Harkon. 'What would you do, Chief, if you heard a couple of really big-time crooks were coming to Megacity?'

Chief Harkon scowled. 'Have 'em picked up at the airport, and find some reason to send them back where they came from.'

'You see?' said Bernice. 'We're halfway there already! Suppose they were technically in the clear – no outstanding charges or anything?'

'I'd try to bluff them. Warn them to keep their noses clean and their stay a short one.'

'But you'd have to let them go?'

'I guess so. The law's the law, and even scumbags have rights.'

'Right!' said Bernice triumphantly. 'So that's what you do to us. Let us go with a stern warning. If you make it nice and public it'll give us some criminal credibility, a chance to investigate the Project from the inside.'

After some more discussion the scheme had been agreed. Chief Harkon had produced a metal box from his desk, unlocked it, and begun pulling out bundles of high-denomination credit notes. Apparently this was the police department slush fund, untraceable money used for paying informants and bribing politicians.

Chris hadn't wanted to take the money at first.

Chief Harkon had insisted. 'If you're gonna do this, you'd better do it right. There's just one way to recognize your big-time crook – conspicuous consumption. They carry cash, big bundles of credit notes, and they throw it around.'

Now, next day, they were established in their new roles, and wondering about their next move.

'The trouble about this scheme of yours is, it puts us in an essentially passive role,' Chris pointed out. 'Investigators investigate – they go round asking questions, stirring things up. We can't really do that. We just have to hang around looking mysterious and enigmatic, and wait for someone else to make the first move.'

Bernice caught sight of herself in a mirror and stood up.

'I can tell you my first move.'

'What's that?'

'When the going gets tough, the tough go shopping. If I'm going to be a Dragon Lady I'd better start looking the part. You need a makeover too.'

Chris looked down at his plain travelling clothes. 'What's wrong with me?'

'You're not nearly gaudy enough. Come on, I assume even Megacity has a shopping district.'

They went down to the dimly lit foyer, where the sad-eyed little desk clerk called them a hovercab.

'Be a few minutes,' he warned. 'They don't like coming downtown these days.'

As they stood waiting a voice from somewhere around knee level said, 'Everything OK, folks?'

They looked down and saw a small, bald-headed, big-eared, hook-nosed figure, the incredibly ugly features contorted in what was apparently meant to be a welcoming smile.

'I'm Louie. I own the joint. They treating you all right?'

Bernice nodded. 'It's everything I expected. You came highly recommended.'

'That right? Where you folks from?'

'Around.'

Louie seemed perfectly satisfied with the answer. It was almost as if it was the one he expected.

'And they heard about Little Louie's Hotel off-planet?'

'In certain circles.'

'You care to tell me who recommended us?'

'No.'

Again, it seemed to be the right answer.

'I can tell you something else they said,' added Bernice. 'They said it was a place where people didn't ask questions.'

'Absolutely,' said Louie. 'No offence, Dragon Lady.'

Bernice raised an eyebrow and Louie said hurriedly, 'Sorry, lady, word gets around. I don't usually run my mouth off.'

'It can be a bad habit,' said Bernice icily. 'Unhealthy.'

Little Louie mopped his bald brow and looked about him for a change of subject, and pointed to an open door leading off the foyer. Decorators could be seen adding the final touches to a bar that occupied one corner of the ground floor.

'We're reopening the piano bar tonight. Hadda close for a while – some drunk wrecked the place.'

'Happen often?'

'Hell, no. Most people got more sense than to cause trouble here. Guy that did it was crazy. He strangled some fence downtown and then got hisself shot by the cops out at the spaceport. Lucky for him they found him before I did.'

The desk clerk called, 'Hovercab's here.'

Bernice jabbed Chris in the ribs. 'Check it out.'

Chris looked blankly at her, Bernice scowled at him, and Chris said, 'Right.' Racking his memory for scenes from old gangster holovids, he slid a hand inside his tunic, glanced keenly around and stalked out into the street.

'Big guy don't talk much,' said Louie.

Bernice said coolly, 'Talking's not what he's best at.'

Chris appeared in the hotel doorway and nodded.

Bernice turned to Louie. 'What's the most expensive store in town?'

'There's a branch of Nieman-Marcus off Central Plaza. Or –'

Bernice cut him off. 'Nieman-Marcus will have to do.' She smiled sweetly down at him. 'We're travelling light. Had to blast off in a hurry.'

Louie nodded understandingly. 'Happens, sometimes.'

Bernice nodded and went out into the street.

Louie stared admiringly after her.

'Some dame, eh, boss?' said the desk clerk.

Little Louie nodded. 'Some dame.'

* * *

The next few hours were heaven for Bernice, and pure hell for Chris. The hovercab took them uptown to the gleaming crystal towers of Nieman-Marcus. Bernice remembered hearing that the store had started out in a place called Texas on Old Earth. Originally it catered for newly rich oil millionaires weighed down with more money than they knew how to spend. Here in Megacity the place was living up to its old traditions. Trailed by a sulky Chris, Bernice glided happily through its scented, air-conditioned atmosphere, surrounded by luxury goods from all over the galaxy.

Fashion was pretty eclectic in Megacity, blending styles from many different ages and cultures. Currently the mode was Earth retro, and Bernice ordered a number of day costumes and evening dresses, all in black, with suitable accompanying floppy-brimmed hats, some with veils.

Ignoring his objections, she ordered a number of outfits for Chris as well. Electronic scanners had already taken their exact measurements, and while they lunched in the store's penthouse restaurant robot tailors were running up their new outfits with unerring precision.

By the time lunch was over, their new clothes were wrapped and ready. Chris insisted on a last-minute visit to the store's flourishing weapons department. In Megacity, as in Old Texas, most people went armed as a matter of course and the store's array of weaponry was comprehensive.

Chris bought a powerful but compact hand blaster and a small hideout blaster. He bought a shoulder rig, and an ankle holster for the hideout weapon. He added a vibroknife and a neuro-sap.

Despite her protests, he insisted on buying a slimline matt-black blaster for Bernice.

'It's Earth retro, madame,' said the Alpha Centaurian sales assistant proudly. 'Modelled on an old projectile weapon, the Beretta automatic. The power pack fits into the butt, like the old cartridge magazine, and you activate the weapon by working the slide. It's a precise reproduction!'

He demonstrated with a flurry of tentacles, sliding the flat power pack into the weapon's handle, and working the slide with a metallic double click.

In addition, Chris bought her a miniature lipstick blaster.

'Short-range of course,' said the assistant. 'But *so* compact! Will that be all, sir, madame? We have some very fine hand-held atomics, state-of-the-art, I assure you!'

'That'll do,' said Bernice firmly. 'It's just for personal protection. We're not starting a war.'

'One never knows, does one, madame?' said the assistant brightly. 'Not in Megacity! Still, if you're sure . . . Shall I giftwrap your purchases?'

'No need,' said Chris. 'We'll wear them.' He slipped off his tunic and strapped on the blasters, put his tunic back on and slipped the vibroknife and the sap in his pockets.

Bernice stowed away the mock Beretta and the lipstick blaster and they headed for the lifts.

'Wonder you don't clank when you walk, carrying all that gear,' she said, as they floated downward in the glass bubble.

'It was your idea to be gangsters,' said Chris. 'The weapons are just necessary accessories.'

'Well, I hate guns,' grumbled Bernice. 'I can use them if I have to but I hate them.'

'A gun is just a tool, ma'am,' said Chris in a deep cowboy voice. 'As good or as bad as the man who uses it.'

'Yeah, and a man's gotta do what a man's gotta do,' said Bernice. 'Toys for boys more like. You loved buying all that hardware . . .'

Still wrangling, they went to pick up their other purchases. Then, with Chris loaded down with packages and parcels and Bernice striding aristocratically ahead, they got the gorgeously uniformed commissionaire to order them a hovercab.

In the weapons department the assistant was talking into a discreet corner comm unit. 'Central? Weapons shop at Nieman here.'

'So?'

'Couple of heavy hitters just came in, and got tooled up. Interested?'

'Go ahead.'

'Usual rates?'

'Sure.'

The assistant gave a full and accurate description of Chris and Bernice, and of the weapons they were now carrying.

'Address?' asked the voice on the other end.

'No, they paid cash down. Seemed to be loaded.'

'OK.'

The comm unit went dead and the assistant went back to his duties. He had no idea who he had just given the information to, or what use they might make of it. Nor did he care. A modest amount of credits would be deposited to his account at Megacity Miners Bank, and that was all that concerned him.

Information was valuable in Megacity – and forewarned was forearmed.

Back in the hotel suite Chris drained his tankard of ale and flopped back in his armchair like a stranded starfish.

'Shopping!' he said bitterly. 'I'd sooner spend six nights in a sewer on a warlock stakeout.'

Bernice pushed Chris's share of the packages towards him. 'Stop grumbling and go and get changed.'

'Then what?'

'A few drinks before dinner. Dinner, and a few more drinks. Then a night on the town.'

Chris groaned. 'How about an early night? Popcorn, a few beers, watch a few old holovids . . .'

Bernice shook her head. 'No chance. The programme for this evening is wining and dining, champagne and caviar, ending up in the most expensive nightspot in Megacity. It's a tough job, but someone's got to do it.'

Chris rose and stretched and yawned. 'It's a helluva way to run an investigation.'

Bernice shrugged. 'What else can we do? Like you said,

we have to hang around looking enigmatic and impressive, and hope someone useful approaches us.'

'I suppose so. We could try dropping a few heavy hints, though.' Loaded with parcels Chris headed for his room. He paused in the doorway. 'About that nightspot . . .'

Bernice was happily ripping open parcels. 'What about it?'

'I think I know just the place . . .'

Little Louie looked around his refurbished piano bar, checking that everything was up and running. The windows were back in again, the walls had been redecorated, and there was a new piano.

There was even a new piano player, the old one having resigned on account of stress – even though Louie had assured him that people hitting other people with his piano wasn't going to be a regular event.

Better get in touch with Murkar, all the same, thought Louie. Get him back on the payroll as doorman, just in case.

Louie looked up as his two latest guests came into the bar.

It was quite a sight. The dame was wearing a long black evening gown with a black silk stole around her shoulders. She was carrying a handbag and wearing a little hat with a flimsy veil. Behind the veil her eyes looked big and dark, and her lips very red.

The big blond guy was all in black too, black suit, black soft hat, black shirt with a white tie. Louie's experienced eye spotted the small but significant bulges that meant the guy was heeled. Couple of blasters at least, and probably a sap as well.

Louie hurried towards them. 'Hey, this is an occasion: first customers since the reopening. Have a drink, on the house.'

He showed them to a corner table. The dame ordered a brandy, the big guy a beer.

'Won't you join us, Louie?' said the dame.

Louie got a beer as well and sat down with them. He raised

his glass. 'Well, *salud y pesetas*!' he looked at their surprised faces. 'It means –'

'I know what it means,' said the dame. 'Health and money!'

'Some guy from New Spain used to come in here,' said Louie. 'Said it all the time.'

The dame took a healthy swig of her brandy. 'There seems to be plenty of money around in Megacity,' she said. 'I imagine health might be in short supply.'

Louie nodded gloomily. 'Place seems to be going all to hell these days. Look what happened to my bar.' He told them of the rising tide of violence in the underworld. Sudden fierce disputes, savage little gangland skirmishes that never reached the ears of the police. 'Now they say there's a turf war brewing up between Nastur and Lucifer,' he finished gloomily. 'Two guys that got along fine for years. Then someone steals a hovertruck full of booze and drugs and takes off into Wolverine territory.'

The big guy looked interested. 'Hijack?'

Louie shook his head. 'Get this – the guy that did the stealing was ripping off his own side! Crazy!'

'How's the Project doing these days?' asked the big guy.

'The how much?'

'The Project. Last time I was here it was just starting up. Word was it was going to be big.'

Louie shook his head. 'Sorry, you lost me. How long ago was this?'

'Quite a while.'

Louie looked from one to the other. 'That why you're here – this Project? To take it over, maybe?' He caught the look in the big guy's eye and said hurriedly, 'Sorry, none of my business.'

'No it isn't,' said the big guy flatly.

'That'll do, Chris,' said the dame sharply. 'Louie's a friend.'

'If you say so.'

The dame smiled at him. 'Someone in your position must hear a lot of interesting things, Louie.'

'I hear all kinds of stuff,' said Louie uneasily. 'I don't pay no attention. I like to mind my own business.'

'Of course you do,' said the dame. 'But if you happen to hear anything interesting about the Project, do let me know.' She put a hand on his arm. 'I can be very grateful. Now can you do me a big favour?'

Louie gulped. 'Sure thing. Like what?'

'Recommend a good place for dinner.'

After a lot of discussion they settled on a canal-boat fish restaurant called the Floating Palace.

'Looks real pretty at night,' said Louie. 'The fish is mostly imported from off-planet so it's safe enough. Take my tip though: stay away from the local speciality – fugora-fish stew.'

The guy called Chris smiled. Suddenly he looked a lot younger.

'You don't have to tell me about fugora-fish stew, Louie. I tried it last time I was here. Took me days to get over it!'

Louie nodded. 'We lose a few tourists every year, but people keep right on ordering it. Beats me.'

The dame drained her glass. 'Let's have another drink before we go. On us, this time, Louie.'

'Wouldn't hear of it,' said Louie. 'You're still my guests. I'll call the Floating Palace, make you a reservation. You'll need a hovercab as well.'

As Louie bustled away Chris turned to Bernice. 'Well, you certainly charmed him!'

'I think it's this outfit,' said Bernice. 'It brings out the *femme fatale* in me. No big-eared bald-headed dwarf can resist me!' She frowned. 'Do you think that blank look was genuine – when you mentioned the Project?'

'Looked like it to me,' said Chris. 'But he'll be curious now and he'll ask around. Maybe word will reach someone who does know something.'

'I like Louie. I hope we're not going to get him killed for asking the wrong questions.'

'Or us,' said Chris grimly. Suddenly he gasped. 'Oh no!'

A giant form had appeared in the doorway and was looking around the bar. The place was filling up by now, and it was obvious that the newcomer was looking for someone.

'What's up?' asked Bernice.

'It's an Ogron called Murkar – and he knows who I am!'

7

THE LAIR

The joint was called the Inferno – it was an underground cellar deep inside Lucifer's territory. It was also Lucifer's HQ.

The doorman was an Ursine thug who I'd had dealings with before. He looked worried when I climbed out of my hovercar and headed for the cellar door.

Flashing red neon from the big INFERNO over the door illuminated his furry scowl.

'I don't know if I should let you in, Garshak.'

'Do you think you can keep me out?'

'I can get help.'

'You'll need it.'

I moved forward and he shrank back. I flashed my winning smile at him, but that only seemed to make him more nervous.

'So what's wrong with letting me in? Aren't my credits as good as anyone's?'

'For one thing, you're a cop.'

'Ex-cop.'

'Mr Lucifer don't like cops. He don't even like ex-cops. He particularly don't like ex-cops who cosy up to that slimy toad Nastur.'

'I talked to Nastur on business,' I said. 'I intend to talk to Lucifer for the same reason – about something that will save him money and trouble. You want to take responsibility for turning me away?'

Reluctantly he moved aside.

I went down the steps and into a noisy crowded cellar. The air was thick with jekkarta-weed smoke, the tightly packed tables were all full, and there was a crowd around the bar at the far end. On a rostrum in the corner, a little band was pumping out jazz. The crowd was mostly human or humanoid with a scattering of Ursines and one or two members of other species. Lucifer was an equal-opportunity crime lord. But they all had one thing in common: they were tough, they were armed, and they were Lucifer's troops. Getting out might prove to be harder than getting in.

Lucifer himself sat alone at a table in an alcove. He was a Demoniac from a planet called Gehenna, incredibly tall and skeletally thin, with jet-black scales. His slanting red eyes were set into a long, narrow skull crowned with two neat horns. Leathery wings folded neatly across his back, and his tail was curled around his feet.

I went over to the alcove. 'May I join you for a moment, Mr Lucifer? I won't take up much of your time.'

He looked up at me, amusement in his red eyes, and decided to respond with equal politeness – which didn't mean he wouldn't have me killed if he changed his mind.

'A pleasure, Mr Garshak. Have a seat. Can I offer you refreshment?'

'A beer would be fine.'

Lucifer raised a claw and a waiter appeared by magic.

'Beer for Mr Garshak,' ordered Lucifer. 'Bring me another bottle of champagne.'

The waiter vanished and reappeared with the drinks almost immediately. I swallowed my beer with a certain amount of relief.

The offering and acceptance of hospitality made me a guest, and in Demoniac culture, as in most others, the guest is sacred.

Lucifer sipped his champagne. 'So what can I do for you, Mr Garshak?'

'I'm here on behalf of Nastur.'

'I am extremely annoyed with Mr Nastur.'

'I think he gathered that when you sent back his last messenger's head.'

'The last messenger was arrogant and overbearing,' said Lucifer. 'I became somewhat . . . irritated with him. Perhaps I was a little hasty.'

I waved the idea away. 'What's an odd head between friends?'

Lucifer smiled. 'You at least seem to be adopting a more civilized approach. What is your message?'

'Mr Nastur very much regrets what happened over the shipment. He'll pay any reasonable compensation. He'd like to resume normal business as soon as possible.'

'Is that all he wants?'

'He'd very much like his hovercab, and its contents and his man Razek back, if I can find them, but that's my problem. Getting things running smoothly again is the important thing.'

Lucifer considered, steepling long thin fingers that ended in razor-sharp claws. 'Very well. Tell Mr Nastur shipments may be resumed – so long as there is no more trouble. I will waive compensation, but in future the toll fee will be doubled.'

'Agreed,' I said. I reckoned Nastur was getting off light.

Lucifer seemed to be getting bored with the whole subject. 'If there's nothing else . . .'

'Just one other thing. If there are any survivors of the shipment business, I'd like to talk to them.'

Lucifer frowned. 'Why?'

'Mr Nastur is very keen that I should find out exactly what happened – so that he can ensure it doesn't happen again. Since none of his people survived the incident – except the thief, that is – yours are the only available witnesses.'

Lucifer raised another finger. The waiter reappeared and Lucifer said, 'Get Zeke.'

Moments later, another Demoniac appeared at the table. His scales were red, not black like Lucifer's. He was half the height and twice the width. Demoniacs seemed to come in a variety of sizes and shapes. This one had the level scar of a fresh blaster burn across the scales of his skull.

'This is Ezekiel, Mr Garshak – Zeke for short. Ezekiel!'

'Boss?'

'This is Mr Garshak. Take him to the bar, buy him a drink, and tell him anything he wants to know about the trouble with Nastur's last shipment.'

Zeke nodded and stood waiting.

I got to my feet. 'Thank you for your time, Mr Lucifer.'

Lucifer gave me a stately nod. 'Drop by any time.'

'I'll try not to trouble you again,' I said. 'I'd hate to become an irritation – I like my head where it is.'

I followed Zeke across to the bar, noticing how he parted the crowds like a battle tank. At the bar he tapped a couple of shoulders and two stools immediately became vacant. Zeke snapped his fingers and two tankards of ale appeared.

He studied me for a moment. 'You're a big one.'

I looked across the crowded room. Nobody was looking at me, but everyone knew I was there. It seemed a long way to the door.

'I'm not as big as a roomful of armed men,' I said.

Zeke nodded. 'Nobody is. So what can I tell you?'

'Tell me what happened. Tell me how you got that burn scar.'

'We stopped the hovertruck on the edge of our territory. This guy Razek was driving, with another guy as guard. Me and a couple of the boys checked the truck and Razek hands over the money. Then suddenly he goes berserk, shoots down my boys. His guard tried to stop him, Razek shoots him, throws him out the truck and takes off.'

'Where do you feature in this?'

'I was round the back of the hovertruck, checking cargo. When I heard blasting I ran round. Razek took a shot at me. He missed, but it was close enough to stun me. Then he took off in the hovercab.'

I looked hard at him, considering his story. 'No,' I said.

'Whaddya mean, no?'

'That's not how it happened. Something must have triggered Razek. You're lying, or at least you're holding something back.'

'You're crazy, that's exactly how it went down.'

'The burn scar doesn't fit the story either,' I said. 'If Razek had shot at you from above, from the hovertruck, the scar would be slanting downwards. But it's dead level. He was on his feet on a level with you when he fired.'

Zeke's hand moved almost imperceptibly towards his pocket.

I laid a hand on his arm, like someone emphasizing a point in a friendly argument. He tried to move his arm off the bar and discovered he couldn't.

'Let me tell you how I think it happened,' I said. 'I think you boys were levying a little extra toll. A few cases of booze, a box or two of drugs, compensation for the guys out on the street. I think Razek saw what was happening and snapped.'

Zeke's eyes were cold. 'You got no proof.'

'Just a theory,' I agreed. 'Would you like to come and discuss it with your boss?'

I smiled at him, let go his arm, and took a swig of beer.

Zeke stared down at the bar for a moment, then looked up.

'OK, you're right, that's how it happened. Whoever was on checkpoint always took a little extra for themselves. Nothing much, nothing official, it just happened. Sort of a local custom.'

'Go on.'

'This guy Razek sees what's happening, jumps out of the truck and goes berserk. Says he's already paid the toll and that's it.'

'And?'

'Like I told you. He blasts down my boys, shoots his own guard when he tries to interfere, blasts me when I come running up. Then he drives away.' Zeke shook his head. 'It don't make any sense – it wasn't even his stuff. And nobody even cared – even Nastur turned a blind eye. And this guy kills three men and takes off into Wolverine territory – all over nothing.'

I finished my beer and stood up. 'You're right, it doesn't make any sense.'

Zeke said, 'Lucifer have to know? About what really happened?'

'I won't tell him if you don't.'

'Thanks, I owe you one. You going after this Razek?'

'Probably.'

'Into Wolverine territory? Into the Lair?'

'If that's where he is.'

'They'll kill you,' said Zeke flatly. 'Kill you and eat you.'

'Ogrons are hard to digest. At the very least I'll give 'em a bellyache.'

'I heard tell they ate a Chelonian once,' said Zeke. 'After that even you'd taste tender!'

I nodded and made my way out of the crowded cellar bar.

Once outside I stood for a moment looking at the neon sign and breathing what passes for fresh air in Megacity.

Well, so far so good. That was phase one completed. Now for phase two. I got into my hovercar and drove towards Wolverine territory.

Sometime later I was bending over the drive section of my hovercar, stopped in a cracked and rutted circular plaza surrounded by gutted and ruined buildings. The old plaza and the ruins around formed a circle of blackness in the perpetual neon haze of Megacity.

This was the Lair, the heart of Wolverine territory.

I had seen and heard nothing as I drove into that circle of blackness. But I had felt something, felt the pressure of constant observation from the surrounding darkness. You could feel the hate and the lust to kill.

When the hovercar choked and stuttered and juddered to a stop, and I got out to check the drive unit, I sensed scuttling movements in the darkness around me.

I ignored them.

I fiddled with the drive for a while, gave it a final thump, and slammed home the cover.

I went back to the front of the hovercar, to the driver's side, reached inside and pressed the starter control. The drive stuttered for a moment and roared into life.

As I started to get inside, I heard the quick patter of clawed feet behind me. The blast of the neuro-sap took me behind the ear and I pitched forward into a black pool . . .

When I awoke I was in the back seat of my own hovercar. There was a cloaked and hooded Wolverine beside me, his blaster jammed into my ribs. Another Wolverine was driving. Their fierce ammoniac smell seemed to fill the hovercar.

I allowed myself to slump sideways, lolling against the Wolverine on the seat beside me. He snarled and thrust me away.

I grabbed the blaster with one hand, bending aside the thin furry arm till the weapon pointed away from me. I clamped my other hand on to the Wolverine's scrawny windpipe, squeezing hard. His body jerked and convulsed and then became still.

The Wolverine in the driving seat realized that something was happening – but by then I'd wrenched the blaster from the dead Wolverine's hand and jammed it into the driver's ear.

'Keep driving,' I said. 'A stolen hovertruck just arrived in your territory. Take me where you're keeping it.' I gave his furry ear another jab with the pistol. 'If I'm not looking right at that hovertruck when we stop, I'll kill you.'

We drove on, following a twisting path through the ruins. Eventually we reached another, smaller plaza. A hovertruck sat in the middle, with half a dozen Wolverines hanging around it.

I wasn't surprised that the driver had done as I asked. He'd probably been heading there anyway. As far as he was concerned he was just driving me deeper into Wolverine territory, to a place where he could count on reinforcements, where he could kill me more easily. He thought he had nothing to lose. He was wrong.

I should have killed him, but I've always been too soft-hearted for my own good. As he brought the hovercar to a halt beside the truck, I smashed him behind the ear with the blaster, then reached out and took his own blaster from inside his cloak.

The other Wolverines had seen one of their own in the driving seat. They must have assumed the pack had made another capture.

They drifted carelessly towards the hovercar, wondering what was going on. I don't know quite what they expected – but I don't think they expected to see me climbing out with a blaster in each hand.

They grabbed frantically for their own weapons but I was already blasting them down. Only two of them lived long enough to fire, and both of them missed. I ran between the still-writhing bodies, jumped up into the hovertruck and stabbed at the controls, hoping Nastur looked after his transportation properly. The truck's powerful big drive unit fired up immediately, and I roared away.

I rocketed the hovertruck between the ruined buildings, doing my best to retrace our route to the old plaza. Once I hit the main highway I headed back for the lights of Megacity.

I was clear of Wolverine territory and starting to feel safe again – as safe as anyone is in Megacity – when I heard a scrabbling sound from the back of the hovertruck. A ghastly-looking figure climbed into the driving seat beside me. It was a broad-shouldered thick-set man, blood-stained, bruised and unshaven, and reeking of booze.

He gave me a dazed hook. 'Wha's going on?'

'Mr Razek, I presume?'

'Yeah, I'm Razek. Who the hell are you? Why are you driving my truck?'

'You lost it, remember? Mr Nastur hired me to get it back.'

Razek rubbed his eyes. 'That's right . . .'

'How much can you remember about what happened? I gather you had trouble with Lucifer's people.'

'I caught them boosting stuff from the truck.'

'What happened after that?'

Razek shrugged. 'I . . . dealt with them,' he said vaguely. 'Then I took off. The Wolverines hijacked the truck. They barred the road with rubble and jumped me when I hadda stop. They beat me up, locked me in the back of the truck and left me there.'

'Lucky they did – you got rescued along with the truck. I assumed you'd already been killed and eaten.'

Razek slumped back in his seat. 'Gotta get the truck back to Nastur . . .'

'Don't worry, I'm taking you there now.'

I drove the truck downtown to Nastur's big warehouse and an astonished Ursine guard opened the gates to let me through. I drove the truck across the yard and into the enormous warehouse. Then I made a few quick preparations, climbed down from the truck and helped Razek to get out.

Nastur sat in his special chair behind a wooden table, boxes and crates and barrels piled all around him.

He looked up at me, orange eyes blinking in amazement.

'Mission accomplished, Mr Nastur,' I said. 'I've spoken to Lucifer and he's agreed you can resume shipments. He wants double toll, but I'm sure you'll agree it's worth it. And here's your truck back, and your driver, both a bit worse for wear.'

'Amazing,' said Nastur. 'You really are an extraordinary fellow, Garshak. Quite extraordinary.'

'All in a day's work,' I said modestly. 'Since the job's completed, I'd like payment in full please – right now.'

To my surprise, Nastur made no objections. 'Of course!'

He snapped his fingers and his Alpha Centaurian accountant appeared. He had an old-fashioned cash box bulging with credit notes clutched in his tentacles.

Under Nastur's directions he counted out everything I was owed, including a handsome sum to cover the loss of my car. I stood watching the notes pile up, hands deep in the pockets of my trenchcoat. When the counting was finished I grabbed the thick roll of credit notes and thrust them into an inside pocket.

'I think I'll go down to Happy Mike's car lot tomorrow morning,' I said chattily. 'He's got a nearly new red sport-hover I've had my eye on for quite some time.'

Suddenly Razek lurched forward. 'This guy gets a load of credits? What about me?'

Nastur stared coldly at him. 'What about you?'

'I stopped Lucifer's guys stealing your stuff. Ain't that worth something?'

'You stumble on a little petty pilfering and for this you kill one of my best men, nearly start a war and then lose an entire truckload of cargo. You're fired.'

'That ain't fair . . .'

'Get out of my sight. You're lucky I don't kill you.'

'We'll see who gets killed,' said Razek thickly. 'I'll kill you, you fat bastard.'

He hurled himself at Nastur.

I didn't even like Nastur, and I didn't owe him a thing now our business relationship was over. Still, it didn't seem right to stand by and watch a recent client get killed.

That old code of the private eye again, I suppose.

I reached out and grabbed Razek. It was like grabbing a live power cable. A few minutes ago he'd been beat up and exhausted. Now he was throbbing with energy. He glared at me for a moment, red flames flickering deep in his eyes. Then he threw me aside – something not easily done – and started out for Nastur again.

I reached out to pull him back but by now Nastur's bodyguards had got their act together. Caught in the crossfire from at least three blasters, Razek's body, still upright, writhed and twisted for what seemed an incredibly long time and then suddenly fell.

I looked down at the body.

'Now there's someone who really had an attitude problem.'

I turned back to Nastur. 'I guess I'll be on my way . . .'

'Not quite yet, Mr Garshak. There is one further item of business to be settled between us.'

There was a nasty gleam in Nastur's orange eyes.

I waited, hands plunged deep into my pockets.

'When I first came to see you, you dealt rather harshly with two members of my entourage. Two Ursines. I employ a good many Ursines, Mr Garshak, and they all seem to feel that the honour of their species has been impugned. They have asked if they might be permitted to pay you back if a suitable opportunity arose.'

'Like now?'

Nastur smirked. 'Like now. After all, in the interests of good employee relations, I can scarcely refuse.'

A bunch of about a dozen Ursines appeared from behind the piles of crates. Some of them carried clubs and neuro-saps.

It wasn't a bad scheme – from Nastur's point of view. There were enough Ursines to give me a bad beating. When I woke up – if I woke up – the bundle of credit notes bulging my inside pocket would have mysteriously disappeared. And if it ended up back in Nastur's tin box, there'd be no way to prove it.

'Just how many Ursines do you think you can handle at once, Mr Garshak?' asked Nastur.

I sighed. Sometimes it's hard to hang on to your faith in sentient species' nature.

'How many can you spare, Mr Nastur?' I asked. 'And are you willing to be the first to go?'

I took my hands out of my pockets, a heavy blaster in each hand. One of them covered Nastur, the other the group of Ursines.

Nobody moved or spoke and I backed slowly out through the big warehouse gates. Once on the other side I started shoving them closed. The Ursine sentries came running up.

'Give me a hand here,' I called. 'Hurry up!'

'What's going on?'

'Mr Nastur's orders. Thieves have broken in – he wants to keep them bottled up in the warehouse. Get these gates shut and locked and blast anyone who tries to climb over. I'm going for help.'

As I ran from the warehouse they were ramming the gates shut. Just as I turned the corner, I heard the crackle of blaster fire. I grinned. I took the two blasters from my pockets and tucked them back in the twin holsters under my arms. I patted the reassuring bulge of the bundle of credit notes and hurried on.

A few streets away I forced a roaming hovercab to stop by standing in front of it and waving my arms. By the usual mixture of threats and bribery, I managed to persuade the driver to take me home.

Back in the office I broke out another bottle of *vragg*, sat on my little balcony and drank to a successful job.

There had been a few hairy moments along the way.

I'd heard about the value Lucifer placed on good manners, and I was pretty sure he'd respond reasonably to a polite approach.

The worst bit had been using myself for live bait for the Wolverines. I knew they took prisoners when they could, sometimes for ransom, sometimes for the pleasure of killing and eating them later. (Apparently they thought the meat tasted better if it was eaten fresh, straight after the kill. Or even before.)

I was pretty sure that they'd underestimate the strength of Ogron resistance to a neuro-sap. Not only are we hard to kill, we're extremely difficult to stun.

Of course they might have used a vibroknife or a blaster, or even a bomb. But they hadn't and I was still here, for whatever that was worth.

I'd even expected a last-minute double-cross from Nastur, and he hadn't disappointed me. I could have tried a fancy fast draw from the holsters, but I'd decided to play safe. When you need a blaster you need it fast, and the best place to have it is right there in your hand.

The strangest thing about the whole business had been the behaviour of Razek. The way he'd snapped at the checkpoint, killed his own man and hijacked his own cargo.

The way he'd gone for Nastur with his bare hands in a warehouse filled with Nastur's bodyguards.

The burning flames in his eyes and the way he'd tossed me – *me* – carelessly aside.

Mulling it all over, I watched the hovertraffic drift by along the street, and the flickering neon signs of the neighbourhood hotels and bars.

I didn't know it was going to be my last peaceful moment for quite some time.

8

MEGACITY STANDOFF

The giant figure had moved into the bar by now, and was looking around. Chris hunched up, trying to make himself small.

Bernice looked at him in surprise.

'Why are you so worried about this character? Who is he anyway?'

'He's called Murkar and he's a cop – at least he was when I last saw him.'

'So why does it matter if he knows who you are?'

'Well, he doesn't really. But he knows who I said I was then.'

Bernice sighed. 'This isn't getting any clearer.'

'When Roz and I were last here we were posing as Pinks.'

'As what?'

'Pinks. Agents of the Interplanetary Pinkerton Bureau.'

'So?'

'Don't you see? We've gone to a hell of a lot of trouble to pretend we're big-time crooks. If Murkar comes along and reveals I'm some kind of a cop . . .'

'But you're not, not any more.'

'I know, but I said I was then!'

'Don't worry,' said Bernice consolingly. 'He'll probably have forgotten you. Aren't Ogrons supposed to be pretty dim?'

'Some Ogrons are brighter than others. From what I remember Murkar's no fool – and you should see Garshak. Oh no!'

Little Louie had left the bar and was coming back towards them. The movement had attracted Murkar's attention. He followed Louie over to them.

'Everything's all fixed up,' said Louie. 'I made the reservation for you – you'll get a good table. Hovercab's on the way. Oh, hi, Murkar. I was going to get in touch with you. Ready to come back to work?'

Murkar nodded. He was staring intently at Chris.

'I know you,' he announced.

To Bernice's astonishment, Chris jumped up and shook Murkar warmly by the hand. 'What a memory! OK, I admit it, I'm the guy! Hey, Louie, you didn't tell me this was a cop bar.'

'Murkar hasn't been a cop for years,' said Louie. 'He works for me now. You two know each other?'

Murkar was still staring at Chris. 'You are called Christopher,' he announced. 'I take you to spaceport after –'

'All right, all right, no need for all the sordid details,' said Chris, still with the same frantic gaiety. He grinned at Louie. 'Last time I was here I got on the wrong side of the police and got booted off the planet. Old Murkar got the job. I must say he was pretty decent about it – for a cop.'

Chris shot Bernice an agonized glance, looked at Louie and made a tiny jerk of the head. Bernice picked up her empty glass.

'Did someone say something about another drink?'

'Coming up,' said Louie and hurried back to the bar.

Chris stared up at Murkar. 'Listen, Murkar, I need you to do me a favour. Don't tell Louie – or anyone – any more than I've just told him. You took me to the spaceport, put me on the shuttle. That's all you know about me.' He sat down again.

Murkar gave him a puzzled frown.

Louie came back with the drinks, including a huge tankard

of ale for Murkar. 'Sit down and join us, Murkar – you're not working yet.' He looked from Murkar to Chris, his face alight with curiosity.

'So you two met before. What had Chris here been up to, Murkar?'

There was a tense silence.

Then Murkar said, 'Don't know. Garshak say take to spaceport, put on shuttle. I take, I put!'

'I guess I'll have to ask Garshak,' said Louie.

Chris reverted to his menacing gangster persona. 'Better not, Louie. Let the dead past stay dead – it's safer that way.'

Bernice gave Louie her menacing Dragon Lady look.

'Like we were saying earlier, Louie – the people who recommended this place said nobody asked questions.'

'Sure, sure, just kidding,' said Louie hurriedly. 'It was just the coincidence. None of my business, right?'

'That's right,' said Chris, and turned to Murkar. 'Is Garshak still around?'

'Still around.'

'You ever see him?'

'Sometimes.'

'I'd like to talk to him. Tell him if you get a chance.'

'I tell.'

Louie's insatiable curiosity got the better of him again. 'I'm surprised you'd want to see Garshak again. I mean, if he deported you . . .'

His voice tailed off under Chris's cold stare.

'Oops, there I go again . . .'

Chris smiled, and Louie relaxed.

'Garshak wasn't so bad,' said Chris. 'He had enough on me to throw me in jail. He let me off the hook – for a price. The only condition was I had to be on the next shuttle out.'

'Sounds like old Garshak,' said Louie. 'I hear things were pretty wild in the old days. This new Chief – Chimp Harkon – you just can't do business with him.'

'We found that out already,' said Bernice. 'He had us picked up at the spaceport when we arrived and tried to give

106

us the bum's rush. He couldn't make it stick, but he won't like it when he finds out we're still here. So let's be discreet, hey, Louie?'

'My lips are sealed,' said Louie. 'How is old Garshak these days, Murkar?'

'Garshak away. Job for Nastur, find stolen hovertruck.'

'If he goes looking in Wolverine territory, we'll none of us see him again,' said Louie gloomily.

'Garshak tough,' said Murkar. 'Tough and smart.'

'That's a good combination,' said Bernice.

Soon after that the hovercab arrived, and Chris and Bernice went away.

Louie ushered them to the door and then came back to join Murkar. He leant forward eagerly. 'Now then, Murkar, have another beer. Tell me all you know about this guy Chris. Oh yeah, and what do you know about something called the Project?'

The Floating Palace lived up to Louie's recommendation. A shining crystal barge, it cruised slowly up and down the waters of Megacity's Grand Canal, mooring at regular intervals to deposit customers and pick up new ones.

Chris and Bernice created a satisfactory stir when they made their entrance. The maître d'hôtel, an Alpha Centaurian, had been told of their importance by Louie in vague but impressive terms. He greeted them as celebrities, and showed them to one of the best tables on the barge.

The imported food and wines were delicious and, on the slowly moving horizon, Megacity by night was an impressive kaleidoscope of glowing, multicoloured lights. And if, as Chris pointed out, the phosphorescence of the canal was caused by an incredible degree of pollution, the barge's glowing bow-wave was no less beautiful for that.

'Why were you keen to see this Garshak again?' asked Bernice over after-dinner brandy.

Chris shrugged. 'Like Murkar said, Garshak's tough and smart. And like you said, that's a good combination. Garshak was Police Chief of Megacity for years. He knows where all the bodies are buried, helped to bury quite a few of them.'

'Would he know about the Project?'

'He'll know if anyone does. And if he doesn't, he'll know where to ask.'

'Can we trust him?'

'If we pay him enough. Garshak was corrupt, but in an honest kind of way. He always gave value for money.'

'And he's an Ogron – like Murkar?'

Chris shook his head. 'He's an Ogron not like Murkar – not like any other Ogron in the universe.'

He told Bernice about the cruel experiments that had increased Garshak's intelligence to such an extraordinary extent.

'Most of the subjects died or went mad, apparently. The few that survived, like Murkar, ended up considerably brighter. But Garshak was the one big success. He got boosted to genius level.'

'So he was lucky then?'

'Was he?' said Chris. 'Garshak was a very flashy character when I met him, fancy clothes and fancy talk. But I always felt there was something tragic about him. Think how alone he is. How would you feel if you were the only really intelligent member of your entire species?'

'I feel like that all the time!' said Bernice. She drained the last of her brandy. 'What now?'

Chris looked around the crowded restaurant. The crowd looked affluent and some of them looked tough. But they didn't, on the whole, look criminal.

'I don't think there's any point staying here – the joint's too respectable.'

'So what do we do?'

'You laid out the programme yourself. Drinks, dinner, then a nightspot.'

'And you said you knew just the place.'

'I used to . . .' Chris raised a hand and the maître d' glided over. 'I visited a nightspot in Megacity, years ago,' said

Chris. 'Place over in Old Town. It was called Raggor's Cavern then, but the name may have changed.'

The maître d' knew the name at once. 'Ah yes sir, Raggor's Cavern. It's called Sara's Cellar these days. I understand that the previous proprietor came to a somewhat sticky end.'

'Extremely sticky,' said Chris. 'I know, I was there.'

The maître d' looked at him in surprise. 'Surely not, sir. It was a very long time ago!'

'Maybe I just heard about it somewhere,' said Chris. 'The bill and a hovercab please.'

The maître d' disappeared, returning minutes later with the bill and the assurance that a hovercab would meet them at the next mooring point.

Chris glanced at the astronomical sum on the printout, and tossed an even larger sum on the table. It occurred to him that Megacity must be one of the few places left where credit notes in hand outranked any other form of credit.

The maître d' gathered the notes with eager tentacles.

'If I might be permitted the liberty, sir.'

'Go ahead.'

'I understand that Sara's Cellar is so expensive that only the more successful among the criminal element can afford it. It has the reputation of being an extremely dangerous place.'

Chris rose to his full height. He yawned and stretched.

'Is that so?' He helped Bernice to her feet.

The maître d' looked up at Chris's massive form, at the expensive clothes and at the cold, hard face.

'But then again, sir, it occurs to me that you yourself might be an extremely dangerous man.'

Chris only smiled. Bernice picked up her bag and gave the maître d' a haughty stare.

'Sure he is – and I'm even tougher than he is!'

The maître d' bowed. 'We're just about to moor.'

He ushered them out of the restaurant, down the departure ramp and into the waiting hovercab.

* * *

Once they'd gone the maître d' returned to the crowded restaurant. He looked around, making sure that everything was under control.

He greeted an arriving mine president and his mistress, handed them into the care of his head waiter, and went to his private office in the bows. He activated a comm unit, punched in a code.

'Sara's Cellar? Get me Sara. It's the MD at the Floating Palace.'

After a moment a voice said, 'Sara. What?'

'Couple headed your way. Could be trouble. Big fair guy, medium-sized woman. Well dressed, big spenders, guy's heeled.'

'Cops?'

'I'd say just the opposite. Something odd. The guy said he was there the night Raggor got it – but he doesn't look all that old.'

'Interesting.' The cool voice sounded amused. 'OK, we'll take care of them.'

'Just thought you might like to know. Professional courtesy.'

'Thanks, I owe you one.'

The comm unit went dead.

The area around the nightclub that had once been called Raggor's Cavern hadn't changed much. The same winding, narrow cobbled alleyway with the same discreet door at the end. The same sort of surly heavy on guard. Only the sign was different. In neat flowing red letters it said SARA'S CELLAR.

Chris paid off the hovercab and pushed past the heavy on the door, shoving a handful of credit notes in his astonished face. He took Bernice's arm, helped her down the steep stone staircase. The last time he'd been on that staircase, thought Chris, it had been choked with broken bodies. He could still hear the screams and the crackle of blaster fire, smell the tang of freshly spilled blood.

Inside it was the same old universal nightclub, the tightly

packed tables, the little stage, the tiny dance floor. Either it was a deliberate attempt at Old Earth retro, or it was, as Roz Forrester had always said, that nightclubs never changed.

The walls were different, though. They'd been painted crimson. Maybe that had been the easiest way to cover up the bloodstains.

A thuggish-looking waiter slouched up and demanded to know if they had a reservation. ''Cause if not, buddy, forget it . . .'

'I've got a reservation, right here,' said Chris, and shoved credit notes at him.

The waiter sniffed. 'Well, I guess we can find you something.' He looked around the crowded room and began ushering them to an obscure table close to the door. Chris shook his head.

'Won't do.'

They were here to establish criminal status, and they weren't going to do that hiding in a dark corner.

Chris pointed to an empty table close to the band. 'That one!'

'That table's reserved for a regular customer.'

'From now on I'm a regular customer,' said Chris. He went over to the table, pulled a chair out for Bernice, sat down himself, shoved more credit notes at the waiter.

'Champagne, best you've got. Make it snappy.'

The waiter shrugged. 'Your funeral, bud.' He moved away.

'We're not overdoing the act, are we?' whispered Bernice.

Chris shook his head. 'Big-time gangsters really do act like this. I used to be a cop – I've watched them. They reckon there's no point to being big-time unless you let everyone know it.'

The waiter came back with the champagne, slopped it into crystal goblets, slouched off.

Chris sat sipping the champagne, looking round, and time rolled back. He'd been sitting here with Roz, sipping some weird drink with live creatures in it, watching an exotic dancer.

111

He heard Bernice's voice as if from far away.

'Hey, come back.'

He looked at her and grinned. 'Sorry, memory overload.'

'What exactly happened? When you were here with Roz?'

'Didn't I tell you – back then?'

Bernice shook her head. 'I was away on Sentarion, living on fruit juice and salad. You told me about Roz and the Project at St Oscar's. But you never said much about what happened here.'

'It was our last night in Megacity,' said Chris. 'Although we didn't know that then. We were looking for a serial killer we called the Ripper, who was really an alien called Karne. He was a shape-shifter, the most skilled of them all. He got stranded after a space battle and he was working his way back to the home planet.'

'I know about Karne,' said Bernice. 'We met later, on Sentarion. Why did he become a serial killer?'

'For travel money,' said Chris. 'As you know, he had vital information for his people and he was desperate to reach his homeworld. He'd establish himself on a planet, find a suitable victim, kill him, rob him and take on his shape. When he'd stolen enough money, he'd move on to the next planet, and start up all over again.'

'And you and Roz tracked him to Megacity?'

Chris nodded. 'He killed a change-booth manager called Sakis, stole his money and his shape. But that wasn't a big enough score. His next target was Raggor, who used to run this place. Raggor was a big-time drug dealer who kept lots of loose cash around. Roz and I were checking out all the likely joints and we finally got lucky. When we were in here that last night, Roz spotted someone who looked exactly like Sakis – and since Sakis was already dead we knew it must be the Ripper.'

Bernice shuddered. 'I'm with you so far, but I don't think I like it.'

'Well, you did ask.'

'I know. Go on.'

'We saw the Ripper go into Raggor's office. He'd spun him some tale about a big deal and got an appointment. There was an Ogron guard on the door – Murkar, working under-cover – and by the time we got past him it was too late.' Chris paused. 'You sure you want to know? This is where it gets nasty.'

Bernice nodded, and Chris went on with the gruesome tale.

'By the time we got in the Ripper had gone back to his Rutan shape. He had to dissect his victims to copy them . . . We arrived just in time to see him slice Raggor open. When he saw us he panicked. He shot out of the office and across the nightclub in a kind of glowing fireball. The place was crowded, like it is now. He carved his way through the crowd and up the stairs, slicing up anyone who got in his way. The place was like a slaughterhouse, blood and body parts everywhere.'

'And?'

Chris shrugged. 'We lost him again. We got ambushed by a pack of Wolverines outside, and that held us up.'

'I can see how it would. How did you manage to survive?'

'Garshak's Ogron police turned up and rescued us. Gar-shak deported us, that same night. Murkar put us on the shuttle.'

'How come you got deported?'

Chris grinned. 'There was some question about what hap-pened to Raggor's loot. Apparently it was still missing – and we were the only ones who knew the Ripper didn't get it. Garshak didn't want us hanging around asking awkward questions.'

Bernice drew a deep breath and took a long swig of champagne.

'I can see why you were so keen to come back here. Blood, mutilation and murder – this place is just choc-a-bloc with happy memories for you!'

Chris swigged his champagne and poured two more glasses. He signalled to the waiter for another bottle. 'It may have been 'nasty, but at least it was simple,' he said grumpily.

'What was?'

'Chasing a serial killer. You knew what you were doing – what you were trying to do anyway. This Project business – do you really think it's connected to all the recent violence, or were you just conning Chief Harkon into helping us?'

'Both!' said Bernice expansively. She was beginning to feel the effects of a long evening's drinking by now. ' "They think they can control it, but they don't realize the danger. Once it gets away from them there'll be blood in the streets. The killing will begin again – and it'll spread from here to a hundred worlds . . ." '

Chris gaped at her. 'Come again.'

'Thass . . . that's what you told me Roz's informant told her. And that's what's been happening, isn't it – blood in the streets?'

Chris frowned. 'I suppose so. It's funny, though . . .'

'What is?'

'What you just said. I hadn't really thought about it before. It's so . . . large-scale. What kind of crime could have that effect? Unless . . .'

A shadow fell across the table. Chris looked up, expecting to see the waiter. Instead he saw an immensely tall black figure standing by the table. It was flanked by two other figures, one red, the other equally black, both much broader, but not so tall.

All three had scaly skins, red slanting eyes, and long narrow heads crowned with neat little horns. Leathery wings were folded cloaklike over their backs.

To Bernice, in her slightly fuddled state, it seemed as if Satan himself, with a couple of attendant fiends, had suddenly appeared beside them. She did her best to look unconcerned. She opened the handbag on the table before her and toyed idly with its contents.

'Excuse me,' said the devil.

Chris was almost as taken aback as Bernice, but he took refuge in his arrogant gangster pose.

'Yeah? What's your problem?'

'I'm afraid you are,' said the tall black figure. The voice was deep and mellow. 'You're sitting at my special table. No one ever sits here but me, my employees and my guests.'

Chris shrugged. 'Looks like you're wrong about that. *We're* sitting here.'

The tall figure sighed. 'I hope we can resolve this without unpleasantness. I am prepared to accept that a genuine mistake has been made. I shall make sure the management finds you another table, equally good if not better. But this table is mine.'

'Not tonight,' said Chris flatly.

'Then you leave me no alternative.'

Chris was tense, ready to make his move. He crossed one leg over the other, so that his hand was near the blaster in his ankle holster . . .

The two flanking devils, clearly bodyguards, were poised.

'One moment,' said Bernice.

The devil raised a clawed hand to halt his bodyguards and turned to her. 'Madame?'

Bernice spoke with exaggerated distinctness. 'My associate and I have come to Megacity on business. It would harm that business if we were seen to be publicly intimidated.'

'I sympathize with your predicament, madame. But –'

'I haven't finished,' said Bernice coldly.

'I beg your pardon.' The devil seemed amused. 'Please go on.'

Bernice touched her lipstick to her mouth. 'This device I am holding appears to be an old-fashioned lipstick. It is in fact a miniature blaster. One end is pointed at my lips, the other end at your heart. If anyone makes a hostile move I shall kill you.'

For a moment no one moved or spoke. Then the devil said, 'I am afraid we have reached an impasse. You see, I am already in business in Megacity. My name is Lucifer. I am a respected crime lord. My reputation and my business too would suffer if I were seen to be publicly humiliated. So I must call your bluff.'

Bernice fought to keep her voice steady. 'It isn't a bluff. I'll kill you.'

'Then my guards will kill you, and your companion.'

'Don't be too sure of that,' said Chris.

'Oh yes, I am sure,' said Lucifer. 'We are three to two. One of you will die, probably both.'

'That won't help you,' said Bernice. 'I told you, you'll be the first to go.'

'Oh, I accept that you mean what you say, madame,' said Lucifer. 'But so do I. It seems we must both die . . .'

9

AMBUSH

Suddenly Bernice realized that all this was real. They were all going to be killed – in an argument over a nightclub table reservation. It was a sobering reflection. She wanted to get up and run – but she saw that Chris was keyed up for combat. He wouldn't back down now.

A cool female voice said, 'Is there some problem here?'

Keeping the lipstick blaster levelled, Bernice flicked a quick glance to one side, before returning her attention to Lucifer.

A tall statuesquely beautiful red-haired woman in a low-cut evening gown had come up to the table.

'Ah, Sara,' said Lucifer. 'Just a little dispute about table reservations. It's about to be resolved.'

Chris, who'd been staring at the woman open-mouthed, hastily returned his attention to the situation – and to Lucifer.

'One way or another,' said Chris grimly.

'Peacefully, I hope,' said the woman with an edge to her voice. 'We haven't had a killing for – oh, it must be several nights now.' She smiled at Chris. 'I'd hate to lose a handsome new customer – or a much-valued old one, of course.'

There was a long tense pause.

Then Lucifer said, 'I offer a compromise – for the sake of the lady with the lipstick.'

'Please go on,' said Bernice.

'One of Sara's minions will bring a chair – two chairs,' said Lucifer. 'And a bottle of champagne. Sara and I will join you at this table. We will share a drink, we will talk for a few moments – then Sara will escort you to another table. Instead of being interlopers, you will have been my guests. Your prestige will be enhanced, mine will not be diminished – and Sara will be spared a most unpleasant scene.'

Before Chris could speak Bernice said, 'We accept. A most generous offer. And I should like to apologize for the rude and uncouth behaviour of my associate. All I can say is that he's still young – he'll learn.'

'If he lives,' said Lucifer. He smiled at Chris, who scowled back – and shot a reproachful look at Bernice.

Sara had already summoned a waiter and two more chairs were hurriedly brought to the table. Sara and Lucifer sat down opposite Chris and Bernice. Lucifer's two bodyguards took position just behind him.

There was yet another tense silence. But then, thought Bernice, it was what you might call an awkward social situation. She turned the lipstick blaster over in her hands.

Lucifer nodded towards it. 'Could you really have killed me with that trinket?'

Unthinkingly Bernice twisted the lipstick case – and blasted the bottle of champagne from the hands of an approaching waiter. He gave a yell of alarm as it exploded, showering him with champagne.

A hush fell on the crowded room – broken by Lucifer's deep laugh. He ordered more champagne and the buzz of conversation started up again all around.

Bernice decided she might as well brazen things out.

'You see?' she said sweetly. 'I could easily have killed you. It's quite an effective little weapon at close range.'

On impulse she tossed Lucifer the lipstick case and he caught it in a long clawed hand. He held it for a moment, the business end aimed at her heart.

'Aren't you tempted to try it?' she asked.

Lucifer smiled. 'It's not really my style. Besides, your

friend already has me covered under the table – with the blaster from his ankle holster.'

He tossed the lipstick to Bernice, who put it back in her evening bag. 'Put the blaster away, Chris,' she said firmly. 'And keep your hands on the table. We're having a truce.'

'A lasting peace, I hope,' said Lucifer smoothly. More champagne arrived. When it was poured, he raised his glass in a toast. '*Salud y pesetas*!'

'*Salud y pesetas*!' said Bernice.

Lucifer refilled the glasses. 'And what brings you to Megacity?'

'You might say it was a special project,' said Chris.

'*The* Project, in fact,' said Bernice.

Lucifer looked blank. He raised his glass again.

'Allow me to wish you every success.'

Another silence.

'I see an excellent table has just become free,' said Sara. 'If you'll come with me?'

She rose, and Chris and Bernice got up to follow her.

Lucifer rose as well. He took Bernice's hand and touched it to his lips. His hand, and his lips, felt dry and warm – almost burning.

'I hope we meet again,' he said. 'I seldom get the chance to talk to a female of your species. Most humans find me rather intimidating.'

'Oh, I wouldn't say that,' said Bernice. 'Personally I prefer a man with a bit of devil in him!'

For a moment Lucifer looked outraged, and Bernice wondered if she'd gone too far. Then he threw back his head and laughed – a deep booming laugh that made heads turn all around.

Sara settled them at their new table, provided yet more champagne, and went to greet some newly arriving customers.

Bernice glanced across the room and saw that Lucifer's two bodyguards had occupied two of the vacant chairs. Lucifer looked up and caught her glance, raising his glass in salute.

She raised her glass back, and took another swig of champagne. After all the recent tension, she was starting to feel nicely relaxed again. She became aware that Chris was scowling at her.

'What's up?'

'Thanks for all the support. "Rude and uncouth" indeed.'

'Well you were. I told you you were overdoing it! But would you listen? Oh no! You had to go right ahead and pick a fight with someone who appears to be Megacity's equivalent of Al Capone!' She chuckled. 'Or is our friend over there really who I think he is?'

'Depends who you think he is!'

'Well, who does he look like? Satan, Beelzebub – Old Nick!'

'He's a Demoniac, from a planet called Gehenna.'

'There you are, then,' said Bernice owlishly. 'The devil himself!'

Chris smiled and shook his head. 'Not really! The planet Gehenna, and the Demoniac species, were originally given those names by explorers from Earth.'

'You can see why!'

'There's a theory that early visits to Earth by Demoniac explorers started a lot of the old myths. Now Demoniacs tend to use those old Earth names when they're dealing with humanoids.'

'Why?'

'Maybe it's some obscure Demoniac joke. Or maybe they reckon it gives them some psychological advantage. It seemed to work with you, anyway.'

'And what does that mean?'

'You were obviously quite taken with him.'

'Yes, I think I was, rather,' said Bernice. 'You know the old saying.'

'What old saying?'

'The Prince of Darkness is a gentleman!'

'I shouldn't rely on it,' said Chris disapprovingly. 'The way you were flirting with him . . .'

'Me, flirting!'

'It's very dangerous to become romantically involved with members of alien species,' said Chris primly. 'Quite apart from the obvious physical problems, there are the cultural ones –'

'At least I wasn't drooling over him the way you were with that red-headed bimbo,' said Bernice truculently.

'Not at all,' said Chris with dignity. 'I had a feeling I'd seen her before. I was just trying to remember . . .'

'Remember! You were committing her contours to memory!'

The beginnings of a promising wrangle were interrupted by the return of its subject. She sat down at their table, poured herself some champagne and studied them both thoughtfully. Or rather she studied Chris, after a brief and dismissive glance at Bernice.

'You know you intrigue me, you really do. What is it, a death wish?'

'Call it boyish enthusiasm,' said Chris. 'I was trying to make a big impression and made a bad start.'

'You nearly made a bad end as well,' said Sara. 'Getting tough with Lucifer, of all people! If he hadn't taken a fancy to your little friend here, you'd be dead by now.'

'His little friend happens to be a full partner and colleague, and the brains of the outfit as well,' said Bernice. 'I'll thank you to remember that!' She looked at the other woman's undeniably impressive figure. 'Though if by the adjective "little" you mean that you could undoubtedly make two, or even three of me . . .'

'I'll make mincemeat of you if I have any more lip,' said Sara in an unexpectedly tough voice.

Chris held up his hands. 'Ladies, please! Haven't we had enough trouble for one night?'

He looked so horrified that both women smiled.

'Sorry,' said Bernice. 'It's been a long night.'

Sara nodded. 'They all are here!' She turned back to Chris. 'I keep getting this feeling that I've seen you before . . .'

'That's just what I was saying,' said Chris. 'Isn't it Benny?'

'It certainly is,' said Bernice.

It's also the oldest chat-up line in the galaxy, she thought, but decided it would be more tactful not to say so out loud.

Sara looked intently at Chris. 'Have you ever been here before? To this club, I mean?'

'Only once, a long time ago.'

'When was that? Perhaps I was here too.'

'You couldn't have been,' said Chris gallantly. 'It was a very long time ago and you're not nearly old enough.'

Sara smiled, clearly pleased with the compliment. 'I'm a lot older than I look. I'm a Rigellian – we have a much longer life span than most humanoids. Besides, there are certain treatments – ask your little friend about them.'

Before Bernice could reply Chris said hurriedly, 'You'd certainly remember if you were here when I was. It was back when Raggor ran the place – on the night he got killed.'

'That's it!' said Sara excitedly. She pointed to a table near the stage. 'You were sitting there – with a small dark-skinned woman. I remember you now. You've hardly changed at all.'

Chris nodded. 'Where were you? I'm sure I'd have noticed you.'

'I'm sure you did. I was on the stage – dancing!'

Chris remembered the gyrating exotic dancer on the tiny stage. He'd been watching her attentively when Roz had spotted the Ripper.

He blushed. 'I'm sorry, I didn't recognize you. You're – you're dressed differently.'

'You mean I'm dressed!' said Sara cheerfully. 'And I'm a lot older as well.' She turned to Bernice. 'I started here years ago, as an exotic dancer. I was a mere child of course!'

'Of course,' agreed Bernice politely. 'I take it that, over the years, you, er, worked your way up?'

Sara looked at her suspiciously, but Bernice kept an expression of polite interest on her face.

'You might say that,' said Sara. 'I moved over to waitressing, head waitress, maître d', finally manager. Eventually they put my name over the door. I don't own the place of course. I run it for a syndicate, but they pay well, and they've given me a few points – shares that is.'

'Fascinating,' said Chris.

Suddenly Sara frowned. 'Weren't you and your friend supposed to have something to do with what happened? You disappeared straight afterwards.'

'We didn't kill Raggor, if that's what you mean,' said Chris. 'We stumbled on the murder and nearly caught the killer. Afterwards the police deported us.'

'There was something about some missing money, too.'

'That's partly why we got deported. The Chief of Police needed someone to blame .'

'Ah well,' said Sara. 'That's all in the past. What about the present? Why are you back in Megacity?'

'We're here because of something called the Project,' said Chris. 'Something that got started back in Raggor's time and has been going on ever since.'

'Never heard of it,' said Sara.

'You're sure?' said Bernice sharply. 'Not a mention or a scrap of gossip? It's very important!'

Sara shook her head. 'Means nothing to me.' She was still looking at Chris. 'You seem to go in for small bossy women.'

Chris looked puzzled. 'I do?'

'Wouldn't you like to try a nice, large, easy-going one, just for a change? Why don't you pick on someone nearer your own size?'

Chris was speechless. He blushed again, a deep tide of red that rose from his neck to his hairline.

The two women watched him interestedly.

'Not too many men can do that these days,' said Sara.

'Oh Chris is multitalented,' said Bernice. 'I'd leave you two alone, but I don't want to go home by myself, and Chris won't let me chat up the demon king.'

'If you're referring to Lucifer, you're too late: he's just left,' said Sara.

'Just my luck.'

'We'd better go too,' said Chris.

'Well, you know where I am now,' said Sara. 'Come down and see me some time!'

They rose. 'Can you call us a hovercab?' asked Bernice.

'Lined up outside. My customers are all known to be big spenders.'

Chris snapped his fingers. 'The bill! All that champagne.'

'On the house.'

'I can't let you do that . . .'

'You can't stop me,' said Sara. 'Pay me next time you come in. We'll work something out.'

'I just bet you will,' said Bernice. She grabbed Chris's sleeve and hauled him towards the steps. 'Come on, Romeo.'

He looked down at her thoughtfully. 'You know, Sara's got something there.'

'What?'

'About small bossy women!'

'Sara's got something all right – and we both know what it is! Home, James!'

As they made their way towards the stairs, Bernice noticed that quite a few tables were empty now. Even Sara's customers had to go home sometime.

'No reactions to mentioning the Project,' said Chris as they climbed the stairs.

'Nothing from Lucifer, nothing from Sara,' agreed Bernice. 'Unless they're both lying, of course.'

Chris shrugged. 'Looked like genuine puzzlement to me. We just drew a blank.'

'So what do we do now? Advertise on the back page of the *Megacity Gazette*? "Wanted, news of large-scale criminal conspiracy, dating back many years. Small reward for finder." '

'We go on looking,' said Chris. 'Most police work is just a lot of plodding around asking questions. Why do you think they used to call them flatfeet?'

They reached the top of the stairs and went outside the club, standing under the glowing sign that read SARA'S CELLAR.

124

The night was hot and oppressive with a thin drizzle of rain. Cabs were cruising around outside, snapping up the departing customers like hungry sharks. There were quite a few people before them, but plenty more cabs around.

Bernice settled down to wait, trying to get some refreshment from the muggy night air. She could see a tall black figure and two smaller ones making their way up the alley. Either Lucifer was walking home, or he was making his way to private transport somewhere nearby.

Maybe he had a fiery chariot parked just around the corner.

'Don't despair,' said Chris, continuing their conversation on the stairs. 'Early days yet. We'll try again tomorrow.'

Bernice yawned. 'I suppose so, I just hope something happens soon.'

Something did.

A rare breeze drifted down the alley towards them and suddenly Chris sniffed the air. Cupping both hands to his mouth he bellowed, 'Look out! Wolverines!'

Drawing a blaster from his ankle and another from under his arm, Chris ran up the alleyway.

Bernice fumbled in her bag, came up with the lipstick, thrust it back, pulled out her new slimline blaster, and ran after him.

Lithe dark shapes had appeared on top of the walls that lined the alleyway. They dropped to the ground and surrounded the three Demoniacs, isolating them in a tight circle.

Caught in a Wolverine crossfire, one of them staggered and fell. With a curious feeling of relief, Bernice realized that it was one of the bodyguards.

Chris opened fire at long range and one of the attackers dropped. At the crackle of blaster fire several of the others swung round. Bernice saw thin wiry figures, hooded and cloaked. She caught a glimpse of fierce red eyes in long-muzzled furry faces, needle-sharp fangs bared in snarls of fury. The Wolverines all carried oddly shaped weapons, like truncated rifles.

Chris was firing steadily, and with half the attackers distracted, the surviving Demoniac bodyguard had drawn his blaster and was returning fire.

Suddenly the ambush turned into a disorganized rout.

Bernice watched Lucifer grab a writhing Wolverine and smash him against the wall. Lucifer's arm flashed out and his claws slashed a Wolverine's throat, producing a spray of red. He was fighting unarmed, she realized. Maybe carrying weapons was beneath him. She saw him stoop, snatch a blaster from the fallen bodyguard and open fire.

A Wolverine, a little to one side, was taking careful aim at an unsuspecting Chris. Suddenly Bernice realized that she wasn't here just as a spectator. She was in a shootout. She raised her blaster and shot the Wolverine down.

Chris fired again, and one of the Wolverines around the Demoniacs fell. The remainder fled, running straight up the steep alley walls like giant spiders and disappearing from view.

Only one giant Wolverine remained, standing between Lucifer and his bodyguard on one side and by Chris and Bernice on the other. It could have fled with the others – it was almost as if it hadn't wanted to escape.

Somehow it had lost its blaster in the struggle but it didn't seem to care. It was stalking towards Bernice and Chris, mad red eyes blazing, foam dripping from its long jaws.

Chris and Bernice raised their blasters, taking careful aim.

Lucifer's deep voice boomed from down the alley.

'Don't shoot! I want to take it alive!'

The hell with that, thought Bernice. One step nearer and I'll blast. She raised her voice. 'You want this thing alive, Lucifer old chum, *you* come and get it.'

Lucifer, she soon realized, was doing exactly that, pounding down the alleyway towards them.

'Don't shoot!' roared Lucifer. 'That one's the leader. I want to know who's behind this. I want it alive!'

As if enraged by his voice the Wolverine turned and lurched back towards him.

Lucifer halted his run, the Wolverine stopped, and the two confronted each other, just a few yards apart.

'You want me alive, do you, devil?' snarled the Wolverine in a saliva-choked, guttural voice.

Lucifer's deep booming tones came in reply.

'Surrender and I shall spare your life – much as it galls me.'

'And afterwards, devil?'

'Tell me who ordered this attack and why, and you shall have your freedom. I give you my word.'

The Wolverine gave a terrible coughing roar.

'You want me alive, devil?' it repeated. 'I want you *dead!*'

In an incredible, almost vertical leap it sprang high in the air, hurtling towards Lucifer.

Before it reached him, three blasters fired at once, catching it in a crossfire while it was still in the air.

The Wolverine's body writhed and twisted for a moment as if supported in the air by blaster fire.

Then it dropped dead at Lucifer's feet.

'Fools!' he roared angrily. 'I told you not to shoot!'

The surviving bodyguard ran up, and whispered deferentially to him. Lucifer looked down at the dead Wolverine.

'My guard very properly reminded me that as the Wolverine was berserk, and almost certainly drugged, it would not, could not, have surrendered and might well have killed me.'

He looked up at Bernice and Chris.

'My apologies, and my thanks.'

Lucifer bowed, and somehow never managed to straighten up again. He toppled to the ground, falling across the dead body of the Wolverine.

10

Shootout on Spaceport Boulevard

It started out as one hell of a nice day.

I woke up to the comforting feeling of plenty of credits in my pocket, and not too much to do except spend some of them.

I got up slowly, showered without even banging my head on the ceiling, as I usually do, and got dressed.

When I came through into the office, Cat was sitting on the balcony sneering at me. Cat was a werecat, a giant, tangled ball of fur, teeth and claws. Werecats are hunters and scavengers, about the only form of wildlife tough enough to survive in Megacity. They're said to be untamable.

Cat wasn't exactly *my* werecat – he took care of his own needs. But he had a taste for booze, and occasionally deigned to accept some of mine. Maybe they wouldn't serve him in the local bars.

There was a little *vragg* left in the office bottle so I took the top off and held it out to him. He jumped off the balcony and I passed him the bottle. He took it in his handlike forepaws, sniffed it as if he was used to a better class of booze, and then emptied the bottle down his throat.

Then he tossed the bottle aside, jumped over the balcony and disappeared. I liked seeing Cat, though it wasn't a close relationship. He was never going to sit on the mat and purr, and if you stroked him you'd probably lose some skin.

I went to the bar across the road for breakfast – coffee, doughnuts and a quick belt of brandy to get me started.

Old Cy the bartender was a wizened little anthropoid, damn near as hairy as Cat.

'See what happened last night, Garshak?' he wheezed as he brought my coffee.

Cy always said that – there was always some bad news to be passed on in Megacity.

'What?'

'Wolverines hit Sara's Cellar, killed some big-time crime lord called Lucifer.'

'You sure?'

Cy nodded to the ever-flickering vidscreen behind the bar.

'Saw it on the news this morning. Blood and bodies everywhere.'

I finished my breakfast, thinking about Lucifer meanwhile. I'd rather taken to him. Still, he was in a dangerous business. He was probably bound to get blasted eventually. I wondered who had ordered the hit. Some business rival, probably.

Maybe even Nastur.

I had another belt of brandy in his memory, and then went back to the office to catch up on my foot-dangling and to plan my day.

A packet popped out of the mail tube.

It held an autoguide disc, nothing else. You put it in your hovercar's guide system and it took you where you needed to go on automatic. Somebody, somewhere, wanted to see me – presumably a client. Only I didn't have a hovercar any more.

The hell with it, I thought – I'd go out and buy one. I could afford it. I'd buy myself some new clothes as well, make a good impression on my new employer.

I had the clothes run up on the autotailor in one of the retro clothes shops at the spaceport. By mid-morning I was strolling along Spaceport Boulevard. I was everything the well-dressed private eye ought to be. I was wearing a new trenchcoat, a new hat, and my pockets were still bulging with credit notes.

It was a fine morning in downtown Megacity – as fine as mornings in Megacity ever get. The acid rain had eased off, and a faint haze of sunshine was forcing its way through the pollution layer.

I drifted into Happy Mike's Second-hand Hovercar Lot on Spaceport Boulevard, looking forward to replacing my old heap with Nastur's money.

Mike's sign originally read:

HAPPY MIKE'S HOVERCRAFT – EVERY HOVER A HAPPY BUY

Long ago some local wit had amended it to read:

EVERY HOVER A HEAP OF TROUBLE

Later someone else had crossed out the last two words.

Happy Mike, the enormous and irritable anthropoid who owned the lot, had never bothered to fix the sign. Maybe he believed in truth in advertising.

Suddenly I saw my own old heap, the one I was about to replace, zooming towards me along the Boulevard – which was pretty puzzling. In fact, considering I'd had to abandon it in Wolverine territory when I got back Nastur's truck, it was downright worrying.

Maybe the Wolverines were returning it out of kindness – but it didn't seem likely. If the Wolverines wanted to give anything back to me, they probably wanted to give it to me right in the neck.

As the hovercar came nearer I saw that it was crammed with cloaked furry figures, all clutching short-barrelled laser rifles, a favourite Wolverine weapon.

Daylight raids like this weren't common, but they weren't completely unknown either. The Wolverines had been known to make a hit on Spaceport Boulevard at high noon before now, striking swiftly and then heading back to the Lair, where no one was going to follow them.

There was only one entrance and exit on the lot, and my

hijacked hovercar was going to make it before I did. I ducked back inside the lot and took cover among the rows of parked vehicles.

Peering round the side of a battered hovertruck, I saw my hovercar thump down across the entrance. A handful of cloaked and hooded figures piled out, and spread out across the lot.

I took a quick look around, assessing my situation. It was lousy. The lot was fenced all round with razor wire, and the fence was high. Mike had strong views on preserving his property. It was impossible to climb into the lot, and just as impossible to climb out. The only way out was through the main entrance, and the Wolverines had left their driver on sentry duty in my hovercar.

Mike would call the cops when he saw what was happening, but response time was never their strongest point, especially when Wolverines were involved. Police policy these days seemed to be to turn up a safe time after the crime had been committed, pick up the pieces, often literally, and arrest everyone who was still around. My Ogron Flying Squad would have arrived a hell of a lot quicker, but they'd been disbanded long ago. The Wolverines would have plenty of time to get the job done and get away before any police hovercars arrived.

I was alone, but at least I wasn't unarmed, not in Megacity. I drew one of my blasters from its shoulder holster and started playing hide and seek around the lot – not an easy game for someone as big as I am.

Every time a Wolverine caught a glimpse of me – or even thought it did – laser fire crackled across the lot. Paint was scorched on some of Mike's best buys, chunks were blasted off, and one or two of the heaps even caught fire. Mike was just going to love this. But at the moment that was the least of my worries.

I wasn't too concerned about being shot at – I was used to that, and as everyone knows Wolverines can't shoot straight. Unfortunately they compensate for this by invariably turning up in force and spraying laser fire across the landscape, on the principle that they're bound to hit something, possibly even their target. Who or what else gets blasted doesn't worry them.

And that was my real problem – I was badly outnumbered. It was time to reduce the odds.

I doubled back among the rows of parked hovercars. Black smoke from the burning vehicles drifted across the lot, providing a certain amount of extra cover. Suddenly I saw a wiry cloaked figure peering through the smoke ahead of me. It was the Wolverine's bad luck that it was peering the wrong way.

I crept up behind it.

Either my creeping up wasn't as good as it used to be, or it sensed or even smelt me. It spun around at the last moment and gave a harsh cry of alarm, cut off by the impact of my blaster barrel smashing across the side of its narrow skull.

One.

The cry alerted another Wolverine, which sprang from behind a burning hovercraft, laser rifle raised. I blasted it down.

Two.

Which left, if my arithmetic was right, three. Plus the one in my car.

My plan, such as it was, was to work my way back to the entrance, killing any Wolverines I encountered, and reach my own hovercar. If I could manage to dispose of the driver, I would repossess my heap and get myself out of there. The hell with any surviving Wolverines – they could walk home.

The plan nearly worked.

I dodged through the rows of hovercars managing to avoid any more Wolverines until I reached a point on the side of the main building close to the entrance. My hovercraft still blocked the way out, and the Wolverine driver was still at the controls, clutching a laser rifle. I could see the Wolverine's narrow head with its long furry muzzle swinging to and fro as it tried to work out what was happening on the lot.

No chance of catching it unawares. I'd just have to charge the hovercraft, shoot first and straightest, haul out the body and hope to jump in and blast off before the rest of the Wolverines realized what was happening.

I poised myself to make the dash – and a guttural voice behind me said, 'Garshak!'

I swung round and found myself facing all three Wolverines and their three laser rifles. I'd been concentrating so hard on what was ahead that I'd forgotten what was still behind me. This time the Wolverines had done the creeping up – and they were a lot better at it than I was.

The central Wolverine snarled, 'Drop blaster!'

Its eyes glinted madly and its muzzle dripped foam. I hesitated for a moment, wondering why I wasn't already dead. They'd have had no compunction about shooting me in the back, which meant they had something else in mind.

At a time like this time slows up; every second ticks by with terrible clarity – and every instant of life is precious.

I could get one of them, that was for sure. Maybe two, though I'd probably be wounded or dying by then. That still left two, the third Wolverine and the one in my hovercar. Too many. They hadn't blasted yet, but they would soon ... Could they possibly want me alive? What for? If they tried to take me prisoner, there was still a chance ...

All this flashed through my mind in the seconds between the Wolverine's snarl and my dropping the blaster.

'Don't move,' said the guttural voice. The Wolverine called out a command to the one in my heap, and the hovercraft rose slowly in the air and moved towards us. Were they planning to take me away in it, back to the Lair? Why bother? If vengeance was their objective, they could kill me here and now. Did they want to interrogate me?

I knew nothing they could possibly want to know.

Maybe they wanted the pleasure of killing me slowly.

I had a sudden vision of myself turning, still alive, on a Wolverine roasting spit. To the Wolverines, the screams of the victim add savour to the meat.

I decided that if they tried to get me into the hovercar I'd grab one of their laser rifles and go down fighting. At the very least, I could make them kill me.

But why bring the hovercar to me, rather than take me over to it? It was near enough . . .

The hovercar roared closer and rose to its maximum height, directly over my head. Still keeping me covered, the Wolverines backed away, leaving me staggering in the blast of the hovercraft's down-jets.

I realized what they were going to do.

They were going to land the hovercar on top of me, crushing me to death. Once again, I couldn't imagine why they'd bother. Sheer nastiness maybe? Or did they hope to make my death look like some bizarre traffic accident?

The problem of their reasons was purely academic.

Speaking practically, my options were pretty lousy. I could stay where I was and be flattened by my own hovercar, or duck out from under and get blasted by three laser rifles.

I'd just decided to jump the nearest Wolverine when a tremendous boom shook the air, and the Wolverine disintegrated into bloody fragments.

I turned and saw Happy Mike, standing on the steps of his main showroom. He looked like a gorilla in mechanic's overalls, which was pretty much what he was, and he was clasping a massive laser cannon with twin barrels the size of subtrain tunnels.

Another boom, another Wolverine blown away.

The third Wolverine swung its laser rifle round on Mike, who was busy reloading. As he stuffed giant shells into the laser cannon's breech, I got out from under, grabbed the Wolverine round its scrawny neck and threw it under the hovercar – just as the driver finally cut the power. The hover thudded down – smothering the Wolverine's final scream.

That left the driver.

As I snatched up my blaster, a laser bolt fired from the hovercar blasted the stonework beside Happy Mike's head.

I don't know how it managed to miss someone as large as

Mike – but, like I said, Wolverines can't shoot straight.

I raised my blaster and took aim, but I didn't even have time to fire. At that range and with that weapon, Happy Mike couldn't miss. There was an enormous double boom and the Wolverine and most of my heap disintegrated in a ball of flame.

Dodging a hail of hot metal fragments, and flapping my hands to clear the smoke, I made my way over to Happy Mike, who was reloading his cannon and looking round for more targets.

'Garshak!' he roared. 'What the hell's going on here?'

'That was my hovercar you just blasted, Mike,' I said reproachfully.

'How the hell was I supposed to know that?'

'You ought to – you sold it to me last year.'

'So what the hell's it doing here full of Wolverines?'

'I was bringing it to you so I could upgrade,' I said.

I nodded towards the still-blazing remnants of my heap.

'How much will you give me on trade-in?'

For a while there I thought Happy Mike was going to blast *me*, but I finally got him calmed down. The story I told him had a lot to do with it. It was a pretty good story, though I say so myself, and some of it was even true.

In this version I'd made a few credits – well, that much was true – and I'd been bringing in my hover so I could upgrade to one of his fine vehicles.

Just as I'd arrived I'd seen a gang of Wolverines sneaking around in his car lot. I'd naturally assumed they were planning to steal all the most expensive vehicles, and, no doubt, to rob and murder Happy Mike himself. As an old friend and a concerned citizen, I'd been unable to stand by and see this happen, and had tackled the villains. In the ensuing shootout, the Wolverines had attempted to steal my hovercar to make their getaway – until prevented by Mike's heroic intervention.

I told much the same tale to the cops when they finally

arrived. At first they were even more sceptical than Mike. They simply assumed I was lying as a matter of routine. Everyone lies to cops – they expect it. Then again they couldn't prove I wasn't telling the whole truth and they didn't much care. My statement gave them a nice simple story so they could wrap up the case and get back to their coffee and doughnuts, which is all most hovercops care about anyway.

They recorded my long lying statement, sent for the blood hoverwagon to cart off what was left of the Wolverines, and went away. At the end of the day there were six Wolverines fewer, which was all to the good.

'Wolverines are getting too damn bold,' said the old sergeant as he got into his police hovercar. 'They hit Sara's Cellar last night, blew away a load of fat cats. Not that they're much loss either.'

The police hover drove away.

After the cops had gone Mike and I got down to some serious haggling. He flatly refused to give me trade-in credit on the smouldering remnants of my old hover. He said he'd have to pay someone to clear the metal scraps away, especially since they were all mixed up with bits of barbe-cued Wolverine.

But he did me a very good deal on a nearly new sport-hover.

It had power-boost, autoguide and air-conditioning, so I came out of it pretty well.

You might even say the Wolverines had done me a favour.

When the deal was done, Mike and I sealed it with a few drinks in the bar across the street. We discussed the state of things in Megacity, and agreed that everything was going to hell. No change there . . . Then I got into my brand-new sporthover, plugged in the autoguide disc and let it take me to see my mystery client.

THE SEA-COAST OF MEGACITY.
Most visitors would be surprised to learn that Megacity

even has a coastline. People seem to think that Megacity covers most of the planet, which, of course, is a ridiculous exaggeration. It does, however, cover much of one of the planet's smallest continents.

Megacity sprawls over much of the island, but it is an island, and it does have a sea coast. There's a big industrial port, which is just an extension of Megacity, but there are also stretches of wild and empty coastline. Empty, that is, except for the castles, châteaux, mansions and manor houses, where the really rich live, when they're not in their penthouses high above Megacity.

Even these unspoilt stretches don't really rate as beauty spots. The coast is bleak and jagged and rocky with long stretches of marshy hinterland. The marsh is quick-marsh — anything that falls in disappears without trace in a matter of minutes.

The sea is dull, grey and sluggish and nearly as polluted as the air and the land.

Still, there are views, of a sort, and the coastal area offers its rich residents ozone mixed with the smog.

The sea provides little in the way of entertainment. Only the toughest and most savage marine life forms have survived. There are none of them that you can eat except, and it's not much of an exception, the highly poisonous fugora fish.

Anything else that lives in the sea will probably eat you.

Nor is the coastline necessarily safe. Since most of their natural food has been poisoned by chemical effluent from the mines, some of the more ambitious amphibians frequently come ashore to devour the too-bold tourist or careless villager.

In fact the sea offers the tourist a choice between being poisoned and being devoured. Beaches are rare, and swimming, or even paddling, is not advised.

from *The Rough Guide to Megerra*

The journey took me clear of Megacity, which is a rare experience for me. My new sports model took me along the rutted freeways, off on minor roads and winding muddy lanes, and finally over rough open country. She flew over the roughest terrain like a bird – I was proud of her.

We came eventually to a castle set on a rocky headland. I recognized the place as soon as I saw it. There'd been an item in the newscasts last time it had changed hands. Now I knew who I was going to see.

Like so many things on Megerra, the castle was a fake, built by some mad mining magnate who later went bust. It had thick walls in the local black stone, along with battlements, turrets, towers and all the usual old stuff you see on historical holovids. It looked as if the original owner had a sense of the dramatic.

There were massive iron gates in front of the castle, which opened silently at our approach. The sporthover moved smoothly up a winding path and stopped at a circular parking area littered with hoverlimos. Just for once I didn't feel my transport was letting me down.

A white-haired butler type in a dark suit pointed to a flight of steps. 'The master is on the terrace, sir. If you'd care to join him?'

I climbed the steep winding stairs until I reached a stone-flagged terrace overlooking the sea.

There at the top of the steps, Lucifer himself was waiting to meet me, black scales gleaming in the feeble sunlight. He looked sinister as hell, as usual, but not one little bit out of place.

'Mr Garshak,' he said. 'I trust I find you well?'

'I'm fine. How are you, Mr Lucifer? I must say you're looking pretty well too – especially since you're dead, according to the vidnews.'

'The reports of my death are gravely exaggerated,' he said solemnly. 'I am allowing them to spread for reasons of my own. In fact I was wounded, but not severely . . .' He paused. 'Forgive me, Mr Garshak – I'm a little preoccupied, but that's no excuse for being a bad host. Have a seat, sir, and a drink.'

138

We sat down at a table at the edge of the railed terrace. Far below us the sea looked like a sheet of lead. The butler type, or another exactly like him, brought our drinks, brandy for me and something purple and fizzing for Lucifer.

I sipped my drink wondering why Lucifer wanted to see me – and why I'd suddenly been upgraded from hireling to honoured guest.

After a moment Lucifer said, 'I hear you have finished your employment with Mr Nastur, Mr Garshak.'

'I guess so. I got his hovertruck and his driver back – though the driver went berserk and he had to have him killed. And as you know, I negotiated an agreement with you.'

'You did indeed, sir, and I was impressed with the way you handled it – and with the recovery of the hovertruck. You're a resourceful fellow.' He paused. 'Tell me, are you particularly bound to the service of Mr Nastur?'

'I don't owe Nastur anything.'

'Are you likely to be working for him again?'

I shook my head. 'We parted on pretty bad terms.'

'Why was that?'

'He paid me off for the job OK, but after that he tried to cheat me. I don't like to be cheated. I had to be pretty firm with him.'

Lucifer smiled. 'I imagine you could do that very effectively.'

I drank some more brandy. 'Forgive me for asking, but why are you so interested in my career?'

'I wish to employ your services, Mr Garshak.'

'To do what?'

'To discover who is trying to have me killed.'

11

CONTACTS

Both Bernice and Chris slept late after the excitement of the previous night. Lucifer's guards had promptly whisked him away in a suddenly appearing black hoverlimo. Chris and Bernice had been left to deal with the Megacity police, who had turned up when all the real action was over.

The police had whisked them away to the local station house to make a statement. Chris had kept it simple. They'd been coming out of Sara's Cellar when they'd seen a fellow customer, who'd left a little earlier, under attack by a Wolverine gang. Naturally they'd gone to help.

The Megacity cops didn't seem to think it was natural at all. They hammered away at Chris and Bernice for ages, together and separately, trying to get them to admit that they were mixed up with Lucifer in some criminal conspiracy. Either that or they'd been in alliance with the Wolverines setting up the ambush.

'Didn't you and Lucifer have some kind of face-off inside the club?' demanded one detective.

'There was a minor misunderstanding over a table reservation,' said Chris wearily. 'It was all cleared up perfectly amicably.'

The detective turned to Bernice. 'I hear you actually took a shot at him.'

'I was showing him this lipstick blaster gadget I'd just

bought at Nieman's,' said Bernice. 'I wasn't too sure how it worked and it went off accidentally. A waiter got a nasty shock, but nobody was hurt.'

When both obstinately refused to change their stories, the police recorded their statements and let them go. It wasn't until the small hours of the morning that a police hovercar deposited them back at Little Louie's Hotel and Piano Bar.

The hotel was still open – nothing in Megacity ever seemed to close – and their arrival had caused no particular stir. As Chris said, it suggested that Louie was quite used to his guests arriving – or leaving – in police custody.

Now they were having a late breakfast in their sitting room, discussing the previous night's events.

Bernice yawned. 'If that's a typical night out in Megacity . . .'

'It doesn't seem to change much,' said Chris. 'Roz and I ran into a Wolverine ambush on the exact same spot, when we were chasing the Ripper. As soon as I caught a whiff of Wolverine . . .'

'The Wolverines were bad enough, but it was the cops who really wore me down.'

Chris, still an Adjudicator at heart, felt compelled to defend the police. 'Don't forget, as far as they're concerned, we're a couple of bad characters Chief Harkon wanted to deport. Being hassled by cops is excellent for our cover.'

'Well, what next?' demanded Bernice.

Chris sighed. 'Have a bit of patience, Benny. I know a lot seems to have happened but we've still only just arrived. We've got to establish ourselves, make a few contacts.'

'You seemed to be making plenty of contact last night.'

Before Chris could reply Louie's voice came from the comm unit.

'Some dame on the comm – wants to talk to Chris. You here?'

Chris shrugged. 'I suppose so.'

Seconds later Sara's voice came from the comm unit.

'Chris? It's Sara. From the club, remember?'

'How could he forget?' muttered Bernice.

Chris glared at her and said, 'Yes, of course I remember.' Rather feebly he added, 'Er, hello.'

'I just wanted to be sure you were all right. I heard about the trouble outside the club, but by the time I managed to get outside you were gone. Someone said you'd been arrested.'

'Not exactly. Just helping the police with their enquiries.'

'And you're not hurt? Not wounded or anything?'

'Not a scratch.'

'I was afraid you might have been killed, like poor Lucifer.'

'What?'

'But you were there. Didn't you know? It was on the news this morning.'

'He collapsed and his own people whisked him away. Right after that we got scooped up by the cops. I didn't know he was dead . . .'

'Well . . .' There was a pause. 'I wondered if you might like to come over to the club for a drink. Or we could have lunch. Another pause. 'And your little friend too, of course – if she's free.'

Chris glanced at Bernice, who was sitting staring straight ahead of her. 'Benny?'

Rapidly she shook her head.

Chris turned back to the comm unit. 'She is not my little friend –'

'Glad to hear it.'

Ignoring this, Chris went on, 'Anyway, she's busy.'

'What about you?'

Chris looked worriedly at Bernice, who nodded vigorously.

'I'm pretty busy too – but I think I might manage lunch.'

'I'll look forward to it.'

The comm unit went dead.

Chris turned back to Bernice. 'I'm sorry, Benny, about Lucifer. You liked him, didn't you?'

'I scarcely knew him, did I? One near fight and a couple of drinks.'

'What about this invitation? Don't you want to go?'

'She wants me there like a hole in the head. You go, Chris.' Bernice managed a grin. 'Like you said, we need to make a few good contacts. You'll do much better at contacting Sara without me around.'

'I can't leave you alone.'

'Oh yes you can. I can always do some more shopping. And I want to do some research as well. There must be a computer library somewhere. This place can't be all mines and nightclubs.'

'What sort of research?'

'Just research. I'm supposed to be a scholar, remember? I can't quite pin it down yet, but I've got a vague idea we might be tackling this whole Project business quite the wrong way . . .'

'Well, if you're sure . . .'

'Go!' said Bernice impatiently. 'It's all in the cause of duty!'

'All right. I'll see you back here later.'

Trying not to look too eager, Chris hurried from the room.

Bernice lingered over her coffee, wondering whether to order a hovercab to Nieman-Marcus, or to try to find a library. She'd just about come down in favour of shopping when Louie's voice came again. 'Call for either you or Mr Chris.'

'Who is it?'

'Party doesn't wish to give his name. Says you met last night at the club.'

'All right, I'll talk to him.'

A deep voice said, 'I was just calling to thank you both.'

Bernice gasped, too astonished to speak.

The deep voice said, 'Hello? Are you there?'

'Somebody just told me you were dead! It was on the news.'

There was a chuckle. 'An exaggeration. It would be more accurate to say I was playing dead. But had it not been for the intervention of you and your friend, the news story would be only too accurate. I was calling to thank you, and to ask you both to come to lunch.'

'I'm afraid Chris isn't here. He's busy.'

'No doubt he has affairs of his own to attend to?'

'Well, I suppose you could put it like that.'

The deep voice said hesitantly, 'Forgive me, I am not familiar with your culture. I don't know if it would be proper . . . If you would care to come alone?'

'I should be happy to,' said Bernice.

'Excellent. It would mean a journey. I'm away from Megacity at the moment, in my place on the coast.'

'I'll be glad to get away. Will a hovercab take me?'

'That won't be necessary: I'll send transport. In about an hour?'

Bernice hurried to her bedroom, and started sorting through her new outfits. After all, Lucifer could be an important contact and she ought to look her best . . .

There's something very strange about going to a nightclub in the daytime, thought Chris. Even in Megacity . . . Still, as Benny says, it's all in the line of duty . . .

He paid off his hovercab at the end of the alley and headed for the entrance. He seemed to be expected. The heavies on the door, two exceptionally thuggish-looking Ursines, bowed respectfully and waved him through.

He went down the familiar stone stairs and into the main room. The place looked quite different by day. It was lighter, and the big room was empty except for the staff, wiping tables, washing floors and polishing glasses.

Sara sat alone on one of the stools along the bar. Chris walked over to her and she rose, took his hands and kissed him on the cheek. She was, he realized, almost as tall as he was.

'I'm glad you could come,' she said.

'Thank you for asking me.'

They smiled at the ridiculously formal phrases.

'Drink? Champagne?'

144

'Beer, please. Anything.'

She went behind the bar and poured him a beer, got herself a glass of white wine, and came back to sit beside him.

She sipped her wine. 'So tell me what happened last night.'

He gave him a brief account of the ambush, playing down his own part.

She gave him a puzzled look. 'Why did you interfere?'

'It just seemed like the thing to do.'

'Lucifer was no friend of yours – you were ready to shoot him yourself in here. Next thing, you're risking your life for him.'

Chris shrugged. 'I was ambushed by Wolverines myself once, on the same spot. When I saw them coming over the wall I just reacted without thinking.'

She studied him thoughtfully. 'Do you do that a lot?'

'React without thinking? I've never thought about it!'

She laughed.

After a moment Chris laughed too. 'Look, I just do what seems best at the time – there isn't always time to think it out.'

'Come and have some lunch.'

She led him to a concealed lift at the back of the room and they rode up to a penthouse apartment. A cold lunch was laid out in a sort of conservatory. They ate among waving green fronds and exotic many-coloured flowers. The food was light and delicious: cold meat and fish, salads, fruits, and there was champagne.

Chris looked around. 'This must be the only green garden in Megacity!'

'One of the few. Everything has to be brought in from off-planet: soil, nutrients, plants, flowers – air! It helps me to endure living in Megacity.'

Chris nodded. 'Sometimes I wonder how anyone stands it.'

'So what brings you here?'

'Why do you ask?'

'I'm interested. Perhaps I can help you.'

'I want to find out about something called the Project.'

'You mentioned it last night. What is it?'

'Something very dangerous. Something that started here a long time ago . . .' Chris told her the little he knew about the Project. 'There's a possibility it's linked to the recent wave of violence, but that's just a theory.'

She considered for a moment. 'I'll see what I can find out for you. I know a lot of people who know a lot of other people. If the Project is as big as you say, someone knows something.'

'Be careful,' warned Chris. 'Years ago it was very dangerous to talk about the Project. Maybe it still is.'

'I'll be careful.'

'You must be wondering why I want to know all this.'

'I didn't ask. If you want to know, I'll try to find out for you.'

'Why?'

She leant forward and kissed him.

Chris drew a deep breath. 'That seems like a pretty good reason.'

She stood up, taking his hands and drawing him to his feet.

'Maybe we can think of a few more.'

Bernice Summerfield had changed her outfit three times, deciding her first choice was best after all, when a worried-looking Little Louie appeared at the door to their suite.

'There's a devil downstairs for you,' he announced.

'I'm sorry?'

'One of those scaly guys – a Demoniac. Most people call them devils. Not to their face, mind you – they reckon it's insulting.'

'Right,' said Bernice. 'I'll be right down.'

Louie gave her a worried look. 'You sure you know what you're doing?'

'I think so. Why?'

'Those Demoniacs are pretty scary. They keep to themselves mostly – and most people like it that way.'

'Thanks, Louie. I'll be all right.'

'Shouldn't you wait for Mr Chris?'

'Mr Chris is busy.' Bernice smiled. 'Urgent private affairs. It's all right, Louie – I'm only going out for lunch with a friend.'

She followed Louie down to the foyer where, as he'd informed her, a devil was waiting. This one was smaller and broader than Lucifer, and his scales, instead of being black, had a reddish tinge. Bernice recognized him as one of Lucifer's bodyguards from the night before. He bowed as she appeared.

'My name is Ezekiel, madame. Zeke, if you prefer. If you will come with me?'

Watched by a still-worried Little Louie, he led her outside to where a big black hoverlimo was waiting. It looked, thought Bernice, uncomfortably like a hearse.

Ezekiel opened the passenger door, settled her in the back, and got into the driver's seat. The hoverlimo zoomed smoothly away.

As Bernice settled back into the luxuriously padded interior of the hoverlimo, Ezekiel's voice came from the front.

'Drinks, drugs, and a variety of light refreshments are available in the locker in front of you, madame.'

'Nothing, thanks, I've not long had breakfast.'

'If you touch the button on the armrest to your right, it will activate the vidscreen.'

'Thank you.'

She touched the button out of curiosity, and a small vidscreen in the partition ahead of her came alive. It seemed to be showing Megacity's version of a rolling news service.

There was a sensational report of the ambush outside Sara's Cellar with a dramatic commentary over after-the-event footage consisting mostly of gruesome shots of dead Wolverines.

Next came an interview with the Mayor, who deplored the rising tide of violence in Megacity, and promised stern measures to deal with the growing menace of the Wolverine street gangs.

This was followed by an interview with Chief Harkon. He deplored the violence as well, and gave a pledge of increased police activity.

Immediately afterwards came reports of another outrage, a Wolverine attack on a used hovercar lot on Spaceport Boulevard.

This featured burning hovercars, and a gorilla-like individual called Happy Mike, brandishing the fearsome laser cannon with which he'd blown the attackers away. When more dead Wolverines appeared on screen, Bernice switched off with a shudder.

'Isn't there any good news in Megacity?'

'Very little, madame,' said Ezekiel solemnly. 'It has always been a dangerous and violent place – and lately things seem to have been getting worse.'

'Can't think why anyone stays on this ghastly planet,' she muttered. 'Perpetual bloodshed, and smoke instead of fresh air.' She was talking to herself, but Ezekiel heard her and replied.

'Profit, madame. There is a great deal of money to be made in Megacity. As for the atmosphere, we Demoniacs feel quite comfortable here.'

'How come?'

'Our homeworld of Gehenna consists largely of active volcanoes. There is just as much smoke in the air, but for different reasons.'

Bernice settled back and watched the smog-ridden streets of Megacity flashing by. Streets gave way to big boulevards, boulevards to freeways, until at last they were streaking through open countryside. The countryside surrounding Megacity was about as scenic as the city itself, thought Bernice. Flat desolate marshland over which rolled banks of grimy fog.

They emerged at last on to a bleak and rocky coastline, ending up at what looked very like Bluebeard's Castle. As

148

they arrived they saw a flashy-looking red hovercar come out of the castle gates. As it passed them Bernice caught a glimpse of a hulking figure at the wheel. Then the hovercar streaked away across the marshlands, disappearing into the fog.

The hoverlimo went through the castle gates, climbed a narrow winding road, and stopped at a round open space.

Bernice got out and followed a white-haired butler up some stone stairs to the terrace, where Lucifer was sitting at a table, gazing out over the dull grey sea.

Lucifer rose, took Bernice's hand and touched it to his lips. As before, his hand and his lips felt almost burning.

He showed her to a seat, and sat down again.

'It was good of you to come.'

'My pleasure. But should you be entertaining visitors? You were hurt . . .'

'Not badly. Apparently a laser bolt grazed my skull. I was stunned, but it didn't take effect until a little later. We Demoniacs have notoriously thick heads.'

It didn't take effect until you *allowed* it to take effect, thought Bernice. You wouldn't let yourself collapse until the fight was over.

'Let me offer you an aperitif,' said Lucifer. He snapped long clawed fingers and the butler brought purple foaming drinks in tall glasses. 'This is one of my planet's wines,' said Lucifer. 'I believe some humans find it quite palatable.'

Bernice found the wine very palatable indeed. It had the tingle of champagne with the kick of an excellent brandy. She drained her glass at once, largely through nervousness, and the butler immediately refilled it from a silver flask.

'I could grow very fond of this stuff,' she said.

Lucifer smiled. 'I am glad. But if I might advise caution? The usual limit for humanoids is three.'

'Then you have to get them down off the chandeliers,' said Bernice. The purple wine was already producing a pleasant mild euphoria. Under its influence, Bernice blurted out the first thing that came into her head. 'Can you fly?'

149

Lucifer rose to his full height, and spread the stubby wings that lay folded on his bony shoulders. 'With these? On this planet, no.' He folded his wings and sat down. 'We manage fairly well on our homeworld, however. The gravity is lower, the atmosphere thicker, and the exploding volcanoes provide constant updraughts of warm air. Flight is one of the things we sacrifice when we leave Gehenna.'

'Don't you miss it?'

'Sometimes.'

'Why leave then?'

'Career opportunities on Gehenna are limited,' he said gravely. 'Not that life is dull. The planet is newly formed in geological terms, and the surface is still changing. But one must expend a great deal of energy in simply surviving. It can get very monotonous avoiding constant earthquakes, suddenly appearing chasms and streams of molten lava.'

'I can see how it might,' said Bernice.

'So some of us leave Gehenna in search of more rewarding lives,' said Lucifer.

'Are you all –' Bernice realized what she was about to say, and suddenly stopped.

'Criminals?' Lucifer shook his head. 'We make good scholars, soldiers, administrators. But this sector of the galaxy is human-dominated, and most humans find us rather intimidating. It tends to hold back your promotion if people faint when they see you. Crime, however, offers rapid rewards – and an intimidating appearance can be a positive advantage.'

'I'm sorry,' said Bernice suddenly. 'All this is really none of my business . . .'

'Not at all. I find your conversation refreshing. As I told you when we first met, I seldom get the chance to talk to human females. The few I do meet tend to be cautious and formal . . .'

'You mean they don't try to steal your reserved nightclub table, threaten to shoot you and ask you outrageously personal questions?'

150

'Rarely! Now, let me ask you some questions of my own.' He leant forward, fixing her with slanting red eyes. 'Why are you and your companion pretending to be desperate criminals when you are no such thing?'

Bernice tried to stall. 'What do you mean?'

'Your act last night was quite convincing. But that was all it was – an act. You are neither a criminal nor a killer.'

'How can you be so sure?'

'I am both,' said Lucifer. 'That's how I know you are neither.'

It would be insane to trust him, to tell him the truth, thought Bernice, and promptly decided to do just that.

'We came to Megacity to uncover a criminal scheme called the Project. We posed as criminals because we thought that might make it easier to find out what we wanted to know.'

'You mentioned this Project last night. What can you tell me about it?'

'Not much.' Bernice told him the little that she knew. 'I hope this doesn't mean we end up on opposite sides.'

Lucifer shook his head. 'This Project is nothing to do with me – I know nothing of it. Besides, it is impossible for us to be enemies now.'

'It is?' Suddenly Bernice felt very pleased – and rather alarmed. 'Why?'

'Because of the blood debt.'

'I'm sorry?'

'You and your companion saved my life last night. Now I am sworn to your service. If I can, I will help you to find your Project . . .'

12

REUNION

—

As I left Lucifer's castle, a human female arrived in a black hoverlimo. She was no one I'd seen before, and as I drove my new red sporthover back towards Megacity, I wondered idly who she was.

Then again, Lucifer's private life was no business of mine. It was his professional life that concerned me – presumably that was why someone was trying to kill him.

I was pretty sure that the Wolverine ambush outside Sara's Cellar was an attempted hit. Assassination to order was a Wolverine speciality, which meant someone had paid for the attack. Which meant, in turn, that someone wanted Lucifer dead pretty badly – a Wolverine hit squad doesn't come cheap. Wolverines are good at their work and Lucifer had been lucky to walk away.

He'd told me a couple he'd met at the club had helped him fight off the Wolverines. He'd been lucky there too – good Samaritans are hard to come by in Megacity.

Lucifer had also told me that the Wolverines' leader was in a weird kind of state. Berserk, he called it. Wolverines are your cool, sneaky kind of killers. They attack when they've got you outnumbered and their style is to hit and run. Their only loyalty is to each other, to the pack. Capture one and offer a deal, and he'll sell out his employer to save his own hide without even thinking about it.

Lucifer said this one had been in a killing frenzy. He also said it looked like a skoob high – only skoob hadn't been around for years. It was one drug at which even Megacity drew the line. I'd pretty well stamped it out during my time as Police Chief, and nobody had dared import it since.

Until now, anyway.

I began thinking about the Wolverine attack on *me* at Happy Mike's hovercar lot. I remembered that one of my Wolverine attackers had mad eyes and a muzzle that dripped foam . . .

I'd assumed it had been a simple revenge attack. I'd hurt their sensitive feelings by recovering Nastur's stolen hovertruck. But then again, that wasn't typical Wolverine behaviour. To them murder is strictly a matter of business.

Sure, they'd hold a grudge. They'd kill me if the chance came up and they could do it safely, and without too much trouble. But to risk mounting an attack in broad daylight on Spaceport Boulevard . . .

Would they do that if nobody was paying them? I started to think about who might want me dead – and about who knew where I might be on that particular morning.

I remembered telling Nastur about having my eye on a red sporthover in Happy Mike's used-hover lot.

At this point in my series of brilliant deductions I noticed I was being followed.

It was a big black hoverlimo and it was gaining on me fast. At first I wasn't particularly alarmed. I assumed it was the one I'd seen delivering the human female to Lucifer's castle.

I assumed that until the black glass window slid down and the Wolverine in the back started blasting at me with a laser rifle.

Luckily for me he was overeager. He fired too soon but not too straight – the laser bolt seared a black line across the red paintwork of my new sporthover.

I spun the sporthover around in a tight turn. Before he knew it I was around behind him. I had my own window open by now, and my blaster in my hand. I zoomed up alongside, fired through the open window and saw the Wolverine slump back.

But there was still the driver. He slammed the big hover-limo into my lighter sporthover, sending me spinning away out of control, off the road and over the marsh.

I fought to regain control, got the sporthover stabilized – and saw the hoverlimo zooming towards me again. I couldn't match it for weight and power. All I had was manoeuvrability.

I hit the rise-jets, shot straight up in the air, and the hoverlimo slid underneath me. I cut the power and the sporthover dropped on to the hoverlimo roof, slamming it down into the marsh.

Pinned down by the added weight of the sporthover, the limo started to sink. That was fine by me – except that I was sitting on top of the hoverlimo, and, unless I got out of there, I was going under as well.

I hit the rise-jet control again – nothing happened.

The hoverlimo sank lower – and so did I.

I heard a frantic squealing from below and looked out of my window. The Wolverine driver was trying to get out of the limo – but it had already sunk too far, and the door was blocked with glutinous mud.

I hit the controls again – still nothing. The jolt on landing must have damaged the circuits.

With a sinister sucking sound, the hoverlimo sank lower. I heard a mud-choked scream from the driver, we sank lower still . . .

The sporthover's power drive caught and we lurched into the air – just as the limo disappeared beneath the mud.

I headed thankfully back for the road, and sent my battered sporthover limping back towards Megacity.

Back in town I headed straight for Happy Mike's car lot. Fortunately, I found him in a good mood. He'd recorded his vidnews interview, and was happily playing it over and over again. With the aid of some of my remaining credits, I persuaded him to let me trade in the sporthover for a nearly new Oldshover. It was grey, beat-up looking, but with an excellent drive unit. I was beginning to see disadvantages in being too noticeable.

I stopped off at a liquor store to replenish my supply of *vragg* and then headed back for the office to do some serious thinking.

Cat was back on the balcony, so I poured him a saucer of *vragg*, and a slug for myself.

I started thinking about the latest attack. They'd picked me up on the way back from Lucifer's castle, which suggested that someone was having the place watched. Someone, maybe, who was worried about Lucifer, worried about me, and doubly worried about the two of us getting together.

I mulled things over for a while and decided I needed to talk to Nastur. I also needed some backup – which meant I needed Murkar back on the payroll.

I knew he'd been working for Little Louie on and off, and decided to go and look for him at Louie's hotel.

When I got there I found Louie in the foyer arguing with a big blond guy who looked vaguely familiar.

'You mean you just let her go off?' the guy was saying.

'So what was I supposed to do?' protested Louie. 'She wanted to go. It wasn't like she was kidnapped. Some devil turned up with a hoverlimo and off she went.'

Suddenly I remembered the woman I'd seen arriving at the castle. I broke in on the argument.

'Are you worried about a medium-sized lady in a black dress with a hat and a veil?'

'That's right,' said the blond guy. 'Have you seen her?'

'If it's the same one she's visiting a Demoniac called Lucifer at his house on the coast.'

'Is she all right?'

'As far as I could tell she was fine.'

The big guy was staring at me. 'It's Garshak, isn't it?'

I looked hard at him and realized we'd met before somewhere. 'That takes care of me. What about you?'

'Chris Cwej,' he said. 'We met when you were Chief of Police.'

Suddenly it all came back to me. This big blond guy and a small dark woman. They'd turned up in Megacity, claiming to be Pinks on the trail of a serial killer they called the Ripper. They'd found him, too, although not until he'd carved up Raggor, and made a shambles of Raggor's Cavern. Their killer had fled the planet and I'd packed them off after him.

It had all happened a long time ago.

I looked at the big blond guy, remembering. The little dark woman had been the boss in those days. I remembered how she'd bullied me in my own office. The blond guy looked older now, and harder. He'd grown up.

'How's your partner?' I asked. 'Tough little dark lady.'

'Dead,' he said briefly. 'I've got a new partner now.'

Suddenly things came together. 'Did the two of you help a Demoniac called Lucifer fight off a Wolverine ambush? Last night, outside Sara's Cellar?'

'That's right. How did you know?'

'I've just been hearing all about it,' I said. 'Lucifer hired me to look into it.'

'Hired you?'

'That's right. I'm a private eye these days.'

The big guy drew a deep breath and turned to Little Louie.

'Is the bar open, Louie?'

'Sure,' said Louie. 'We never close.'

'Can I buy you a drink, Mr Garshak?' the big guy asked.

'By all means, Mr Cwej.'

'Is this a private party?' asked a female voice. 'Or can I come too?'

The woman I'd seen at Lucifer's castle had come into the lobby. Outside, a big black hoverlimo was pulling away.

The big guy grabbed her shoulders. 'Benny! Are you all right?'

'I'm fine,' she said coolly. 'I've just been having lunch with Lucifer. I thought you were the one in danger. How are you?'

The big guy blushed. 'Fine, fine,' he said hurriedly. 'Sara was very helpful . . .'

'I just bet she was.'

'This is Mr Garshak, Bernice. Roz and I met him when we first came to Megacity. He was Chief of Police then. Now he's a private eye. He's working for Lucifer. Mr Garshak, may I introduce Bernice Summerfield – sometimes known as the Dragon Lady.'

She looked at me and nodded. 'I saw you. You left just as I arrived.' She turned to the big guy. 'Lucifer wants to help too, Chris. He says he owes us a blood debt.'

'Maybe we can all help each other,' I said. 'How about that drink, Louie?'

'Come this way,' said Louie, and ushered us into the bar.

It was empty at this time of day, and we settled ourselves at a corner table. Louie brought the drinks, *vragg* for me, ale for Chris, white wine for the lady, and discreetly made himself scarce.

We raised our glasses in a silent toast, sipped our drinks and looked thoughtfully at each other.

I turned to Chris. 'So who are you chasing this time?'

'I wish I knew,' he said. 'It's all rather vague.'

The woman, Bernice, said, 'Have you ever heard of the Project?'

I shook my head. 'What Project?'

Chris sighed. 'That's part of the problem.'

He told me how his old partner, Roz Forrester, had picked up something about some big-time scheme or scam or conspiracy called the Project, when they first came to Megacity. How they'd had no time to follow it up then, but he'd come back to look into it now.

'Why?' I asked.

'I promised Roz we'd come back and check it out some day. She can't now, so I have. It was unfinished business.'

I looked at Bernice. 'And you?'

'I've been friends of Roz and Chris for a long time. I didn't want to get involved at first. But as soon as I so much as talked to Chris someone tried to kill me – and killed a young friend of mine instead. I got fired from my job and framed on trumped-up charges. Now it's personal.'

'We'd like to hire you as well,' said Chris. 'Can you help us find the Project?'

I shook my head. 'Against the private eye code. One client at a time. Unless . . .'

'Unless what?' asked Bernice.

'Unless there's a connection.'

Chris frowned. 'Why should there be?'

'Lucifer was attacked by Wolverines – so was I. You know Lucifer, I know Lucifer, I know you.'

'Chance, surely?'

'Or serendipity,' I said. 'Sometimes I think there's no such thing as coincidence.'

'Something else,' said Bernice. 'Senseless violent crime has been rising steadily ever since Chris and Roz were first here. I think it's got something to do with the Project.'

'Why?' I asked again.

'Instinct! Post hoc –'

'Is not necessarily propter hoc,' I said.

Chris looked baffled.

Bernice explained. 'Because something happened *after* something else, it doesn't necessarily mean it happened *because* of that something else.'

'Maybe not,' said Chris. 'But Roz Forrester's informant, the one who mysteriously committed suicide, said the Project was bound to get out of control and there'd be blood on the streets. He also said it would spread to hundreds of other worlds.'

I downed my *vragg* and signalled to Louie for another round.

When the drinks had come and Louie had gone I said, 'You were talking about senseless violence.'

Chris nodded. 'So?'

'If it is getting worse – and I agree with you, it is – I can think of a possible reason.'

158

Bernice leant forward. 'Let's hear it.'

'Did you ever hear of a drug called skoob?'

Bernice looked blank but Chris said, 'Yes of course – skoob! I've heard of it, but I never encountered it. I went to some lectures on the history of it when I was . . . when I was in my old job. It had been stamped out on my homeworld by then.'

'It was supposed to have been stamped out everywhere,' I said. 'Nowhere would tolerate it, not even Megacity.'

Bernice said, ' So what is this stuff?'

'It was discovered on some godforsaken jungle planet,' said Chris. 'Extracted from the root of some rare plant. The natives used it in their religious ceremonies.'

'And what does it do to people?'

'Produces an immediate incredible high, followed almost at once by acute withdrawal symptoms,' I said. 'The addict will pay any price, do anything, to get more. If he can't he goes paranoid.'

Chris said, 'But even if he does get more, he passes into a state of even more violent paranoia. Skoob spread right through this section of the galaxy, but it caused so much havoc that every planetary government cooperated in stamping it out.'

'Even the drug lords banned it in the end,' I said. 'What's the use of customers who are likely to kill you if you don't supply them, and almost certain to kill you if you do?'

'And you think someone's smuggling it in again?' asked Bernice.

'It's possible.'

Chris shook his head. 'It's hard to see how. The plant would only grow on this one planet – something to do with unique soil make-up. The problem was so bad that a number of planetary governments formed an alliance to deal with it. They invaded the planet, rooted out and burnt every last skoob plant, and put the planet under permanent quarantine.'

'That was a long time ago,' I said. 'Maybe they missed a plant or two and the stuff re-established itself. Maybe the quarantine authority grew lax, or got corrupted, and a nice quiet little skoob industry started up again.'

Bernice leant forward eagerly. 'Or maybe someone discovered how to synthesize, the stuff, manufacture it artificially. Perhaps that was the Project! Maybe they thought they'd found a way to control the side effects. That could have been what Roz's informant meant. So they used Megacity as a test market – but the side effects started creeping back.'

'Steady on,' said Chris. 'It's a nice little theory, but that's all it is, a theory. We haven't a scrap of proof.'

'We might be able to get some,' I said.

'Where?' demanded Bernice.

'A while ago a nasty piece of work called Nastur lost a shipment of booze and drugs,' I said. 'He lost it because one of his own men went berserk. It went missing in Lucifer's territory, and ended up in Wolverine hands – after which a number of Wolverines went berserk. Nastur was desperate to get the shipment back – which was why he hired me. Since then attempts have been made to kill Lucifer – and to kill me.'

Chris looked baffled. 'Why?'

'As for Lucifer, could be a lot of things – he's not short of enemies. But for me – maybe just because I knew about that shipment. Maybe because someone was afraid I'd found out too much.'

'So where is this shipment now?' demanded Bernice.

'Nastur's warehouse. I recovered it, and gave it back to him.'

'What did you do that for?'

'That was what I was paid for. At the time I thought it was just a routine shipment. Perhaps it is.'

'And perhaps it isn't!' said Bernice. She looked from me to Chris, her face alive with excitement. 'I think we ought to find out, don't you?'

'Wonderful!' I said. 'I suppose you're going to turn up at his warehouse and have a little chat with him?'

'Yes,' she said. 'That's exactly what I'm going to do.'

13

RAID

The brown-furred Ursine on guard outside Nastur's warehouse slumped against the doorpost and yawned. A big black hoverlimo slid quietly around the corner. Hurriedly the guard straightened up, tried to look tough and alert. Could be someone important, and it wouldn't do to be caught slacking. Things were pretty tense around the place these days. For some reason old Nastur was in a hell of an evil mood – and that same bad mood had spread all the way down the chain of command.

The limo sighed to a halt and a big fair-haired human got out of the back seat. He opened the door and a female got out. Like the man, she was dressed all in black.

The big man slapped the roof of the hoverlimo and it drifted away. The woman looked at the guard and said, 'Nastur.'

He gaped at her and the big man said, 'The lady wants to see Nastur, dummy. Go and tell him she's here.'

The Ursine guard gaped some more. 'Listen, I don't think –'

'You're not equipped to think,' said the woman coldly. 'Just go and tell Nastur he's got a visitor.'

The guard reached out for the touchpad in the post, giving the signal that opened the small door set into the large one.

The door opened and he went inside.

* * *

In the big floodlit yard a black-furred Ursine, one of the sub-bosses, was checking packing cases against a list.

He looked up. 'So why ain't you outside?'

'Visitors for Mr Nastur, boss,' said the guard importantly.

'Names?'

'They didn't say.'

The sub-boss sighed. 'They didn't say. Number?'

'How's that?'

'How many?' said the sub-boss wearily. 'You did count them? Or were there more than three?'

'No, just two,' said the guard, relieved. 'Humans, a big guy and a small dame.'

'They got an appointment?'

'How's that, boss?'

The sub-boss sighed again. 'I know, they didn't say. Why don't you just chase them off? Mr Nastur doesn't want street bums coming round bothering him.'

'These aren't bums, boss. They arrived in this big black limo and they're dressed real sharp. They look like they're important.'

The sub-boss frowned. He was no more anxious than the guard to make any mistakes, not with Nastur in his present foul mood.

'You're sure there are only two? Maybe they've got an army hidden in the limo.'

The guard shook his head. 'They sent the limo away.'

'OK, let's take a look at them. Send them in.'

The guard went out, and the sub-boss called over two human bodyguards. 'Visitors. Watch 'em.'

The bodyguards nodded, picked up their laser rifles and stood flanking the door.

The sub-boss watched as the two strangers came into the yard. The sentry retreated outside, closing the door behind him. The visitors, whoever they were, were trapped. They might find getting out a lot harder than getting in.

The sub-boss studied the two strangers. The woman, clearly the one in charge, glanced casually around the

162

yard. She didn't seem impressed. The big man, standing protectively behind her, looked around as well, but his survey was very different. The sub-boss saw him checking the number of guards, their position, the weapons they carried, escape routes and cover in case of trouble. This was a professional.

The sub-boss said bluntly, 'You armed?'

The woman said, 'Of course we're armed.'

He nodded towards a nearby packing case. 'On top of the case there. Slowly.'

Covered by the two bodyguards, the woman took a slim blaster from her bag and tossed it on to the packing case. The big man took a heavy hand blaster from under his arm and put it carefully beside the woman's one.

The sub-boss approached and without being told the big man raised his arms, holding them out from his sides. Quickly and efficiently the sub-boss patted him down. He turned to the woman. 'You too, lady.'

The woman raised her arms. 'You can look but don't touch.'

The sub-boss walked around her, until he was satisfied that there was no sign of the bulge of even the smallest of blasters.

'OK. Now what do you want here?'

'We want to see Nastur.'

'Who does?'

'We'll tell him that.'

The sub-boss shook his head. 'It doesn't work like that. I gotta have a name the boss will recognize. Your name, a contact name, whatever.'

The woman said, 'Tell Nastur Miss Dragon and Mr Christopher are here to see him. Tell him we come from Emil Malek.'

The sub-boss said, 'You better be telling the truth, lady.' He turned and walked into the cavernous warehouse.

He found Nastur is his usual place in the back, sitting in his special chair, surrounded by boxes, crates and barrels. His two underbosses, both human, were with him. Some kind of conference was going on.

Nastur glared at him with orange eyes. 'Well?'

'Something's come up, Mr Nastur.' Briefly he told of the arrival of the two strangers. 'The dame calls herself Dragon, the guy's called Christopher.'

'Two people walk in off the street and you expect me to see them?'

'You want them thrown out, I'll throw them out. You want them killed, I'll have them killed. Only . . .'

'Only what?'

'They look convincing, they sound convincing and they gave Malek's name. It's up to you, boss.'

Nastur pondered, blinking furiously.

As she stood waiting for Nastur's hairy henchman to return, Bernice Summerfield wondered what the hell she was doing here. It was all the more puzzling, since the whole scheme had been her idea – she'd had to talk the others into it.

She was reminded of the old story about the man who took off all his clothes and jumped into a patch of stinging nettles. Asked afterwards why ever he'd done such a thing, he replied, 'Well, it seemed a good idea at the time!'

And there was the other story about the man found fast asleep in a blazing bed. Asked if he knew how the bed had caught fire he said, 'Hell no, it was on fire when I got in.'

Now, belatedly, she was wondering if her scheme would really work. It all depended on whether she could keep this Nastur character convinced and interested for long enough. Garshak had warned her she wouldn't even get an audience without a contact name. Reluctantly, he had given her one – that of the legendary Emil Malek, rumoured to be the current head of the equally legendary Combine.

A loose amalgamation of the Mafia-type organizations on a hundred worlds, the Combine was the largest known criminal organization in the galaxy. The Capo di Tutti Capi

– the Combine was deeply conservative and clung to the old Mafia terminology – was a shadowy figure called Emil Malek. Even to know his name was a kind of criminal credential.

So far the Combine had left Megacity alone. Murderously efficient where it had to be, the Combine preferred to make its money as peacefully as possible, and Megacity had been considered too violent and undisciplined. But Megacity was also immensely profitable and, again according to Garshak, a Combine takeover was something every Megacity crime boss dreaded.

Claiming to come from Emil Malek was a dangerous gambit. It just might buy them a hearing and even a measure of protection. Or it might, of course, provoke immediate execution, depending on how paranoid Nastur turned out to be.

The henchman appeared in the doorway of the warehouse and summoned them with a jerk of his head. Dropping back into her Dragon Lady persona, Bernice stalked towards him, Chris following behind. The two bodyguards fell in behind them both.

Their guide led them through an enormous shadowy warehouse, stacked with boxes, crates and barrels of every shape and size. Filled, presumably with stolen goods, thought Bernice. Hovertrucks were parked around the sides of the warehouse area and she kept an eye out for the one they were interested in. Garshak had described it as well as he could – old, grey, dirty, battered and scarred with laser burns. But one old hovertruck looks much like another, and the warehouse was full of them.

'I can tell you exactly where you'll find that hovertruck,' Garshak had said. 'Right next to Nastur himself. If I'm right about what's in it, he won't let it out of his sight.'

They came up to a little group of figures, gathered under a light-globe in the centre of the warehouse. Dominating the group was the extraordinary figure of Nastur. Gross, slimy, toadlike, he sat in his specially made chair, which, according to Garshak, he never left, and was staring at her with huge orange eyes.

Not far away, to Nastur's left and her right, was a battered old grey hovertruck, its sides scarred with laser burns.

So far, so good, thought Bernice.

She and Chris came to a halt just before Nastur's chair. He waved the henchman away, but the two armed bodyguards remained.

Bernice met Nastur's orange glare with her best Dragon Lady stare and inclined her head very slightly. 'Mr Nastur? I bring greetings from Emil Malek.'

Nastur made no reply. The eyes blinked once, that was all.

Bernice plunged ahead with her carefully prepared spiel.

'Mr Malek feels that it is time for him to extend his operations to Megacity. For this reason he has dispatched me to initiate discussions with certain prominent local businessmen such as yourself.'

Nastur spoke for the first time in a wheezing, unctuous voice that fully matched the unpleasantness of his appearance.

'I am honoured indeed, Miss . . . Miss Dragon? But what if I do not wish for the privilege of allying myself with Mr Malek?'

Bernice gave him her most sinister smile. 'Mr Malek tends to take the position that those who are not with him are against him.' She paused to let this sink in and went on, 'He prefers, where possible, to follow a policy of friendly association. But if this is not possible there is an alternative policy that serves equally well.'

'And that is?' hissed Nastur.

'Extermination.'

There was an angry growl from Nastur's henchmen. He held up a broad flipper-like hand to silence them.

'Mr Malek has been happy to ignore events in Megacity for many years. May I ask what has caused this change in policy?'

'You must ask Mr Malek himself,' said Bernice. 'I imagine,' she added casually, 'that recent increases in Megacity's

166

profitability, due to the Project, might have something to do with it.'

'The Project?'

Nastur seemed genuinely puzzled – just like everyone else, thought Bernice. 'You could scarcely hope to keep something of such scope as the Project a secret for ever,' she persisted.

'I know nothing of any Project,' said Nastur dismissively.

'Just as you know nothing of the trade in the drug skoob?'

Nastur's eyes flicked towards the battered old hovertruck.

'That is another matter. What do you know of skoob?'

'There is very little that Mr Malek does not know.'

Nastur examined her thoughtfully. 'I think you are lying . . .'

Garshak drove the big black hoverlimo around the back of the warehouse yard and sat it down close to the fence. He grinned to himself, remembering what a job it had been persuading Happy Mike to let him hire it.

'Bad things happen to hovers when you get your hands on them, Garshak,' Happy Mike had growled.

Garshak had promised to return the hoverlimo the very next day – without a scratch.

He got out of the limo, climbed carefully on to the roof and took a flying leap over the fence, clearing it by millimetres. He hit the ground on the other side and rolled over into a patch of shadow. He crouched there for a moment, waiting, hoping nobody had heard the thud he'd made on landing.

Somebody had.

He heard a nervous voice from somewhere nearby.

'You hear that?'

A bored voice said, 'Hear what?'

'Sounds like something jumped over the fence.'

'Werecat probably.'

'Hell of a big werecat.'

The nervous one appeared around the corner of the building, a human guard with a laser rifle. Garshak let him get past the patch of shadow, reached out and grabbed his ankle and

167

yanked him off his feet. The guard gave an astonished squawk. As he hit the ground a huge fist hit him behind the ear and he collapsed.

The squawk brought the second guard running. He tripped over his friend's body, and as he scrambled to his feet Garshak rose up out of the shadows and chopped him down again. After dragging both bodies into the shadow, Garshak moved on. Good thing they were both humanoid, he thought. Rabbit-punching an Ursine was like hitting a tree.

Garshak knew exactly where he'd originally left the truck and was hoping Nastur hadn't bothered to move it. If his theory was right, Nastur wouldn't want to risk drawing attention to that particular shipment. Garshak had decided that Nastur was probably keeping the skoob-smuggling operation secret from most of his own people, hiding the stuff in everyday shipments.

Garshak moved silently forward between parked hover-trucks and stacked bales and boxes until he heard Bernice's voice. He edged nearer until he was close enough to see her. She and Chris were standing in front of Nastur and a group of his people. Just to one side of them was an old grey hovertruck scarred with laser burns. The truck he'd hauled out of Wolverine territory.

Garshak listened for a moment. Bernice was putting on a pretty convincing act, he thought.

'It's no use your asking me any more questions, Mr Nastur,' she was saying. 'I have no intention of answering them. I have delivered my message. If you are not interested in Mr Malek's proposition, there are others who will be. I have been instructed to contact a Mr Lucifer next.'

She was playing it pretty cool, thought Garshak admiringly, but it just wasn't working. Nastur was still suspicious and he wasn't buying her pitch.

'You will contact nobody,' hissed Nastur furiously. 'Certainly not that vile and unspeakable devil Lucifer.' He managed to calm down. 'To be honest I am not sure what to make of you, Miss Dragon. You know too little to be what you claim you are, and too much about my affairs for your own good. I am not sure what your real purpose is, but you will tell me. Oh yes, you will tell me. In fact, before very much longer, you will be begging to tell me. I can be most persuasive.'

Garshak bared long fangs in a silent snarl. He had already seen victims of Nastur's powers of persuasion, some dead, some still alive. They all had vital parts missing. Nastur liked to use a vibroknife.

Garshak glanced quickly across at Chris, to see his reaction. Chris didn't move or speak, but he looked poised, ready. He'd better be, thought Garshak grimly.

He started creeping towards the hovertruck . . .

Nastur glared angrily at the human female before him. He was sure she was lying. But if she was not what she claimed to be where did she find the courage to defy him? It actually seemed as if she was not afraid of him – which was utterly ridiculous. Everyone was afraid of him!

'I warn you not to do anything foolish, Nastur,' she said contemptuously. 'Allow us to leave now or you will be very sorry.'

Nastur's temper snapped. 'It is you who will be sorry. Seize her and bring her over here to me. If the man moves, kill him. And bring me a vibroknife . . .'

The hovertruck drive unit roared into life and several things happened very quickly.

As the nearest guard reached for the female she reached into the bag she carried, produced a small shining object and shot him in the head.

The big man stooped with incredible speed, rose with a blaster in his hand and shot down the second guard.

As Nastur's two underbosses clawed for their blasters, a heavy hand blaster boomed twice from the hovertruck cab and they both fell.

A massive figure leant out of the open cab door, blaster in hand, and a hated voice roared, 'Chris, Bernice, over here!

Anyone else moves and I'll smear Nastur all over this warehouse!'

Nastur quivered with fury. 'Garshak!'

The two humans sprinted for the hovercab and jumped inside.

Doors slammed and the hovertruck gathered speed.

Trapped in his chair, surrounded by the dead bodies of his guards, Nastur watched helplessly as the hovertruck zoomed across the yard and straight through the still-closed gates.

Amid a shower of wood and metal fragments, the hovertruck vanished into the night.

Nastur began screaming orders. 'Personal bodyguard squad, here to me. I want the gate guard and his sub-boss. The rest of you, get after them. Take anything that moves but catch them. Kill Garshak and the two humans and get that hovertruck back.' He grabbed a trusted aide by the arm. 'You – go to the Lair and hire every Wolverine you can find. Same orders for them. I want Garshak and his friends dead and the hovertruck back here. Tell them I'll pay top rates, whatever they want!'

Hovercars, hovertrucks and even the odd hoverbike began roaring through the shattered gates.

When everyone had gone, the warehouse was silent and half empty. Nastur sat in his chair, bodyguards around him.

Before them stood the two Ursines – the gate guard and his sub-boss.

Nastur's orange eyes turned on the gate guard.

'You let them in.'

The sub-boss said, 'He checked with me, boss. It's not really his fault.'

The implacable orange eyes turned on the sub-boss. 'You brought them to me.'

Resigned, the sub-boss said, 'He checked with me, I checked with you, you said bring them in. Your decision, boss.'

'So it was all my fault,' said Nastur. 'I suppose all I can really say is, be more careful next time.'

170

The sub-boss didn't speak. Black-haired Ursines are brighter.

The brown-furred gate guard said, 'Thanks boss, we sure will!'

'No you won't,' said Nastur.

'Boss?'

'There won't be any next time,' said Nastur.

He waved to his bodyguards and they blasted the two Ursines down.

14

GARSHAK'S STING

As the hovertruck rocketed along the highway, Bernice said indignantly, 'This wasn't the plan, you know!'

Garshak glanced over his shoulder, alert for the inevitable pursuit. 'It wasn't?'

'You were supposed to sneak into the hovertruck, check it for this skoob drug, take away a sample and sneak out, while I made a dignified exit!'

'The only exit you were going to make would have been in a body bag,' said Garshak. 'Probably several different body bags! I saw it was all going wrong so I improvised.'

'Just as well you did,' said Chris. 'He saved both our lives, Benny.'

'I know,' said Bernice. 'I'm babbling because I'm still scared.' She touched Garshak's huge hairy hand where it lay on the steering wheel. 'Thanks.'

'My pleasure.' Garshak glanced over his shoulder again. 'The question now is, where do we go? My place and your hotel will soon be swarming with Nastur's boys. We need somewhere safe where we can check out this truck and plan our next move.'

'Lucifer's castle,' said Bernice instantly. 'We'll be safe there if anywhere.'

'You think he'll take us in?' asked Chris.

'Of course he will,' said Bernice confidently. 'Garshak's

working for him, isn't he? And if this drug business is behind the attack on Lucifer – he's involved in this as much as we are. Besides, he owes us, remember? All that blood-debt stuff.'

'Right,' said Garshak. 'Lucifer's castle it is.'

He swung the hovertruck at the next junction, heading out of Megacity towards the marshlands.

Back at the warehouse, Nastur's men were slowly trailing back.

To Nastur's rage they all told the same story of failure. The stolen hovertruck had got away too quickly – they had lost the trail.

There was no sign of the hovertruck or its passengers anywhere near Louie's hotel or Garshak's office.

Nastur's aide reported that the Wolverines were out in force looking for Garshak and his two accomplices. 'They were very keen,' said the aide. 'They hate Garshak so much I think they'd kill him for free.'

'They'll have to find him first,' snarled Nastur.

The truck stood in the floodlit circular area below Lucifer's castle. Bernice, Chris and Lucifer watched while Garshak made a swift and efficient search of the cargo.

It didn't take him long to find what he was searching for. One of the bales of jekkarta weed had already been torn open, and in a hollowed-out nest inside there were traces of glowing green granules. Garshak produced a long knife and ripped open another bale. Inside this was a smaller, tightly packed parcel. He punched a hole in it with his knife and green granules trickled out.

Garshak jumped out of the hovertruck and handed the package to Lucifer. 'Skoob,' he said. 'One drug smuggled inside another. Someone opened that first bale and got at the skoob. First Nastur's man, then later the Wolverines. It sent them berserk. But there's plenty more skoob left in the cargo, millions of credits' worth. No wonder Nastur was so desperate to get his hovertruck back.' He turned to Lucifer. 'I think he was afraid your men had stumbled on the secret, too, at the checkpoint. That's probably why he tried to have you killed. Me too. When I'd got the truck back, he was afraid I might have looked inside and discovered his secret.'

Lucifer nodded gravely. He looked at Chris and Bernice.

'It looks as if we have found your Project. Nastur must have been smuggling this filth into Megacity for years.'

In the baronial dining hall of Lucifer's castle the butler served drinks and a variety of food.

Lucifer raised his glass of foaming purple wine. 'To the end of the Project!'

They all drank.

Bernice said, 'I'm more than happy to drink to that. How are we going to achieve it?'

'I shall achieve it,' said Lucifer grandly. 'I shall destroy Nastur, take over his organization, find and cut off his source of supply. From now on it is war between us.'

'Why not let the police do it?' suggested Chris. 'Skoob smuggling is something no administration can afford to tolerate, not even in Megacity.'

Lucifer looked shocked. 'My dear Christopher, I am a professional criminal. I couldn't possibly go to the police.'

'We can,' said Bernice. 'You needn't be involved at all. Chris and I can go to Chief Harkon and tell him we've got proof that Nastur has been smuggling skoob.'

'There's a slight problem with that,' said Garshak.

'Which is?'

'All the evidence of skoob smuggling we've actually got is currently outside there in the courtyard. We don't want to get Mr Lucifer arrested, do we? After all, he's your friend and my employer.'

There was a moment of baffled silence.

Then Bernice said, 'In that case we shall just have to get the evidence back where it belongs – won't we, Mr Garshak?'

Garshak groaned.

* * *

Next morning Chris and Bernice sped to Megacity Police HQ in one of Lucifer's hoverlimos, accompanied by several armed guards.

Chief Harkon received them in the ornate office that had once belonged to Garshak.

'I was wondering when I'd be hearing from you two. Are you getting anywhere at all? As far as I can see, things have got worse, not better, since you arrived! The Mayor's giving me more grief as each day goes by.'

'How would you like to bust up a skoob-smuggling racket, Chief?' said Bernice. 'Wouldn't that make you the hero of the hour?'

'Sure it would,' said Harkon. 'But skoob hasn't been seen in Megacity for years.'

Chris took a small plastic-wrapped packet from his pocket and handed it over. 'Careful, there's a little hole in the top there.'

Harkon shook the packet and a few shining green granules trickled out into his hand.

'Skoob!' he whispered. 'Where did you get this?'

'We think someone's been smuggling it into Megacity,' said Bernice. 'It may account for the outbreaks of violence.'

'Who's doing this?' demanded Harkon. 'Where can I find him?'

'We can tell you who he is and where he is,' said Chris. 'Catching him with the goods might be a little more difficult.'

'Why will it be difficult?' said Harkon, seeing his triumph slipping away. 'What's going on?'

'Don't worry, Chief,' said Bernice. 'I've got a plan.'

Nastur's warehouse was in a state of siege. The shattered main gate had been barricaded and there were armed guards everywhere – as many as could be spared from the task of hunting Garshak and his two human associates.

Nastur sat in the warehouse yard in his usual chair, raging at his men as they made their useless reports.

'They must be somewhere,' he snarled. 'I know they've not left the planet – we've had the spaceport watched by the Wolverines.'

As if on cue a cloaked and hooded figure emerged from the shadows.

'Well,' hissed Nastur. 'Have you found Garshak yet?'

'No, Garshak,' said the Wolverine. 'Search clubs, bars, hotels, spaceport, everywhere. No Garshak.'

'Useless fools!'

Under the hood, thin lips drew back from the long muzzle in a low snarl.

'I'm sorry,' said Nastur hurriedly. 'I know you're doing your best. This matter is very important to me.'

You had to watch your step with Wolverines. They were good servants and efficient killers, but they were touchy. Offend them and you might find yourself on the receiving end of their attentions.

'Not find Garshak,' said the Wolverine. 'Find man and woman.'

Nastur leant forward eagerly. 'Where?'

'Police headquarters. Go to see Harkon.'

Nastur felt a pang of unease, and then told himself he had nothing to fear. Garshak's friends were in no position to complain to the police. Hadn't they destroyed his property, stolen his truck, killed his bodyguards? All the same, it was worrying . . . In the old days there had been few problems with the Megacity police that a bundle of credits wouldn't solve. But Chief Harkon had a disturbing tendency towards honesty.

Nastur was still brooding over this new development when one of his bodyguards said, 'Boss?'

Lost in thought, Nastur didn't reply.

'Boss!' said the bodyguard again.

'What is it? Can't you see I'm trying to think?'

'Sorry, boss, but I thought you were keen to find Garshak, and that hovertruck he took?'

'Well, of course I am! What about it?'

'I think that's the truck coming down the street right now. And it looks like Garshak's driving it.'

The bodyguard pointed, and Nastur stared in astonishment. Through a gap in the barricade he could see the missing hovertruck coming slowly down the road towards him.

Nastur raised his voice. 'Guards, here, all of you! Cover that hovertruck!'

A dozen armed bodyguards came running out of the warehouse and took positions grouped around Nastur, laser rifles trained on the hovertruck. It stopped outside the improvised barricade.

Garshak stuck his head out of the window.

'Well, are you going to shift that barrier or what?'

Nastur's bodyguards looked at their boss for instructions.

'A couple of you move the barrier,' ordered Nastur.

Once he got Garshak and the truck safely back inside his warehouse, he mused, neither would ever be seen again.

When the barrier was clear Garshak drove the hovertruck slowly forward. Halfway through the gap where the gate had been the truck stopped.

'What are you doing?' screamed Nastur. 'Move it in here!'

Garshak leant out of the cab. 'First we need to talk.'

Nastur glared balefully at him.

'Well?'

'We need to discuss my finder's fee.'

'Finder's fee? You have already been paid once – overpaid. You steal my hovertruck, bring it back and expect to be paid again?'

'Different fees for different jobs,' said Garshak blandly. 'You hired me to get your hovertruck back – I got it back. First job, first fee. The two strangers hired me to steal it from you, so I stole it. Second job, second fee. I stole the truck from the strangers. Now I'm offering to sell it back to you. Third job, third –'

'All right, all right,' said Nastur. 'Get that hovertruck in here. I want it off the street and out of sight.'

Garshak shook his head. 'First I want your promise that you'll call off your people – and the Wolverines as well. No point in earning another fee if I don't live to spend it.'

'Very well, I give you my word. Now will you get that hovertruck in here?'

'We still haven't agreed a fee.'

'How much do you want?' snarled Nastur.

'Ten per cent of the value of the hovertruck's cargo,' said Garshak. 'And I mean ten per cent of the real value – the stuff that's hidden inside the jekkarta crates.'

'Ten per cent!' screamed Nastur. 'That's outrageous, Garshak. That – that stuff is worth millions –' He broke off. After all, it didn't really matter how much he promised. He had no intention of paying Garshak anything at all. He was going to kill him at the very first opportunity.

Nastur smiled horribly. 'You drive a hard bargain, Garshak, but I agree. Just bring the hovertruck into the yard, will you? There's a good fellow.'

Infuriatingly, the truck still didn't move.

'Maybe I ought to keep the stuff and sell it myself,' said Garshak thoughtfully. 'Why settle for ten per cent when you could have a hundred per cent? I mean, I don't even know for sure that the stuff in the hovertruck is really yours.'

'Of course it's mine,' screamed Nastur, goaded beyond endurance.

'You're quite sure about that?'

Nastur's scream became a bellow. *'Everything in that hovertruck is mine, smuggled in by me and me alone, and paid for with my own credits. I own it and I intend to be the one who sells it!'* He calmed himself with an enormous effort. 'Now – get that hovertruck in here.'

'If you insist,' said Garshak. He drove into the yard, and halted the hovertruck just in front of Nastur's chair.

Nastur smiled again, rubbing flipper-like paws together. He raised his voice in a stream of orders.

'Get the barricade back in place. Get the hovertruck inside the warehouse – *and kill Garshak*!'

There was a crackle of blaster fire, and Garshak ducked back inside the hovertruck. The firing, however, came not from Nastur's bodyguards, but from the blasters of the squad of Megacity police who jumped from the back of the hovertruck.

Several of Nastur's bodyguards fell dead or stunned, and the rest turned to run back into the warehouse. They found themselves facing the blasters of still more police, who came pouring from inside. Some of the guards tried to resist. Caught in a crossfire, they were immediately shot down. The survivors threw down their rifles in surrender.

A police hoverwagon drove into the yard. Chief Harkon, Chris and Bernice got out, accompanied by still more policemen.

Chief Harkon stood in front of Nastur, looking down at him, hands on hips. 'I've waited a long time for this, Nastur.' He cleared his throat. 'I hereby arrest you on charges of smuggling the noxious drug known as skoob, with intent to distribute it in Megacity . . .'

'You are making a mistake, Chief Harkon,' said Nastur calmly. 'I have no idea of the contents of that truck – and whatever they are, they have nothing to do with me.'

'Is that so?' said Chief Harkon. 'And how do you account for its presence here in your warehouse yard?'

'Some rogue called Garshak just drove it in here. He told me the truck contained skoob, and offered to sell it to me for an outrageous price.' Nastur did his best to look virtuous. 'Naturally I told him I wasn't interested.'

'Is that the truth now?'

'My guards will testify to it – those you haven't already killed. As I said, Chief, you are making a terrible mistake. I'm afraid I shall be forced to sue the administration.'

'Will you, now?' Harkon raised his voice. 'Mr Garshak!'

Garshak jumped down from the hovertruck. 'Chief Harkon?'

'Do you have the prisoner's confession?'

'I do, Chief.'

'Nonsense,' said Nastur indignantly. 'I made no confession.'

Garshak produced a police recorder from his pocket, held it up and touched a control. Nastur's angry voice boomed out. *'Everything in that hovertruck is mine, smuggled in by me and me alone, and paid for with my own credits. I own it and I intend to be the one who sells it!'*

Garshak switched off the recorder and handed it to Harkon. 'That will do nicely, Mr Nastur,' said Harkon. 'Admission of ownership and confession of intent to distribute.'

Nastur made one last desperate attempt to wriggle free.

'I think you'll find that recording is useless to you, Chief Harkon. Such a confession is admissible only if recorded by an authorized police official, and Garshak is no longer –'

He broke off as Garshak turned back the lapel of his coat and revealed a large and battered star bearing the word 'Deputy'.

'Take him away,' said Harkon. Four policemen picked up Nastur's chair and carried it and the now speechless Nastur over to the waiting police hoverwagon.

Chris and Bernice were congratulating Garshak.

'Well done!' said Chris.

'Brilliant!' said Bernice.

Garshak surveyed the battered hovertruck. 'I'll be glad to see the last of that thing. It's caused me a lot of trouble.' He looked down at Bernice. 'And as for this latest mad scheme of yours . . .'

'Well, it worked, didn't it?' said Bernice triumphantly. 'I think we deserve a celebration. Any chance of a lift back to Louie's hotel, Chief?'

'With pleasure,' said Harkon. 'I shall have to detain Mr Garshak a little longer. I need a statement from him – and for today at least, he's still a deputy.' He reached up and patted Garshak on the shoulder. 'An excellent piece of undercover police work, Mr Garshak. Would you care to consider rejoining the force in an official capacity?'

* * *

Later that evening, the celebration was in full swing. After an excellent dinner Chris and Bernice adjourned to the piano bar.

'Hear about Nastur?' asked Louie as they came in. 'Busted for dealing skoob!' He shook his head disapprovingly. 'Serve him right too – that stuff's murder!'

Murkar, back on duty as doorman, nodded solemnly in agreement.

Bernice ordered champagne, and she and Chris went on discussing the skoob affair.

'You know,' said Chris, 'I'm still not positive this skoob smuggling really is the Project – the one Roz got on to.'

Bernice didn't want anything to spoil the celebration.

'Oh come on, Chris, it must be. Everything fits! The crime-against-humanity bit, the upsurge in violence.'

'Still several loose ends, though,' said Chris argumentatively.

'Such as?'

'Nastur couldn't have been selling skoob back when Roz and I were first here. According to Garshak, he wasn't even in Megacity.'

Bernice shrugged. 'Maybe someone else was just setting the racket up then. Nastur could have taken it over later.'

'Maybe so,' said Chris. 'But what about the St Oscar's connection? Why such a big reaction when they discovered we were coming to Megacity to look into the Project?'

'The Advanced Research Department is involved somehow,' said Bernice positively. 'Maybe they were the ones synthesizing the drug, or trying to. Just the sort of thing they would do. I only hope the police come up with the link. If I can prove they're involved in drug trafficking, I can make them drop all those fake charges and reinstate me.'

Garshak appeared in the doorway, stopped for a few words with Murkar and came over to join them. He ordered a mug of ale, drained it, and immediately ordered another.

'Harkon's been working me to death,' he said. 'He wants me to come back on the force.'

'Will you?' asked Chris. 'You must miss the job. I do.'

'I'm not sure. I was only a poor corrupt police official, Chris, not a noble Adjudicator like you. And I've come to enjoy my freedom.'

Bernice took a swig of champagne. 'Garshak will know,' she announced, looking defiantly at Chris. She turned to Garshak.

'How long has this skoob-smuggling racket been going on?'

'It hasn't,' said Garshak. 'We stopped it before it even got started.'

They looked blankly at him.

'How can you be sure?' asked Bernice faintly.

'This was the first and only shipment. The only one in existence as far as we know. Somehow it got overlooked when the United Planets had their big purge. Nastur found out somehow and managed to get his hands on it. His Alpha Centaurian accountant made a full confession. They planned to sell off most of it, and keep some back to try to synthesize more.'

'Did you come across any mention of St Oscar's University on Dellah?' asked Bernice hopefully. 'Was something called the Advanced Research Department involved in the synthesizing?'

Garshak shook his head. 'The synthesizing part was just in the planning stage. They needed to sell off some of the drug first to finance the research.'

'So there's no way the skoob smuggling could have got started back when we first met?' asked Chris. 'Or be the cause of the upsurge in violent crime?'

'I don't see how,' said Garshak. 'It's all very recent, and not enough of it got out.'

Chris sighed. 'You know what this means, Benny?'

'Oh yes,' said Bernice bitterly. 'We've been charging up a blind alley – risking our necks playing crimebuster – and it's all for nothing.'

'Not nothing,' objected Chris. 'We've helped to break up

182

an ugly racket and save a lot of lives.'

'We haven't tracked down Roz's mysterious Project, which is what you came here to do,' said Bernice gloomily. 'We haven't got the goods on St Oscar's either – which I need to do if I'm ever going to get my job back.'

'We'll just have to start all over again,' said Chris. 'Chief Harkon will help – he owes us now.'

Bernice brightened a little. 'Lucifer will help as well. So we've got the cops and the robbers on our side!'

'I'll even help as well,' said Garshak. 'I suppose I come somewhere in between!'

'We need a break,' said Chris broodingly. 'A thread to pull on that will untangle the rest.'

'Hey Chris!'

He looked up and saw Louie calling from the bar.

'Call for you on the comm. Some dame.'

'Excuse me,' said Chris. He got up and went to the bar.

'Now then,' said Garshak. 'Tell me all about this Project.'

Bernice swigged more champagne. 'It's a long story. It all started when Chris and Roz first came to Megacity . . .'

Chris followed Louie's directions to a corner comm booth and said, 'Chris here.'

'How've you been, Chris?' said a female voice. It was Sara.

'Busy,' said Chris rather guiltily. 'I've been meaning to call . . .'

'I thought you might like to come over and see me,' said Sara.

'I'd like to, Sara, I really would, but I'm pretty busy just now.'

There was a moment of silence.

Sara said, 'If it's any inducement – I've found someone who knows something about the Project . . .'

15

THE BREAK

It was late when Chris arrived at Sara's Cellar, and once again he was greeted as an honoured guest. Word seemed to have got around among the staff that he and the boss were more than just good friends. The heavies on the door waved him through and when he went down the stairs the maître d' greeted him with a bow.

The place was packed, every table full, and a group of assorted life forms were pounding out strange alien rhythms from a dais in the corner. They finished their number and a buzz of conversation filled the room.

'Madame Sara is expecting you, sir,' said the maître d'. 'You'll find her by the bar.'

Sara was perched on a stool with her back to the bar. Elegant in a silver evening gown, her red hair piled high, she was surveying the crowded room with a professional eye.

Chris slid on to the stool beside her and kissed her briefly and a little awkwardly on the lips.

She smiled at him. 'Ale or champagne?'

'Champagne,' said Chris. 'Definitely a night for champagne.'

Sara glanced over her shoulder. 'Ramon!'

The hovering barman brought a bottle, opened it, filled two silver tankards and slid discreetly away. Chris looked at the tankards in mild surprise.

'If you're going to drink champagne, drink it,' said Sara cheerfully. 'No point in sipping at the stuff.'

She took a swig from her tankard and Chris did the same. The cool, sparkling wine was delicious and Chris felt a sudden surge of wellbeing. He smiled – and then immediately frowned.

Sara cocked her head. 'What is it?'

'I was thinking it's nice to relax. Life's been a bit stressful lately.'

'So why the frown?'

'I seem to be getting a taste for the high life!'

'What's wrong with that?'

'I've still got a job to do. I can't afford to get too relaxed.' He winced as the group broke into another noisy number.

'What do you think of the band?'

Chris raised his voice above the incessant pounding noise. 'Very . . . striking! I particularly like the octopod on the double bass.'

'They're the Antares Hot Five – they play something called jazz. Old Earth retro is all the rage just now.'

Chris nodded. He leant forward, his lips close to her ear. 'You said you had some information for me.'

'Relaxing time over already?'

'I'm sorry . . .'

'That's all right. I like a man who keeps his mind on the job.' Sara drained her tankard. 'Come along.'

Chris swigged down the rest of his champagne, burped, and followed her. To his surprise she led him behind the bar and down a steep flight of stone steps.

He found himself in a long cellar which ran under the whole of the nightclub. The walls were whitewashed, the floor stone-flagged. Stone pillars, worn smooth with age, supported the roof.

The cellar was stacked with wine racks, liquor crates and beer barrels, some in plastimetal, others in old-fashioned wood. Nearby, a stooping figure in a leather apron was lifting a wooden barrel on to a trestle. Chris saw that the man was thickset, broad-shouldered and beetle-browed, with a heavy jaw. He was very old, his brown face seamed and wrinkled, his massive skull bald except for a fringe of snow-white hair. Judging by the way he handled the heavy barrel he was still immensely strong.

Chris looked around the cellar. 'Very impressive.'

'You're standing in just about the oldest place in Megacity.' Sara explained that the club had been built on the site of an old native tavern. The cellar had survived all the changes of name and ownership. They went over to watch the old man.

'Sam here's my cellarman,' she explained. 'He's the only one knows how to look after traditional Earth Ale.'

The old man knocked a wooden bung from the top of the barrel, picked up a plastic jug, and began pouring a colourless liquid slowly into the barrel.

'What's he doing?' asked Chris.

The old man looked up. 'This stuff's called finings,' he said. 'Made from fish guts. You pour it into the beer, let her settle, and it works through and clears out all the impurities, leaves her clear and sparkling.' He gestured scornfully at the plastimetal barrels. 'This modern stuff comes all ready-refined, but you need the old ways to get the real flavour. They've been doing it this way on Earth for hundreds of years.'

Carefully he tipped in the remains of the jug.

'Fascinating,' said Chris politely. 'It's very kind of you to let me see your cellar, Sara . . .'

'I didn't bring you down here to see the cellar,' said Sara. 'I brought you here to see Sam.' She smiled at his look of puzzlement. 'I asked everywhere about this precious Project of yours. Either nobody knew, or nobody was talking. And all the time the answer was right here under my feet! I'd better get back upstairs. I'll leave you and Sam to talk. Come and say goodbye before you go.'

She went back up the stone steps, leaving Chris staring dubiously at an old humanoid stooping over his barrel.

What could an old codger like this possibly know about the Project?

The old man straightened up, arching his back to relieve the strain. 'Don't recognize me, do you?'

Chris shook his head. 'I'm sorry. Should I?'

'We met once. Not for long, and a long long time ago. Seems like I've changed a lot more than you have.'

'I'm sorry,' said Chris again. 'When did we meet?'

'A long long time ago, back when you first came to Megacity. In a beer hall downtown, remember? Four drunk miners came in and started getting tough with your lady friend.'

'Yes, I remember,' said Chris slowly. He looked at the old man. 'Were you –'

'I'm the one your lady friend kicked in the balls,' said the old man bluntly. He laughed wheezily. 'I couldn't walk upright for a week! Then you came back from the bar and clobbered two of the others and me and Sev made a run for it.'

Chris didn't quite know what to say. 'I'm sorry I didn't recognize you at first. I never really got a good look at you.'

'I saw all I wanted to of you – and your lady friend. Say, that was one tough little dame. How's she doing?'

'Dead,' said Chris briefly.

'Dead, eh?' said the old man. 'Tough.'

Chris decided it was time to get down to business. 'Sara said you knew something about the Project.'

For a moment the old man didn't reply. He cleared his throat. 'Thirsty work, talking.' He took two tankards from a shelf and went over to another barrel. 'This one should be about ready by now.' He turned the spigot and drew off two mugs of ale, passing one to Chris. They both drank. The beer was cool and delicious and Chris found himself draining the tankard at one swallow.

'Best part of my job, testing the ale,' said the old man. 'Good stuff, hey?'

'Best I ever tasted,' said Chris. 'About the Project . . .'

The old man finished his beer and refilled both tankards.

'Give me some time, boy. I've been clammed up about the Project so long I got to work my way round to it. I wouldn't be talking to you now if Miss Sara hadn't asked me to.' He took another swig of beer. 'Back in those days Megacity was a lot wilder, and so was I. I came here to work in the mines, made good money for a while. Then I got fired for drinking and fighting. I hung around in bars till I'd spent all my savings, then I drifted into being pretty much of a lowlife. Robbery, mugging, stuff like that. I'd always been stronger than your lot so I ended up working mostly as a leg-breaker.'

Chris nodded. He was familiar with the pattern from his Adjudicator days. 'Who for?'

'Whoever. Mind you, I was never a killer. Just low-level, hired muscle, when the big boys wanted somebody leant on.' The old man shrugged. 'I got tired of it in time and got out. Started working behind the bar instead of leaning on it, and ended up down here.'

Chris sighed. Probably the old boy didn't get much chance to talk about the old days. He was quite capable of telling Chris his entire life story.

'The Project,' Chris prompted gently.

'Around the time you was here first, there was a sudden upswing in the leg-breaking business. There was something big called the Project starting up and everyone was talking about it. Then word came down that everyone hadda *stop* talking about it. Quite a few people were killed just to make an example – lot of hovercabbies, barmen, guys like that. Anyone who was still talking about the Project after that got a beating. If they didn't learn from that, they were killed.'

'And did it work?' asked Chris. 'I'd have thought it was impossible to stop people from talking.'

The old man chuckled. 'It took a while, but it sure as hell worked in the end. Came the day nobody was talking about it – from then till now.'

'Where did we come in?'

Sam shrugged. 'The guy who hired me, Sev, told me you'd

been asking too many questions. At first they were gonna kill you, but they were afraid to do it because you were Pinks. So Sev hired me and a couple of others to discourage you. As you know, we didn't do too well at it.'

'Did anyone report back what had happened?'

'I sure as hell didn't. I just laid low till I could walk upright again.'

'Perhaps nobody did – and soon after that we left anyway,' said Chris thoughtfully. 'Maybe they thought we'd been scared off . . .' It was time, he thought, to ask the really important questions. 'So, what was this Project? Who was running it?'

'No idea,' said old Sam.

Chris's heart sank. Was his only lead about to fizzle out?

Sam saw his disappointed face. 'Look, all the guys doing the shutting up had strict orders to shut up themselves – about what they were doing, and why they were doing it.'

'What about this Sev, the one who hired you? Did he know?'

'Maybe he did know and talked too much. He was found in a back alley with his throat ripped out not long after. Mostly they used Wolverines for the killing.'

'And you never heard a name? Some big crime lord or gang boss?'

'Never. Except . . .'

'Except what?' asked Chris eagerly.

'I heard rumours an outfit called Custodiex was providing some of the hired muscle for the beatings. Big private security setup. Worked for them myself for a while.'

Chris drained his tankard and handed it back to the old man.

'Thanks, Sam.'

'Sorry I couldn't tell you more.'

'It's a start,' said Chris. 'Maybe it'll lead somewhere.'

He reached in his pocket but the old man shook his head.

'No need. It was a favour to Miss Sara.' Sam grinned reminiscently, shaking his head. 'That was some kick – I can still feel it now. Pity about that little lady friend of yours.'

'Yes,' said Chris. 'It is.'

The old man went back to his work, and Chris went upstairs to find Sara. She was sitting back at the bar and she looked up eagerly as he approached. 'Was Sam any help?'

'Quite a bit. He's given me somewhere to start, anyway.'

Sara glanced at the still-hovering barman. 'More champagne?'

'I'd better not. I need to get moving on this.'

'I'll be working here till the small hours,' she said. 'After that I need my sleep. If you'd care to come round one afternoon. Afternoons are the best time here.'

'Afternoons are wonderful here,' said Chris. 'I'll come as soon as I possibly can.' He leant forward and kissed her hard.

'You're getting better at that,' she said.

'Practice,' said Chris solemnly. 'I need much more practice.'

He turned and moved away through the crowded bar.

Quite a few people besides Sara watched him go.

'So there you are,' concluded Chris. 'As you can see, he didn't really tell me much.'

'I don't know,' said Garshak. 'He may have told you more than he realized – more than you realized as well, come to that.'

It was next morning, and they were having an early drink in Louie's bar – to counter the effects of all the late-night celebratory drinks they'd had the night before. Garshak, who had ended up sleeping in the hotel, had joined them.

Bernice swigged her coffee and brandy and shuddered. 'Stop being so bloody enigmatic, Garshak,' she said irritably. 'I can't cope with that and a hangover. Who told who more than who realized about what?'

'I've been thinking,' said Garshak calmly.

'Well I'm glad somebody has. The rest of us don't seem to be too good at it.'

'Please explain, Mr Garshak,' said Chris, polite as ever

190

despite a pounding head. Champagne and old ale just didn't mix well, he decided. Especially when you were drinking both by the tankard.

Garshak beamed at his haggard audience. One of the many irritating things about Ogrons is that they don't get hang-overs.

'Just look at the people – the three most important people – who you've been asking for information about this mysterious Project,' he said. 'Lucifer. Sara. Me.'

Bernice nodded and immediately wished that she hadn't. 'So?'

'A crime lord,' he said. 'A lady who runs the nightclub patronized by the criminal elite. And me, an ex-police chief and present-day private detective.'

'Get on with it, Garshak,' muttered Bernice. 'What's your point?'

'We none of us knew anything about it!'

'Yes, we realize that,' said Bernice through gritted teeth. 'That's our problem, rather, isn't it?'

Chris frowned, wishing his brain didn't feel like setting plasticrete. 'Are you saying we've been asking the wrong people?'

Garshak shook his head. 'Not at all,' he said infuriatingly. 'In a sense, you've been asking exactly the right people. Lucifer, Sara and I are probably three of the best-informed people on criminal affairs in all Megacity. But not one of us knew anything about the Project. Surely you can see what that single fact tells us?'

'No I bloody well can't,' snarled Bernice. 'And if you don't tell me right now in simple language –'

Garshak slammed a huge hairy hand on the table, making the glasses, Chris and Bernice all shudder and jump in the air.

'*If the Project was any kind of straightforward criminal scheme we'd have known about it!* One of us would have heard of it for certain, and probably all three. But we haven't!'

There was a moment of silence.

Then Bernice said, 'Hang on. Are you saying the Project isn't a criminal scheme.'

'Yes – or rather, yes and no.'

'Garshak!'

'Obviously something that can be called a crime against humanity, something that's going to cause blood in the streets, must be in some way criminal. But not in the sense you've been using the word – the everyday professional sense.'

'What you're saying,' said Chris slowly, 'is that, although the Project is a criminal scheme, it isn't necessarily something devised by or operating among professional criminals – like Nastur, or even Lucifer?'

'That's right,' said Garshak. 'Except in a fringe kind of way on the lowest levels – as demonstrated by the involvement of your friend Sam.'

'So, not criminals, but people prepared to employ criminals?'

'Precisely. All that grandiose stuff about suppressing any mention of the Project – it's just not the way criminals think.'

'Then who does?'

'Governments,' said Garshak. 'Or very large and powerful corporations who think like governments. Run by people who don't commit crimes with their own hands, but who are perfectly prepared to pay others to do the dirty work – if the stakes are high enough.'

'Of course!' said Bernice. 'We've been looking in the wrong direction. Down in the gutter with the killers and drug smugglers, instead of up in the penthouses with the fat cats.'

'Who do you think might be involved?' asked Chris.

Garshak shrugged. 'Almost any of the leading citizens of Megacity. The City Council is stuffed with the rich and powerful – and they didn't get where they are by being overscrupulous.'

Bernice nodded. 'There's an old saying – "There's no

completely honest way to make a billion credits"!'

'Something else,' said Garshak. 'Didn't you say Sam mentioned Custodiex?'

Chris nodded. 'What are they?'

'Executive security for millionaires and top corporations. Custodiex would never stoop to working for ordinary criminals – ordinary crooks don't earn enough to pay Custodiex fees!'

'Well, we can investigate Custodiex for a start,' said Chris. 'Anyone else?'

'We could try the Wolverines,' said Garshak. 'They don't keep written records – but someone in the Pack might remember and be willing to drop a name for a price. One thing about Wolverines is they're consistent – they'll sell anyone out to anyone!'

'We can't talk to Wolverines though,' objected Chris. 'You especially, Mr Garshak!'

'I can if I can figure out a way to stay alive long enough!'

'You know what I'm going to do?' said Bernice. 'Research! I've been so caught up in all this macho derring-do I forgot I'm supposed to be a scholar. I'm going to research the fat cats – millionaires, politicians, big corporations.'

Garshak looked sceptical. 'Research? How will that help?'

'Well, if we accept your theory, and I think we must, we know two things about the people behind the Project. They're rich and powerful – and they're in trouble.'

'Roz's informant said the Project was bound to go wrong,' said Chris.

'Exactly. I can research that informant's death as well – and all these other violent crimes. Oh, and I can also check for anyone with a link to St Oscar's . . .'

Bernice felt ideas coming thick and fast now.

'Garshak, you've got us back in the game. You're a genius!'

'I know,' said Garshak modestly.

'You know what this calls for?' said Bernice. 'Champagne!' She waved towards the bar. 'Champagne, Louie!'

'Coming right up,' said Louie. 'Call for you, Chris, that dame again.'

Chris went off to the comm booth and Louie brought and poured the champagne.

When Chris returned to the table his face was grave.

'What's happened?' asked Bernice. 'Is Sara all right?'

'Yes, but old Sam isn't. Someone went down into the cellar last night and smashed in his head with a mallet . . .'

16

INVESTIGATION

The Megacity cops were there in force when Chris and Murkar arrived in the cellar of Sara's Cellar. As a tribute to Sara's importance, Chief Harkon himself was in attendance. He was surveying the crime scene, Sara by his side, when Chris came down the steps.

Chris had stood for a moment at the top of the steps, taking everything in.

A white-overalled crimetech crouched by Sam's body. The old man lay face down in front of one of his own barrels. He was sprawled out in an untidy heap, a pool of blood around the shattered skull.

Nearby lay a wooden mallet, its head sticky with blood. Chris remembered seeing that same mallet in old Sam's hand the night before. A couple of overturned ale mugs lay on the floor nearby.

Chris felt suddenly envious of Chief Harkon and his men. The study of the crime scene, the waiting for forensic evidence, the search for methods and motives. Above all the questioning of witnesses and suspects, the flicker in someone's eyes that told you he was lying – but could you prove it? The old game of good cop and bad cop, to persuade someone to talk when it was clearly in his own best interests to clam up . . .

Violent death was always a tragedy, but to an investigator

it was the start of the hunt. And once a cop . . . But he wasn't an Adjudicator any more. Investigating Sam's death wasn't his job.

'Just another motiveless murder, I'm afraid, Miss Sara,' Harkon was saying, as Chris and Murkar reached the bottom of the stairs. 'We seem to get more and more of them these days. Some drunk sneaks into your cellar to steal booze, Sam catches him, the thief grabs the mallet . . .'

Chris greeted them both, and introduced the giant figure at his side. 'I want you to take Murkar on for a while, Sara,' he said.

Sara looked puzzled. 'Why? What for?'

'To keep an eye on you. I'll take care of his salary – I just want you to keep him around for a while.' Before she could argue, Chris turned to Chief Harkon. 'With respect, Chief, I can't agree with you about the crime.'

Not surprisingly Chief Harkon took immediate umbrage.

'Is that so, young man? And how much experience do you have of police work?'

'I was an Adjudicator for several years, remember.'

Harkon glared suspiciously at him. 'Being an Adjudicator is a job for life, isn't it?'

'Usually.'

'So why did you leave?'

'Corruption. Not mine, other people's.'

Harkon nodded. 'That can happen. So what's your theory?'

'I don't think someone just came in off the streets and killed Sam. Sara's security is pretty good.'

'Someone already in the club, then?' argued Chief Harkon.

Chris shook his head. 'Not likely. Sara knows most of her customers. Some of them are criminals, but they're not thugs or lowlifes. Isn't that so, Sara?'

She nodded. 'This place is neutral ground – people just don't cause trouble here.' She smiled at Chris. 'Well, not usually.'

Harkon looked dubious. 'Not all your criminal clients are so high-class. Miss Sara. What about bodyguards, hangers-on, people like that?'

196

'That's quite true, I couldn't guarantee all of them. All the same, I don't think they'd dare – their own bosses would kill them.'

'There's something else,' said Chris. 'Old Sam was a tough nut. He'd been a hard man in his time, and he was still pretty strong. I got the impression that mallet was never far away. If someone had broken in, I'd bet that the thief would be the one who ended up with a split skull.'

Harkon sighed gustily. 'So how did he get himself killed?'

'By someone he knew,' said Chris. 'Someone he trusted. Sam was very proud of his ale, and I imagine he always offered visitors a drink – just as he did me last night. I think Sam turned away to fill a mug and his visitor snatched up the mallet and killed him.'

'So you had a drink with him last night, did you?' snapped Harkon. 'Maybe it's you I ought to be arresting!'

Chris just stared at him. He was so used to being on the investigating end that he'd never even thought of himself as a possible suspect.

He looked so comically dismayed that, despite the tragic circumstances, Sara laughed outright.

'It's all right, Chief Harkon, I can vouch for Chris. I came down to see Sam after Chris left, to thank him for helping, and he was alive and well and in the best of spirits.'

'I'm not sure you're an unbiased witness,' grumbled Harkon. 'Did anyone see Sam at all after that? No one noticed he hadn't gone home?'

Sara shook her head. 'Sam pretty well lived in the cellar. He often slept there. He did his work in his own time – sometimes nobody saw him for ages.'

'So he could have been killed any time in the night.' Harkon swung round on to Chris. 'This help he was giving you . . .'

'Remember when Professor Summerfield and I first came here? We told you we were were looking into something called the Project – that was why false charges had been

trumped up against us? We thought it might even be responsible for the rise in violent crime in Megacity.'

'I thought we'd solved all that with the skoob bust.'

'Unfortunately not – that was a blind alley. The Project is
something else and it's still going on. Sam knew something
about it – not much, but something. I think he was killed just
for talking to me.'

'Is that so? And would you happen to know who by?'

'I know that too,' said Chris calmly. 'Give me some
authority and I'll prove it to you.'

'What kind of authority?' asked Harkon suspiciously.

'Make me a special deputy, the way you did Garshak.'

Harkon thrust his hand into his pocket and took out a
battered silver star.

'It just so happens I've got Garshak's badge right here, him
having no further use for it.' He tossed the star to Chris.
'Raise your right hand . . .'

A few minutes later, Chris was duly sworn in as a
Megacity Special Investigator.

Chief Harkon gave him a satirical look and said, 'All right,
Sherlock – get started!'

Chris turned to Sara. 'Is your barman still on duty – the
one who served us champagne last night?'

'Ramon? Yes, he'll be clearing up the bar ready for
tonight. Why?'

'Could you send him down here, please? Take Murkar
with you. Oh, and Chief, can you lend me your recorder?'

Harkon unclipped the black box from his belt and handed
it to Chris, who slipped it into his pocket. While Sara was
away the crimetech came over to them.

'Anything?' asked Harkon.

'No DNA on the mallet – according to the molecular
scanner whoever used it was wearing thin plastic gloves.
Blood coagulant factor says he died nine hours ago.'

'Couple of hours after I talked to him,' said Chris.

Ramon, the barman, came down the steps, followed by the
giant figure of Murkar. Chris studied the man thoughtfully.

Slim, dark, shiny-haired and soft-footed, he was the perfect barman, efficient and almost unnoticed. He was nervous now, but perhaps that was natural.

'What's all this about? It's terrible what happened to Sam, but I don't know anything about it. I was upstairs, all evening. People saw me, lots of people . . .'

'It's all right, sonny,' said Chief Harkon soothingly. 'Just routine enquiries. We'll be talking to everyone – just so happens you're the first.' He smiled encouragingly at the nervous barman. 'Between you and me we think some varmint sneaked in off the street and killed him.'

Chris stared grimly at the barman. 'Unless it was someone closer to home. When did you last see old Sam?'

'Fairly early last night. I came down to get a case of champagne. He was fine then, fiddling about with one of those old wooden barrels. Sam sure loved his ale.'

'And that was the last time you saw him?' asked Harkon mildly.

'Afraid so, Chief.'

'Then take a look at him now,' snarled Chris. Grabbing Ramon by one thin shoulder he dragged him over to the body. Ramon looked down, shuddering at the sight of the shattered skull in its pool of blood. 'No, please . . .'

'What's the matter? Don't you like looking at your work?'

Ramon backed away. 'I don't know what you're talking about – I didn't do this.'

'No? We'll find the bar gloves, Ramon – wherever you've hidden them. Then we can match the gloves to the mallet and your DNA to the inside of the gloves.'

'That's impossible –' Ramon broke in suddenly.

'Impossible because you destroyed the gloves? Fed them into the garbage-shredder?'

Ramon made no reply.

'I'll tell you exactly how it happened,' Chris went on. 'You came down here late last night when the place was closed. You had a chat with Sam and he gave you a mug of that ale he was so proud of. You emptied the mug. When Sam turned round to give you a refill you grabbed the mallet and smashed his head in.'

'Why would I do that? Sam was a friend of mine.'

'You killed him because he talked to me about the Project,' said Chris. 'What I want to know is, who told you to do it – and who paid you?'

'I don't know what you're talking about.'

Chris grabbed him by the arm and dragged him into a quiet corner of the cellar.

'Listen, I'm going to give you one last chance to save yourself.' He nodded back towards Harkon, who was chatting to the crimetech. 'Chief Harkon's old and lazy. You heard him: he'd just as soon write this off as murder by some unknown robber. Just tell me who set the killing up. I'll tell him you're innocent and you'll walk.'

Ramon brooded for a moment. 'I heard you and Miss Sara talking last night, about this Project. Don't mean nothing to me, but I called it into the Grapevine.'

'The what?'

'You don't know about the Grapevine? How long you been a cop in Megacity?'

Chris grinned. 'First day on the force. Tell me about this Grapevine.'

'It's a kind of central information service, all computerized. Been around for years. How it works, if you hear something interesting you call it in. Could be anything, gossip, scandal, a job being planned, a deal going down. Customers call the Grapevine to see if there's any info on record they might like to hear. If they want the info they buy it, and the Grapevine pays the supplier a percentage.'

'How?'

'The credits appear in your account – could be big, could be small, depends on the info.'

'So you called the Grapevine.'

'That's right.'

'And?'

'Couple of hours later I get a call back, not from them but

from the customer. They want me to – take care of Sam.'
Ramon shrugged. 'I'm in big financial trouble. I got gambling debts, a bit of a habit . . .'

'So what did you do? Say it!'

'OK, OK . . . So I went down to the cellar and bashed his head in with his own mallet. I hated to do it – I liked the old guy. But I had to kill him. It was him or me, right?'

'Who was this customer? Who paid for the job?'

'No idea.'

Chris grabbed him by the lapels and shook him hard.

'Don't lie, Ramon. Even a louse like you wouldn't commit a murder for someone he didn't know, someone who might refuse to pay up or even turn him in. You knew who you were dealing with all right.'

'OK, OK,' gasped Ramon. 'I'll tell you.'

Chris let him go. 'Well?'

'It was a big security outfit called Custodiex. They knew I worked here. I'd done a few jobs for them before. It's all their fault – they made me kill old Sam. I didn't dare refuse – they know too much about me. Don't tell them I told you or I'm dead.' He grabbed Chris's arm. 'You'll fix things with Harkon for me, like you said?'

'We'll go over and see him now.'

They walked back over to Chief Harkon.

'Well?' he asked. 'How did your little chat go?'

'It went fine, Chief. Ramon here made a full confession.'

'That's not true, Chief, I denied everything.'

Chris took the recorder out of his pocket and touched a control. Chris's voice came out, followed by Ramon's:

'So what did you do? Say it!'

'OK, OK . . . So I went down to the cellar and bashed his head in with his own mallet. I hated to do it – I liked the old guy. But I had to kill him. It was him or me, right?'

Ramon stared at him in outrage. 'You promised!'

'I lied,' said Chris.

He switched off the recorder and slipped it back in his pocket. Chief Harkon called over a policeman and Ramon was dragged away, still protesting.

'Well done,' said Harkon. 'How did you know it was him?'

'I was pretty sure Sam was killed because of the Project. Ramon was the only one close enough to overhear Sara mention it to me. Can you give me a lift in a police hover, Chief? I've got to go and see a man about security . . .'

'It was a big security outfit called Custodiex. They knew I worked here. I'd done a few jobs for them before. It's all their fault – they made me kill old Sam. I didn't dare refuse – they know too much about me. Don't tell them I told you or I'm dead.'

Chris switched off the recorder.

The managing director of Custodiex, a plump, well-groomed man called Siros, sat back in his chair and gazed around his luxurious penthouse office as if for inspiration.

'I'm shocked, officer, absolutely appalled. Naturally the poor fellow must be deranged.'

'Don't give me that, Siros,' snarled Chris in his bad-cop voice. 'When that record comes out in evidence, your outfit's in a world of trouble.' He paused. 'If it comes out, that is.'

Siros raised an eyebrow. 'Is the matter in any doubt? Perhaps some accommodation could be reached . . .'

Chris pretended to consider. 'Well, we need the record – but not necessarily all of it. Ramon confesses to the actual murder earlier on. I'm pretty clumsy with these things – I might accidentally erase the bit that mentions your company's name.'

Siros smiled understandingly. 'Of course! Perhaps a contribution to the Police Benevolent Fund? No doubt credit notes would be more convenient?' He reached for his wallet. 'Let's say –'

'Let's say nothing of the kind.'

'Then what do you want?'

'For a start, I want the name of your client. The one who hired you all those years ago to suppress any talk about the

Project. The one who keeps you on a retainer to stamp out any more talk that comes up.'

There was a long pause. Then Siros said carefully, 'Naturally, the affairs of this company are highly confidential.'

'Naturally.'

'However, if I were to mention, in passing, the name of one of our oldest and most valuable clients . . .'

'Go ahead and mention.'

Siros spoke a name. 'You said for a start,' he added. 'Is there something else?'

'Don't tell your clients about my visit or our deal. You got rid of old Sam, but Ramon was clumsy and got caught.'

'Agreed.'

'And don't take on any more Project work. No more beatings, no more murders. If I hear about anyone else being hurt or killed for talking about the Project – and if it happens I will hear – I'll know where to come.'

'What do we tell our client?'

'Just stall. The Project will be smashed soon.'

'Indeed!' Siros lowered his voice. 'You don't happen to know what the Project actually is, do you, officer?'

'Don't you?'

'All we were given was the name. It's a condition of our employment that we make no attempt to find out.'

Chris rose to go. 'Oh, just one more thing. You'd better start praying for the health of the lady who runs Sara's Cellar – the place where Sam and Ramon used to work.'

'And why should I do that?'

'Because if anything happens to her, anything at all, I'll come back here and kill you.'

17

BLOOD FEAST

Bernice Summerfield sat at Chief Harkon's desk in the faded luxury of Garshak's old office surfing the Meganet. Information of every aspect, past and present, of the city's life could be found there. Business, politics, crime, scandal. Files of the *Megacity Gazette* from the very first issue to the latest edition. Police records, company records, financial records. Some of the more confidential items were code-protected but the police computer could gain access to almost every file.

It was Garshak himself who had suggested that she make use of police facilities. He had driven her to police headquarters in an old hovertruck he'd acquired and persuaded Chief Harkon to let him install her at the computer.

Harkon had agreed with remarkably little persuasion. Since the great Nastur skoob bust, Harkon's credit with the Mayor had improved no end, and the Chief knew how much of that success he owed to Garshak, Chris and Bernice.

Now Chris had just helped Chief Harkon to catch a murderer, so he and his friends stood even higher in Harkon's favour.

Garshak had helped to design the police information-retrieval system in his days as Chief of Police and he had an unrivalled knowledge of the way it worked.

He had given Bernice a thorough grounding in the system,

and then left, saying, rather puzzlingly, he had some shopping to do.

Before leaving he'd warned Bernice not to try to access any files for the Project.

'You'll just be told that no such files exist,' he told her, 'but you'll set off a warning system at the same time. If they trace the origin of the enquiry, someone will call round with a bomb or an atomic bazooka, and I don't want my old office blasted – or you either, of course.'

Bernice settled down to her work. She punched up the statistics for violent crime at the time of Roz and Chris's first visit to Megacity. As she studied the stream of data she thought that this was the kind of detecting she liked, sitting comfortably at the computer in an office surrounded by policemen.

She wondered how Garshak was getting on out there on the mean streets of Megacity . . .

I was kind of relieved when me and my hovertruck reached the Plaza in one piece. I kept thinking of Happy Mike's remark that bad things happened to hovercars in my hands. He'd repeated it with colourful emphasis when I'd returned his precious black hoverlimo. Unfortunately two of Nastur's heavies had used it as a barricade in a shootout with the cops during the raid. It had been slightly damaged by blaster fire. Well, quite extensively damaged actually. It hadn't been easy persuading Happy to hire me the hovertruck but I needed it for my plan – such as it was.

It might seem strange to feel relieved when I'd just driven into the single most dangerous place in Megacity, but I'd been worried that the Wolverines might try to take me and the hovertruck out with mines, bombs or heavy artillery. It's hard to have a meaningful discussion with a laser cannon.

I reckoned they'd held off so far because they were curious about what I was up to. Wolverines hate anything they don't understand. They're always afraid you might somehow be putting something over them.

I looked around me. My surroundings weren't any more cheerful than they'd been on my last visit. The same cracked and rutted circular plaza surrounded by gutted buildings. The Plaza and the ruins all around formed a great circle of blackness, dimly lit by the glow from the surrounding neon lights of Megacity.

I got out of the hover, peeled off my trenchcoat and threw it inside. Underneath I was wearing the traditional costume of my people – coarse open shirt, leather trousers and jerkin, and high boots. It's best to feel comfortable when you may have to fight hand to hand. I'd left my twin blasters behind – they'd be no use to me here – and I had a big fighting knife at my waist.

I made, though I say it myself, a splendid barbarian figure. I folded my arms across my chest and waited.

The Wolverines appeared out of the darkness. Soon I was surrounded by a great circle of them, thin, sinuous, cloaked figures, teeth and eyes shining beneath their hoods. There looked to be about fifty of them, maybe more, which meant several packs had gathered. It was more Wolverines in one place than I'd ever seen before, or wanted to see again.

They all stood there, glaring hate at me. They all had sharp claws and long yellow fangs, and there were knives and blasters and laser rifles beneath those cloaks.

They studied me for a long time, trying to work out what was going on. One of them called, 'Time to die, Garshak!'

As the snarling crowd surged forward, I bellowed, 'I claim the Blood Truce!'

That stopped them in their tracks. I'd appealed to an old Wolverine tradition.

Some people regard Wolverines as no better than savage beasts, claiming they have no culture – but they're wrong. The Wolverines have a primitive culture of their own, and a few basic traditions to which they cling very strongly.

One of them is the Blood Truce. Its purpose is to provide a way for Wolverines to settle disputes other than by the traditional method of violence. When Wolverines fight each other, they fight so savagely that battles go on till there's no one left alive. In primitive times on their home planet of Lupus II, the Wolverines came close to wiping themselves out.

Hence the Blood Truce.

The Wolverines broke up into angry arguing groups. As far as I could tell, some packs felt that the Blood Truce only applied between Wolverines, others that a custom was a custom and it was wrong to go against it. This dispute raged for some time. Wolverines have a reputation for being taciturn but they can be incredibly garrulous among themselves. They chewed over the problem for some time. I waited patiently. It was better than having them chewing over me – which might still be their next move.

Then someone shouted, 'No Blood Truce without Blood Offering!'

Others joined in. 'Blood Offering! Where is Blood Offering?' Once again they began moving forward menacingly.

This was what I was waiting for. 'Wait!' I called.

I went to the back of the hovertruck and threw it open. Inside was the finest and fattest marsh ox available that morning in the Megacity meat market. I heaved the body on to my shoulders – no easy feat even for me – staggered to the centre of the Plaza and threw down the carcass with an almighty thud. As soon as I got my breath back, I gave the ritual cry. 'I bring the Blood Offering!'

That really started a riot. Wolverines will eat anything, including, some say, each other, but they really *love* marsh ox.

More arguments broke out. The Wolverine packs I'd never really tangled with were all for taking the Blood Offering and tucking right in. Some of them even started building a fire.

(Wolverines don't really cook, but they like to char the outside of their meat as a gesture towards being civilized.)

Wolverines from the packs I'd reduced in numbers over the years – there were quite a few of those – felt no Blood

Offering could wipe out the debt. The pack who'd set up the ambush at Happy Mike's place were yelling the loudest.

Finally someone shouted, 'The Old One! Let the Old One speak!' Old Wolverines are pretty much a rarity. As soon as a Wolverine gets too old to fight, some other Wolverine kills him. But one or two survive as pack elders, revered for their wisdom and experience. Presumably, the old white-furred Wolverine who moved creakily forward into the firelight was one of them.

'Garshak!' he croaked. 'The blood of those who died at the hovercar place cries for vengeance. You must fight their pack-brothers. If you live, you may make the Blood Offering!'

If I died they'd eat my marsh ox and me as well, probably, but it would have been tactless to say so. Each Wolverine is linked in a special brother-bond to one or two others. The main question was, how many pack-brothers had survived?

Three Wolverines stepped forward. All three carried laser rifles. I had no blaster, and I'd have stood no chance in a firefight even if I had. Immediately I drew my fighting knife, tossed it aside, and stood looking at them expectantly.

They'd have shot me down if they dared but custom decreed we fight on equal terms – well, three-to-one equal terms anyway.

All three threw down their laser rifles.

The leader of the trio sprang at my throat. I clamped my hands around his windpipe and choked him to death.

So far so good – but the process gave the two survivors time to attack, one from the front one from behind.

I grappled with the one in front, holding fangs and claws away from me. Meanwhile the one behind was clamped to my shoulders, trying to tear through the stiff collar of my leather jerkin and get his teeth into my neck. If he managed to bite through an artery I'd bleed to death in minutes.

I threw myself high in the air and landed on my back, my attacker underneath. The impact of my weight stunned him and broke his grip. I rolled free, grabbed the Wolverine in front and snapped his neck. Whirling round, I grabbed the still-dazed one on the ground and did the same to him. Then I snatched up my knife, cut the head off the dead marsh ox at a single stroke and tossed it on to the fire.

Wolverines crowded round, knives appeared from under cloaks and soon the carcass was cut into bloody fragments and tossed on the fire. The cooking technique, such as it was, was to chuck your bit of meat on to the blaze, watch it sizzle for a bit and then lift it out with your knife. Getting badly burnt was all part of the fun.

I speared a choice chunk from the flames and tossed it to the Old Wolverine. Knocking another Wolverine aside, I speared a smaller chunk for myself and crouched beside the Old One, who was tearing eagerly at his charred and bloody meat with his few remaining teeth.

Heat from the blazing fire beat against our faces and all around eyes and fangs and knife blades gleamed in the firelight.

I tore at my chunk of charred and bloody marsh ox. 'Long ago, perhaps when even you were young, men paid the Wolverines to kill other men who spoke of a thing called the Project. Do you remember this?'

Munching a chunk of meat, he nodded silently.

'I want the name of the one who ordered the killings.'

He went on chewing, staring at me with glazed old eyes. There was no particular reason why he should answer. But there was no particular reason why he shouldn't. What did a batch of long-ago contract killings mean to him?

He croaked a name. 'The man was called Kragg.'

I tossed him the rest of my chunk of meat, rose and strolled casually towards my truck. Nobody tried to stop me. For tonight at least I was an honorary Wolverine.

I got in the hovertruck and drove carefully home. Nobody bothered me, nobody tried to kill me. I called a police contact, got him to check a name on the files, and changed into more civilized clothes. I had a date to meet the others at Louie's bar and compare notes. I was feeling pretty good.

Just before I left I went out to the borrowed hovertruck, to pick up my coat. After searching the whole truck from top to bottom I realized that, Blood Truce or no Blood Truce, you can never trust a Wolverine.

One of the hairy bastards had stolen my brand-new trenchcoat.

Bernice sat at her corner table in Louie's bar, full of pride and brandy, and looked smugly at her two friends. 'Well, how did we all get on?'

They looked equally smugly back at her.

'You first,' said Chris politely. 'How did you get on? You seem to have been celebrating already!'

'How did you manage with my computer?' asked Garshak.

'Pretty damned well,' said Bernice smugly. 'I checked figures for violent crime around the time of Chris and Roz's first visit to Megacity. They held steady – high but no higher than usual – for quite some time. Then they started to climb, slowly at first and then faster, and they've been climbing ever since.

'I checked the violent offenders and found that they were nearly all miners or ex-miners. I checked again and found that a statishtically – *statistically* – higher proportion of them came from just one company. Oh, and I checked a suicide, a jumper, who landed in Mineral Plaza. He was a scientist in the service of the same company.'

She looked triumphantly at the table. Chris and Garshak looked back with expressions of polite interest.

'I ran some more checks on that particular company and found an interesting pattern. It's one of the oldest companies on Megerra. It was in the lead for a time and then it got a bit stagnant – it was falling behind. Then it had a sudden upsurge, started making fantastic profits. Then it levelled off, then it started to decline. Now it's really struggling again. Bad labour relations, high turnover, huge unexplained research expenses, lots of workers fired for fighting, or going berserk and smashing company equipment.' She paused impressively. 'And the name of that company is –'

'The Devlin Mining Corporation,' said Chris.

'Commonly called DevCorps,' added Garshak.

'Bugger!' said Bernice. 'How the hell did you two smart-arse Sherlocks come up with the right answer as soon as me?'

They mollified her and explained.

Garshak gave an account of his expedition to Wolverine territory, playing down the horrifying risks he'd run.

'The old Wolverine told me a man called Kragg had ordered the original wave of killings – the ones that started while you were still here, Chris,' he added. 'I checked him out on police files and discovered he was Security Chief for DevCorps.'

Chris told of his detection of old Sam's murderer, and of the way he'd blackmailed the truth out of Siros.

'He said DevCorps had been paying Custodiex to suppress all talk of the Project for years. Still are.'

'Why didn't DevCorps use Custodiex to hire the Wolverines as well?' asked Bernice. 'Why risk using their own man?'

'They had to,' said Garshak. 'Custodiex will hire human thugs – even killers – discreetly at several removes. But even they draw the line at dealing with Wolverines. DevCorps had to handle that direct – probably still do.'

'Did you get anything out of the Wolverines, about the Project itself, what it actually was?' asked Bernice.

Garshak shook his head. 'The Wolverines weren't even interested. They don't care why they kill people, just as long as they get paid.'

'How about you, Chris?'

'I'm pretty sure Siros was telling the truth. Even Custodiex don't know what the Project actually is.'

'Neither do we,' said Bernice. 'But we're going to find out.'

'How?' asked Garshak.

'DevCorps is due for a visit from the Interplanetary Business Inspectorate.'

Chris looked baffled. 'And what might that be?'

'You're looking at it,' said Bernice.

18

TOUR OF INSPECTION

They had to take Bernice's plan to the Mayor in the end. Harkon flatly refused to mess with anything as rich and powerful as DevCorps without the sanction of higher authority.

Chris and Bernice went with him to the Mayor's office next morning to plead their case.

His Honour Markos Ramarr, Mayor of Megacity, listened to Bernice's exposition with a worried frown on his handsome face.

When she'd finished outlining her theories he turned aggrievedly to Chief Harkon. 'I thought we'd cracked this violent crime problem, Chief. I thought it was all down to skoob smuggling?'

Harkon wished desperately that this were true, but he came through loyally in support of Bernice's theory.

'Only a few cases, sir, and those the most recent. If the lady's right the long-term rise is down to this thing they call the Project – run by DevCorps.'

'And this Project does what?'

'That's what we want to find out,' said Bernice.

'But DevCorps is one of the oldest and most respected firms on the planet! I can't believe they'd do anything criminal.'

'Three different leads point to them, Mr Mayor,' said Chris. 'You know what they say: "Once is happenstance, twice is coincidence – but three times is enemy action!" '

Bernice leant forward persuasively. 'All we're asking you to do is let us take a look. If there's nothing there, then that's what we'll find and we'll go away.'

'So, you want me to say you're from this . . .'

'Interplanetary Business Inspectorate,' said Bernice. 'Megerra's in the Interplanetary Union, isn't it?'

'Well, nominally,' said the Mayor. 'We've never really had much to do with them.'

The Union was a loose confederation of planets in this sector of the galaxy, set up to foster good relations and restore trade after the chaos and confusion of the war. The Union had prospered and now some members were in favour of closer federation, and a common credit system. Some even advocated planetary union. Megerra, however, clung on to independence, ignored most of the Union directives from New Brussels, and occasionally threatened to pull out altogether.

'So much the better,' said Bernice. 'The Union is always spawning daft directives and crackpot committees. All we want you to do is call DevCorps – do you know their president?'

'I most certainly do. Joseph Devlin is an old friend of mine.'

'Call Mr Devlin then, and tell him that the Interplanetary Union have saddled you with a couple of bureaucrats on some kind of inspection visit. Ask him if he'll talk to them and show them around, just to keep them happy and get them out of your hair.'

Ramarr still looked dubious. 'I don't know . . . Look, who are you people anyway? I don't know if you're crooks, cops, or what! Who do you work for? Hell, I don't even know your names!'

'My name is Christopher Cwej, and this is Professor Bernice Summerfield. We're just private citizens, sir.'

'And what's your interest in this Project?'

'A long time ago I came to Megacity with a friend and she

214

stumbled across the Project. We had some urgent business at the time and we had to leave, but I promised her we'd come back someday and look into it.'

'And you're not a cop?'

'Not really, not any longer, though I used to be an Adjudicator. Recently, I've been working for Chief Harkon as a temporary deputy.'

Ramarr turned to Bernice. 'And you're this friend, right?'

'No, Mr Mayor. The friend Chris mentioned is dead now. He asked me to help him to look into the Project. In a way I'm taking her place.'

Ramarr shook his head. 'A daring duo of freelance crime fighters!' He sighed. 'Chief Harkon tells me you gave him a lot of help on the skoob business, so I guess we owe you something for that. All the same, I don't like the idea of prying into the affairs of a long-established and perfectly respectable mining company . . .'

A message flashed up on the readout screen set into his desk.

Ramarr stood up. 'Urgent call. If you folks will excuse me . . .'

Harkon stood up. 'Would you like us to leave, Mr Mayor?'

'No, no, stay where you are. I'll take it in the sanctum.'

Ramarr rose, opened a concealed door in the panelling behind his desk, and disappeared.

Chris looked at Chief Harkon. 'Do you think he'll go for it?'

Harkon sank back into his chair. 'I'm not sure. He's not too happy about the idea.'

'He's a politician,' said Bernice. 'No politician likes to risk upsetting the fat cats.'

The wait seemed to drag on for a very long time. At last the Mayor emerged, his face grave. He studied them for a moment and then his face broke into a politician's warm smile.

'Well, this must be your lucky day! That was Joe Devlin on the comm link, calling me about something quite different. In a moment of weakness I just casually mentioned this visiting committee ... He said fine, send them along. He's out at the mining complex today, so we fixed an appointment later this afternoon.'

'That's splendid,' said Bernice. 'Could I ask you one more favour?'

'Well?'

'Could you possibly lend us one of the mayoral hover-limos – just to make us look more official?'

'OK, OK, if that's what you want. Now if you'll forgive me . . .' Clearly anxious to be rid of them, he ushered them to the door. 'I'll send the limo round to your hotel this afternoon,' he said. 'See my secretary in the outer office. She'll make all the arrangements.' Giving them all a warm smile and a hearty handshake, he bustled them out of his office.

The mayoral hoverlimo parked outside Louie's Hotel, and a tall, thin, fair-haired chauffeur got out, and walked into the gloomy foyer.

An ugly dwarflike creature approached him and the chauffeur said, 'Am I in the right place? Little Louie's Hotel?'

'Correct. I'm Louie.'

'I'm supposed to pick up a couple of VIPs. You sure this is the right place?'

'Yeah, yeah, they won't be down for a while yet. The dame's still getting ready.' He reached up and grabbed the chauffeur's elbow and steered him into the empty bar. 'You got time for a quick belt.'

The chauffeur looked tempted and worried at the same time.

'I can't afford to get booze on the breath.'

Louie winked, and reached for a tall white bottle of colourless liquid. 'Don't worry. Got a bottle of Algolian vodka here. Hell of a kick, not a whiff of liquor.'

He poured the chauffeur a generous slug, handed him the glass and went to the door and peered out. 'Hey, better knock it back quick. I think I hear your VIPs coming.'

216

The chauffeur emptied the glass, gasping as the vodka, ice-cold and fiery at the same time, spread its warm glow through his body.

Louie came hurrying back into the bar.

'False alarm. Time for another!'

He poured the protesting driver a second big drink, nipped back to the bar door and called, 'Quick, they're coming!'

Automatically the chauffeur drained the second glass. This time the glow seemed to rise into his brain and he felt consciousness slipping away.

He saw a massive figure coming towards him and saw with bemused surprise that it too wore a chauffeur's uniform. It was like looking at himself in a magnifying mirror. His other self caught him as he slid gently towards the ground . . .

Garshak lowered the unconscious chauffeur on to a couch.

'When he comes round, tell him he had a few drinks too many so you covered for him and found the VIPs another driver. Tell him no one will say anything if he doesn't.'

'Right,' said Louie. He looked up at the massive figure incongruous in the chauffeur's uniform. 'What's the caper, Garshak? Payroll? Bank job?'

Garshak patted him on his bald head with a massive hairy hand.

'Believe me, Louie, you don't want to know!'

Chris and Bernice came into the bar.

Bernice looked down at the unconscious chauffeur. 'It worked then?'

'Sleeping like a babe,' said Louie. 'Good old Mickey Finn gets 'em every time.'

Garshak touched his cap. 'Your carriage awaits!'

Bernice was wearing a sober, grey costume. Her hair was scraped back and she wore large old-fashioned glasses. Chris wore a dark suit this time with a white shirt and a black tie.

It had been easy enough fitting themselves out in these rudimentary disguises. Getting Garshak's uniform made to measure in time had been more of a problem.

They followed Garshak out of the hotel and he opened the passenger door of the hoverlimo. They got in, he got into the driver's seat, and the hoverlimo purred smoothly away.

As the hoverlimo sped north, Chris and Bernice studied reels of flimsy computer printouts – hard copies of all the information about DevCorp Bernice had been able to extract from the files.

'They'll only show us what they want us to see, remember,' said Chris. 'We'll get the standard sanitized VIP tour.'

'We'll just have to find a way to see the things they don't want to show us,' said Bernice. 'This is the only way we can get inside. DevCorps' security is massive.' She nodded at the massive figure in the front seat. 'Don't forget our ace in the hole!'

The big hoverlimo sped on and on, and even Megacity was left behind at last, the neon-lit streets thinning out and vanishing until they were driving through bleak and rocky countryside.

The marshes and the sea of the south had been desolate enough, thought Bernice, but the north part of the continent was a thousand times worse, bare rocky landscape, ripped and churned by years of opencast mining. She knew from her researches that the DevCorps mining complex was the nearest to Megacity itself, embedded in the range of black mountains that cut off the northern end of the continent.

The road began to climb, and at last they could see the range of jagged black mountains, looming up before them. The road rose even more steeply, winding to and fro across the mountainside.

Finally Garshak called, 'There it is!'

The DevCorps Mining Complex was a grim and forbidding place. The road led steeply up to massive metal gates set into the mountainside itself. The gates swung open as they drove up, and then closed behind them.

They found themselves on the edge of a massive complex of buildings, a miniature city built on to a mountain plateau.

218

An elegantly dressed young woman was waiting to greet them.

'Welcome to DevCorps. If you will come with me . . . Your chauffeur can park over there, in the company garage.'

The hoverlimo moved obediently away and the aide led them to a waiting groundcar, a small, glass-walled, buglike vehicle.

'This is our VIP tour vehicle,' said the aide. 'Everything is fully automated and there is a full audio commentary.'

Chris and Bernice looked at each other in dismay. They knew that their freedom of action was going to be limited. But they had hoped for a tour on foot, with a chance for at least one of them to slip away and investigate anything that looked interesting. They'd get nowhere locked inside a glass bubble.

'This is all very kind,' said Bernice, 'but it isn't exactly what we came for. We are Interplanetary Union officials, not tourists. We had hoped to have a meeting with your president to discuss the economic situation, and the present business climate in Megacity.'

The aide went on as if she hadn't spoken. 'At the conclusion of the tour the vehicle will deposit you at a lift. The lift will take you to the presidential suite, where Mr Joseph Devlin the Third, our company president, will be waiting to meet you.'

Bernice looked at Chris, who shrugged. There seemed to be no way out. They got into the little groundcar and it sped away.

'Well, it's all down to Garshak now,' said Bernice. 'We're trapped in this flying goldfish bowl.'

'Garshak can do it,' said Chris. 'He won't let us down.'

They were speeding past row upon row of identical little houses, each one with its identical patch of artificial grass.

'Welcome to DevCorps,' said the glass bug in an unbearably sweet voice. 'We are now passing through the workers' housing area, where there is accommodation and excellent recreational facilities for hundreds of DevCorps workers and their families.

'At the heart of this area is the famous Medcorps Complex, where generations of our miners, their wives and their children have been able to benefit from the finest of medical care . . .'

'Oh shut up,' said Bernice.

The tour bug was remorseless. It took them through vast engineering workshops where massive pieces of mining machinery were serviced and repaired. It took them through rock-processing factories where the ore was crushed and minerals were extracted.

It took them to the rock face where machines drilled and ripped and tore the heart out of the mountain itself.

They saw long lines of grim-faced miners climbing into shuttle trains that took them into the heart of the mountains to drive and maintain the machines.

They saw other trains deposit weary men, helmeted and overalled and grimed with rock dust, who climbed wearily from the carriages and trudged towards showers and dormitories.

They saw jostling crowds of men waiting for the hover-buses that would take them into Megacity for their long-awaited good time. Many of the men looked dour and angry and once or twice they saw fights break out.

All the time the tour bug's unbearably sweet voice bombarded them with interesting mining facts and fascinating production statistics until their brains felt numb.

At last, at long, long last, it stopped in front of a set of lift doors in a rock wall. 'I hope you have enjoyed the tour,' shrilled the bug, and its door slid open.

Wearily, Bernice and Chris climbed out. The lift doors slid open, revealing a luxuriously decorated interior. They exchanged glances, went inside, and sat down on comfortably padded benches.

The lift doors closed and the lift shot upward for what seemed to be a very long way. When it stopped, the doors slid open and they got up and stepped out into a large and luxuriously furnished anteroom. There were soft carpets, silk-draped walls, fine paintings and valuable antiques.

There were also three black-uniformed security guards who were covering them with blasters and a very large hard-faced man in plain clothes who seemed to be in charge.

'Stand very still please,' said the large man. 'Just a formality.' He searched first Chris and then Bernice with rapid impersonal efficiency.

'This is ridiculous,' snapped Bernice in her best civil service voice. 'We are Interplanetary Union officials. Why should we carry weapons?'

The big man ignored her, nodding towards a set of double doors on the far side of the room.

'Through there – the boss is waiting for you.'

On the other side of the doors was an even more luxurious office with a picture window on one side overlooking the mining complex. There was a massive desk at the far end of the room. Over the desk hung a floodlit full-length portrait of a neat, plump little man in old-fashioned formal clothes.

Behind the desk sat a neat, plump little man in formal clothes of a more modern cut. He rose and bowed.

'Professor Summerfield? Mr Cwej? I am Joseph Devlin the Third, president of DevCorps.'

He saw that Bernice was looking at the portrait.

'You admire the painting, Professor Summerfield?'

'It's a very good likeness.'

'It is – but not of me. That is Joseph Devlin the First, founder of DevCorps. Incidentally, the gentleman who escorted you in is Mr Simeon Kragg, a direct descendant of the Simeon Kragg who was my grandfather's chief security officer.'

'Fascinating,' said Bernice. 'A real family business.'

She had an obscure feeling that things had somehow gone wrong. Nevertheless, she launched into her cover story.

'It's very good of you to see us, President Devlin. We are here on behalf of the Interplanetary Business Inspectorate . . .'

'Nonsense,' said Devlin. 'Don't waste my time with

pathetic lies.' The plump face looked suddenly vicious. 'You are here on behalf of nobody but yourselves. A daring duo of freelance crime fighters – prying into something that doesn't concern you.'

Chris took a step forward and the three security guards raised their blasters. They had positioned themselves so that he and Bernice could be caught in a triple crossfire – a crossfire that would not endanger Devlin or Kragg. Chris relaxed, waiting.

'If you knew who we were, why did you let us come here?'

'I was curious to see you,' said Devlin. 'Just once.'

'Fair enough,' said Bernice. 'But did you have to subject us to that incredibly boring tour?'

'I wanted you to see the grandeur of the institution you were insolent enough to attack,' said the little man seriously. 'Sadly, you seem to lack the intelligence to appreciate it.'

'Your glorious institution is in trouble, isn't it?' said Chris. 'Ever since the Project started going wrong?'

'The Project made this company the greatest on Megerra,' said the little man furiously. 'Once the glitches are sorted out, it will do so again!'

'And how are you going to sort out these glitches?' asked Bernice. 'Are those Advanced Research Department people at St Oscar's being much help?'

'They assure me that in time –' Devlin broke off, staring hard at Bernice. 'You're fishing, Professor Summerfield. You know nothing about the Project.'

'We've a very good idea of the harm it's done,' said Chris.

Devlin laughed. 'Perhaps you do. But as to what it is, how it works, what it can do – you know nothing!'

'Enlighten us!' said Bernice.

Devlin shook his head. 'You'll just have to go on guessing in the short time you have left.'

A comm unit bleeped on Kragg's wrist. He held it to his ear.

'We've got another berserker, sir – in the computer centre. Seems to have smashed the place up.'

'Find the man responsible and punish him,' snapped Devlin. 'But first I want you to deal with these two.'

'What do you want me to do with them, sir?'

'Oh, just take them down to the gates, escort them well clear of the premises . . .' Joseph Devlin smiled. 'Then kill them.'

'With the greatest of pleasure, sir,' said Simeon Kragg.

He smiled at Bernice in a way that made her shudder, and she looked at him in horrified fascination.

A little red flame seemed to dance deep in his eyes.

19

DOWNLOAD

I drove slowly over to the enormous garage and parked the hoverlimo in the first space I found. I sat there for a moment. No one seemed interested in me so I got out of the limo and looked around.

There was a brightly lit, glass-walled waiting room in a far corner of the garage and I walked over towards it. There was a desk with a comm unit with a man in an overall behind it. Men in chauffeurs' uniforms were sitting about talking – waiting till their bosses needed them.

I went to the doorway and said, 'Computer room.'

The man behind the desk looked up. 'Yeah?'

I took a disk from my pocket. 'Computer room. Boss forget disk. Important. Computer room. Where?'

'Give the poor guy a guide stick,' said one of the chauffeurs. 'Otherwise he'll be wandering around for a week.'

The man took a plastic rod from a rack in the wall, slotted it into the comm unit, punched in coordinates, took the rod out and handed it to me. 'There you go. She's set for the computer complex – it's through that door over there. Loud beep right way, no beep wrong way, OK?'

'OK,' I said. I took the rod and went off in the direction he'd indicated. As I moved away I heard one of the chauffeurs say, 'I knew the city once used those guys as cops, but chauffeurs! I'm surprised they can even drive.'

I heard their raucous laughter as I moved away.

I let the guide stick take me along a maze of corridors until I came to an inner complex within the complex, with the words COMPUTER DIVISION on a locked door. I waited by the door until someone opened it to come out. I moved into the space and took him by the arm. 'Computer boss?'

'Sorry?'

'Boss computer man here?' I squeezed his arm, hard enough to hurt.

'OK, OK, no need to break the arm. The head of the Computer Division is over there – in his office.'

'You take.'

'You can't just go in there –'

I squeezed again and he yelped. Sometimes I don't know my own strength. 'Important message for computer boss,' I said. 'You take.'

'All right, all right, I take!'

I took his arm in a firm but friendly grip and he led me across a long room filled with computer banks to a corner office with an opaque glass door.

He tapped on it and an irritable voice said, 'What is it now?'

My unwilling guide opened the door and said, 'Sorry to disturb you, Professor, this – this driver insists on seeing you.'

'You go – message private,' I said. I let go of his arm and he scuttled thankfully away.

Inside the room, a tall thin man with a long neck and a bald head was working at a computer terminal. He looked up irritably.

'Well?'

I closed the door and went inside the room. 'Computer boss?'

'I am Professor Taine, head of the Computer Division, and I am very busy. Now, what do you want?'

I stepped close to the desk, reached out and clamped one hand around his scrawny windpipe. 'You!' I said. I squeezed

– not too hard, humans are very fragile – and he went first red and then purple. I relaxed my grip and he sucked in air.

'I have a very simple proposition for you, Professor,' I said. 'Do exactly as I tell you and you continue to breathe. Disobey me and you stop. Is that clear? Just nod.'

He nodded as best he could. Retaining my grip, I moved round until I was standing behind him at the terminal.

'Do you have the access codes for the Project?'

He sounded shocked. 'Those codes are all highly classified. You shouldn't even –'

He broke off as I squeezed, a little harder this time.

'You're forgetting the proposition, Professor,' I said reprovingly. 'Do you have the Project codes?' He nodded. 'All of them?' He nodded. 'And this is the master terminal?' He nodded again.

'Excellent!' I said. 'Let's go to work.'

I must say, the professor really did very well. He followed my instructions exactly – I hardly had to squeeze at all. When someone tapped on the door and asked if he was all right he shouted, 'Go away, I'm busy!' without any prompting from me.

The task I was giving him was both complex and unorthodox and even with his full cooperation it took some time. Finally, however, it was finished.

I sent, or rather had the professor send, a final message: 'All data received?'

After a worryingly long delay the reply came back: 'All data received and transferred.'

I gave a sigh of relief.

'Well, we're done. Thank you for all your help, Professor.'

I let go of his neck and he fainted, which was just as well, really. He'd had a very trying time, and I'd have hated to distress him further.

I picked up his chair and smashed his computer to smithereens.

Still carrying the chair I went out of the office and walked quickly through the main computer room smashing every computer I could reach. I left the computer division and hurried back towards the garage, hoping I'd memorized the return route correctly.

Alarms were ringing all around now and a squad of armed security guards were pounding towards me. I stepped back into a doorway and pointed back the way I'd come.

'Thank goodness you've come,' I squealed in as high and nervous a voice as I could manage. 'He's in the computer room. Hurry! He's smashing the whole place up!'

They pounded away and I moved on towards the garage.

I wondered if I'd make it.

I wondered what was happening to Chris and Benny.

In a sense it didn't matter – the job was done now. But it would be nice if some of us made it back alive!

There was a glint of triumph in Bernice's eyes as Kragg and his three guards marched her and Chris towards the garage.

Something told her that Garshak had done it. Live or die, they'd already won. Of course, it would be nice to live. But they weren't dead yet – and Garshak was a survivor if ever there was one.

When they arrived at the car, Kragg was suspicious to find no chauffeur in the driver's seat.

'Where's your chauffeur?'

'No idea,' said Bernice. 'He knew we'd be a while – I expect he went off to look for something to eat or drink.'

Kragg glared suspiciously at her. 'Is the chauffeur one of you? Was he in on this?' A sudden thought struck him. 'Is he the one who smashed up the computer room?'

Chris shrugged. 'I doubt it. He was just the Mayor's chauffeur. He came with the car.'

'What was he like?'

'Tall, thin, fair-haired,' said Bernice. 'Bit standoffish and finicky.'

Kragg nodded. 'That's Toler, the Mayor's regular driver. He knows his way round here. Check the refectory and the bar.'

The man started to move away, but Kragg called him back.

'No, wait, this way's better. No reason Toler should get it for nothing — it'd upset the Mayor.'

'The crash'll look all wrong without the chauffeur,' objected one of the guards.

'No it won't,' said Kragg triumphantly. 'It happened like this. We escorted our guests back to the Mayor's hoverlimo — no Toler. The lady got stroppy, refused to wait while we found him, ordered the guy to drive her back to Megacity. Dangerous road, strange limo, guy can't handle it, they go off the edge. Tragic accident! Much less believable if Toler's driving — he knows the road backwards.'

'The gate guard will see this guy's not driving,' said the second guard.

'The gate guard will see what he's told to see,' said Kragg. He turned to the third guard. 'You drive. Take them to a dodgy spot in the road, put the big guy in the driver's seat, blast them both and send the limo over the edge.'

'Very neat,' said Chris.

Bernice nodded. 'Old Toler had a lucky escape.'

'Glad you approve,' said Kragg. 'Get in!' He looked at the three guards. 'Do it quick and neat and get back here on foot.'

He studied Chris and Bernice almost hungrily, and once again they saw the red flicker in his eyes.

'Wish I could come with you but I've got to sort out this computer maniac.'

Their murders efficiently arranged, he strode away.

Menaced by the blasters of the guards, Chris and Bernice got in the back seat. The mayoral hoverlimo was so large that there was plenty of room for them to sit in the middle, leaving room for a guard on either side. There was even another equally roomy passenger seat behind them. The third guard got into the driving seat, and soon the hoverlimo rose and glided away. The gate guard saluted the mayoral crest as the gates opened and the limo glided through, lurching out on to the steep and winding road.

Bernice looked out of the hoverlimo and shuddered. It was a good spot for an accident . . .

Chris decided it was time to make his move. He stood a better chance in the relatively cramped conditions inside the limo than out in the open where the guards would have a clear field of fire. If he could grab one of those blasters . . .

Suddenly the head of the guard to his left jerked forward, rabbit-punched by a huge hairy fist.

Seconds later the head of the guard on Bernice's right did exactly the same.

Huge hairy hands caught each one by the back of the neck and hauled them over the back of the seat into the rear section.

Concentrating on the dangerously winding road, the driver became aware that something was going on.

'You OK?' he called, and a vague grunt answered him. He drove on until he reached a narrow curve over a steep drop.

He set down the limo.

'This will do, right? Don't want to take them too far. We gotta walk back, remember!'

Receiving no reply, he turned, and almost fainted from shock.

There was no sign of his fellow guards but his two passengers were still there – with a huge and monstrous third passenger grinning at him from between them.

With a yell of fear the guard reached for the door.

As he got it open, something hard hit him behind the ear, and he fell out of the car.

Chris rubbed his knuckles. 'My turn, I think.'

'You're welcome,' said Garshak. 'I'll just get out and chuck these three over the edge.'

'Just out,' said Bernice.

Garshak paused. 'What?'

'Just chuck them out of the car, not over the cliff edge.'

'It's what they were going to do to you.'

'We're not them.'

Muttering something about sloppy human sentimentality, Garshak dragged the other two guards from the back of the car and tossed them carelessly beside their fellow. He jumped back into the driver's seat and the big hoverlimo zoomed away.

Suddenly realizing what had happened, Chris thumped Garshak between the shoulder blades. 'Hey, we did it!'

Bernice jumped up and kissed him on the top of his bald skull.

The hoverlimo lurched dangerously.

'Stop that!' yelled Garshak. 'Or there really will be an accident!'

He threw the hoverlimo round the steep curves, heading back towards Megacity.

'How did you get back there?' asked Bernice.

'I'd just reached the garage when I saw you being marched back under guard. I thought the front seat wouldn't be too safe so I sneaked into the back section. Lucky it's such a big limo.'

Suddenly Chris remembered. 'Did you get the Project data?'

'I did.'

'All of it?'

'As far as I know.'

'What did you get?' demanded Bernice.

'Damned if I can tell you. I was too busy sending it to scan it. Medical stuff, mostly I think.'

'What kind of medical stuff?'

'I don't know, I tell you. Let's get back to the station and find out.'

The hoverlimo rocketed onward through the darkness, and soon the great blur of multicoloured light that was Megacity appeared ahead.

'Never thought I'd be so glad to see the place again,' said Bernice.

'Nothing much wrong with old Mega,' said Garshak. 'You just have to know it to love it!'

He drove the hoverlimo straight to police HQ and grabbed the first available policeman.

'Take this limo back to the Mayor's garage, returned with thanks. That's all you say. You haven't seen anyone. You don't know a thing.'

'Not too far from the truth,' grumbled the cop. But Garshak was still a legend in the Megacity Police and he obeyed cheerfully enough, jumping into the limo and driving away.

Garshak led them up the stairs at a run to his old office, where they found Chief Harkon pacing to and fro.

'What the hell's going on, Garshak? I've got orders from the Mayor to arrest you all on sight. Did you really smash up DevCorp's computer room?'

'Me?'

'You fit the description!'

'I do?'

Harkon glared at him. 'You do! How many Ogrons in a chauffeur suit do you see running around?'

'Coincidence,' said Garshak blandly. 'Did we get the data?'

'How the hell do I know?'

'Didn't you check the computer?'

Harkon shrugged. 'I set things up for downloading the way you said. I've been kept busy fielding angry calls from the Mayor since then!'

Garshak went back to his old desk and punched codes into the computer. Data began to flood across the screen. He touched a control and hard copy began whirring from the printer.

The three of them studied it as it streamed out. There was so much data that it took them quite some time to absorb it all. The whole story of the Project was there from first conception, through early success, down to present disaster.

'So that's it,' said Garshak at last. 'Fascinating.'

Benny's head was swimming – and her spirit was chilled. Beneath the flood of immensely complex technical data the full horror of the Project was beginning to emerge.

'Fascinating and horrible,' she said. 'However did you get hold of all this stuff, Garshak?'

'Simple. I persuaded a nice computer professor to give me all the necessary access codes, and then introduced a self-replicating polymorphic virus protocol. It created a wormhole in their firewall so that the packets of data were accepted as low-grade routine security transmissions and downloaded without question.'

'Garshak, you're a genius!'

'I know!'

'I still don't understand it,' complained Harkon. 'Chromosomes, genomes, dominant and recessive genes . . . What the hell were these medical guys actually doing?'

Bernice tried to explain. 'You know of genetic engineering, of course, Chief?'

'I've heard of it – don't mean to say I know what the hell it is. Dammit, I'm a cop, not a scientist.'

'It's the direct modification of chromosomes to produce permanent changes in a species. You can modify existing organisms, even create entirely new ones . . .'

Harkon held up his hand. 'You lost me already, lady. All I want to know is what were these guys doing, and how come it bumped up my violent-crime statistics?'

'Look at it this way,' said Garshak. 'All intelligent life forms evolved from some kind of primitive species, right?'

'I guess so . . .'

'And back in those primitive days, you had to be savage to survive. It was kill or be killed.'

Harkon nodded.

'Right,' said Garshak. 'Now, that kill-or-be-killed reflex is overlaid, controlled, by what we call civilization. But it's still there in all of us. What the Project did to those who were experimented on was to boost it, make it dominant again. Any kind of threat produced a sort of throwback, a savage who only knew one way to respond – by killing.'

Harkon was horrified. 'So that's it!'

Garshak nodded. 'It's a simplification, but that's basically it. I think the reaction must produce some kind of chemical imbalance. The subject's whole perception of reality must change. And of course, the reaction would be hereditary.'

Bernice shuddered. 'It's even worse than I thought.'

'Worse than anyone *could* have thought,' said Chris. 'No wonder they were prepared to go to any lengths to cover it up.'

'So what do we do now?' said Garshak. 'How do we handle it?'

Bernice fished through the reams of computer paper. 'See this? There's a board meeting here in Megacity in a few days – at DevCorps' head office in Mineral Plaza.'

Chris frowned. 'Doesn't Devlin own the company outright?'

Bernice rooted through more paper. 'He certainly acts as if he does, doesn't he? But according to this he sold forty-nine per cent of the shares to a consortium of Megacity businessmen just a few years ago. It happened when the company got into serious financial difficulties and he was desperate to raise money.'

'So now he's got a board of directors to answer to,' said Chris.

'And just look who's on it, Chief!' said Garshak. He showed Chief Harkon a familiar name on the list.

'I think we ought to attend that meeting,' said Bernice. 'There are one or two things about their company and its president that the board members ought to know.'

The others listened attentively as she explained her plan.

'But it all depends on you, Chief Harkon,' she said.

Harkon had fallen silent, stunned by the sheer scale of the horror they had discovered.

'Me?' he said. 'What the hell am I supposed to do?'

'I know you're the one with most to lose,' said Bernice. 'But we can't really do it without your help. The question is – are you with us?'

20

Payback

The DevCorps annual board meeting was held in the boardroom at the top of the DevCorp Tower overlooking Mineral Plaza.

A group of Megacity's richest and most important businessmen were gathered around the long table, listening to President Joseph Devlin's address. The president stood at the head of the table. As always, Simeon Kragg, his chief security officer, stood deferentially behind him.

The directors were not a happy group. They had invested their money largely because of the Devlin name, and because of the company's astounding success in the past. This year, however, as for so many years before, profits were down, dividends reduced. Yet President Devlin continued to promise them vast profits, next year, always next year, and to patronize them as if it was a positive privilege to be allowed to lose your money by investing it in the oldest firm in Megacity.

'And so,' Joseph Devlin droned on, 'I can assure you that in the future, the very near future –'

A clear female voice rang through the boardroom. 'I shouldn't make any more extravagant promises for the future, President Devlin. I don't think you have one.'

The astonished directors saw that a strangely assorted group had appeared in the doorway of the boardroom.

There was a smallish, smartly dressed, dark-haired female, a very large, fair-haired young man, and, of all things, an enormous Ogron in a long trenchcoat.

Next to them was Chief Harkon in full dress uniform.

President Devlin stared at the group disdainfully.

'I take it these criminals are under arrest, Chief Harkon?'

'No one's under arrest as yet, Mr Devlin – though some-one may well be very soon. For the moment, I simply wish to warn you all that my men are guarding the exit. No one will be allowed to leave this boardroom until Professor Summer-field has finished what she has to say.'

Mayor Ramarr leapt to his feet. 'What the hell's going on here, Chief Harkon?'

'Sit down, Mr Mayor. You're here because you're a director of DevCorps and you'll listen with the rest.'

'This will cost you your job, Harkon.'

'*Sit down.*'

Slowly Ramarr sat.

Harkon turned to Bernice. 'Professor Summerfield?'

Bernice had been elected spokesperson by the others on the grounds that, as an academic, she was used to lectur-ing people. Now she surveyed the astonished DevCorps directors as if they were a class of exceptionally dim first-year students.

'I propose to deliver a brief lecture on the history of DevCorps,' she said crisply. 'Please pay attention. The infor-mation I am about to give you is of vital importance to you all, to Megerra, and to many other planets. The subject is complex, but for the moment I shall try to be as simple and as concise as possible. Later, hard evidence and complex scien-tific proof will be provided for everything I intend to say.'

She paused, gathering her thoughts, and then began.

'As you all know, the Devlin Mining Corporation is one of the oldest firms on the planet. For a long time it was one of the most prosperous, but, as old firms will, it began to stagnate. To revive its fortunes the president's grandfather, father and currently President Devlin himself have had recourse to one of the most abominable of crimes – illicit genetic manipulation. Hiring Professor Vashtar, a scientist whose work had been banned on every civilized planet, they began a programme of interference with the DNA of their workers, and of their workers' unborn children.'

There was a low murmur of astonishment. Bernice went on.

'Even Professor Vashtar himself finally realized the dangers of his work. He attempted to confess to an associate of Mr Cwej. Professor Vashtar died that same day. He threw himself, or was thrown, from a window in this very building.'

Instinctively every director looked at the long-since-repaired window. Then they returned their gaze to Bernice.

She smiled grimly and went on with her lecture.

'The horrifying programme of genetic manipulation continued. It was carried out, without the knowledge or consent of the workers concerned, under the cover of an elaborate programme of medical care.'

A tall, white-haired man interrupted. 'This is a monstrous allegation. Why would anyone, any company, do such a thing?'

'Profit,' said Bernice crisply. 'After all, that justifies everything, doesn't it?'

The tall man fell silent, and Bernice continued.

'The original intention was to create the ideal miner, someone capable of working longer and harder than any normal man. This vile scheme was code-named "The Project" and its very existence was shrouded in secrecy. In the early days garbled stories somehow leaked out, and rumours inevitably began to spread, especially among Megacity's thriving criminal community. They were intrigued because they believed the Project to be some incredibly profitable crime – which indeed it was, at least at first, though not in the way they thought.

'In a relatively short time, however, these rumours were ruthlessly suppressed, by a sustained campaign of intimidation and murder.

'For a time the Project actually succeeded. The productivity and the profits of DevCorps soared – until an atavistic mutation occurred. A dominant killer gene appeared. As a result, workers were created who were not only stronger and more determined than others, but completely savage and ruthless. Men capable, under certain pressures, of killing. Men who reacted to *any* frustration with savage violence.'

Bernice paused again, looking around her fascinated and horrified audience.

'Such men do not make good employees, gentlemen. They fight with their supervisors and their fellows, and eventually they have to be discharged. They often drift into crime. But even hardened criminals have little or no use for men like these – men who kill not for profit, but for pleasure, or for no reason at all. Thanks to the Project, a considerable number of these men are now at large in Megacity. They are largely responsible for the brutal and senseless crimes which you hear of every day, and for the tide of violence which Chief Harkon and other police chiefs have struggled in vain to hold back. Others of these men have left the planet. Since the killer gene is dominant, it will almost certainly be passed on to their children and their children's children – to spread the killer strain on hundreds of other worlds.'

Again Bernice paused. Devlin stood white and silent.

'Faced with potential disaster, you might expect any normal man to abandon such a scheme. President Devlin has not done so. He has poured company money – your money – into the Project, in an attempt to make it successful again.'

An angry murmur ran around the boardroom. Bernice realized that at last she was hitting the directors where it hurt.

'Most recently President Devlin has hired amoral research scientists at St Oscar's University on Dellah, my own university, in an attempt to salvage this mad plan. I believe that illegal experiments have been conducted on human subjects in an attempt to bring the killer gene under control. Like President Devlin, these scientists have not hesitated to defend the secrecy of the Project with cold-blooded murder.'

The tall white-haired man jumped to his feet. 'I am Aled Klamath, vice-chairman of this board. Is this incredible story really true?'

By now Joseph Devlin had recovered from his shock.

'Of course it isn't,' he sneered. 'These ridiculous allegations are based on stolen data, illegally obtained and misinterpreted by those too ignorant to understand them. A jumped-up teacher, an off-world adventurer and an Ogron! Will you take their word against mine?'

Aled Klamath looked steadily at Bernice. 'I'm sure I speak for my fellow directors when I say we find ourselves quite unable to accept such wild accusations. I suppose it is possible that some well-meant attempts at medical welfare went a little awry, but I'm sure the errors can be corrected. If we avoid overreaction this great company can still survive . . .'

Bernice shook her head. 'You people don't give up, do you?' she said. 'It's over, I tell you. We have proof – unassailable, incontrovertible proof.'

'I find it very hard to believe that.'

'Try!' said Chris. 'We have full and detailed evidence, held on the computer files of the police. Everything can and will be proved.'

'You're a part of this mess now, all of you,' said Bernice. 'Now you have to help clear it up.'

'And what, exactly, are we supposed to do?' Klamath asked.

'Close down the Project at once. Trace everyone who has been subjected to genetic manipulation. Warn the authorities on other worlds where necessary. Finance research to see if the condition can be cured, or at least alleviated.'

Aled Klamath looked outraged. 'Do you realize the sheer complexity of what you are asking us to do?'

'Oh yes,' said Chris cheerfully. 'It's an enormous task. But then, the Project is an enormous crime.'

Klamath glanced around the table at the horrified faces of

238

his fellow directors. Then he shook his head. 'It's out of the question. The expense alone would bankrupt the company.'

'It's certainly going to cost an enormous amount of money,' said Bernice. 'The sale of the assets of DevCorps will cover some of it, but all the rest of you will have to contribute. I'm sure the Megacity Council will help – won't it, Mr Mayor?'

Ramarr shook his head determinedly. 'It will do no such thing. This is purely a commercial matter.'

Bernice Summerfield was beginning to lose patience. 'I think it's about time you all stopped whining about what it will cost you to put things right, and started thinking about what it will cost you if you don't.'

'And that is?' asked Klamath coldly. 'Suppose we ignore your demands?'

Garshak spoke for the first time. 'We are prepared to put this information out on the Meganet, to make it instantly available to every planet in this sector of the galaxy.'

'Do you think they will believe you?' asked Klamath.

'Are you willing to gamble that they won't?'

'Do you think tourists will still come to Megacity where any passer-by may suddenly turn into a murderous maniac?' asked Bernice. 'Will investors put money into companies whose miners may turn killer?'

Chris Cwej spelt it out for them.

'The tourists will stop coming. The investment funds will dry up. This city – and this planet – will die.'

There was an appalled silence.

After a moment Klamath said, 'If the problem can be tackled on a city, indeed on a planetary level . . . Mr Mayor?'

'It would have to be discussed in full council,' said Ramarr slowly. 'But if the wellbeing of the whole planet is involved, then I suppose . . .'

Bernice sighed inwardly with relief. They were seeing sense at last. It was going to be all right.

Suddenly Joseph Devlin screamed, 'Don't listen to her, you fools! The Project is still viable – it just needs more time, more work. We're close to a solution. The situation can still be saved.'

For a moment, if only because the directors so desperately wanted to believe him, it looked as if he might sway them back to his side. Devlin pressed home his brief advantage.

'The effects of the Project were never as bad as she's claimed. All this talk of murderous maniacs . . . Hysterical nonsense!'

'Is it?' said Bernice. 'And what if I were to tell you that one of these genetically manufactured maniacs, one of these killers created by the Project, was here, in this very boardroom?' She pointed to Simeon Kragg. 'This man is Devlin's security chief. Yesterday he arranged to have me and my associate murdered on a word from his boss – and he enjoyed doing it! *Look at him!* He'd like to kill me now.'

The horrified directors watched as Simeon Kragg stalked towards her, hands reaching for her throat, red flames flickering deep in his eyes.

Benny sensed Chris and Garshak tense beside her – but it was Joseph Devlin who diverted Kragg's attention.

'Kragg, no! Keep away from her, you fool. You're just playing into her hands.'

It was a fatal mistake. Kragg swung round on his employer.

'You stupid, arrogant little idiot!' Kragg's voice was strained and hysterical. 'Don't you see it's all over? I tried to warn you, my father tried to warn your father, but none of you listened. None of you damned Devlins will ever listen.'

He glared at the horrified directors, the red flames burning brighter in his eyes. 'If you want proof of what she's been saying, look at me! My father was the result of one of his damned experiments. Do you know he was so loyal, so devoted, that he actually volunteered? And what happened? They turned him into a killer. He murdered my mother and then killed himself. But first they produced me – a child of the Project!' He laughed. 'She's quite right. I've killed for DevCorps time and time again. Killed and enjoyed it.'

'Be silent, Kragg,' screamed Devlin.

Suddenly Kragg leapt forward and seized Devlin from behind, his forearm locked around the plump neck. Chris and Harkon tried to pull him off but Kragg, in his killer frenzy, scarcely seemed to notice their efforts.

Bernice looked up at Garshak. Surely he had the strength to wrest Kragg away from Devlin?

Garshak looked back at her impassively. He didn't move.

Kragg thrust his knee into Devlin's back and jerked hard once, snapping the little man's neck with an audible crack. He hurled the body to the ground.

Police flooded into the room, and Kragg was dragged struggling away. Devlin's body was hauled out like a sack of garbage.

Garshak looked down at Bernice. 'Congratulations – a very convincing demonstration.'

Bernice gave him a horrified look. 'I didn't mean to get anyone killed.'

'Perhaps not. But all the same, Devlin's better out of the way – and I rather think we've finally made our point! They're beginning to accept the situation.' He grinned savagely. 'As the old Ogron proverb has it, "When you have them by the balls, their hearts and minds will follow!" '

Klamath rose and said unsteadily, 'Due to the sudden and unexpected demise of President Devlin, I declare this meeting closed. I suggest we reconvene in a few days to discuss what measures we can take to deal with this terrible situation.'

He looked appealingly at Bernice. 'I am not sure what your role is in this unhappy affair, Professor Summerfield, but you seem to be exceptionally well informed. I trust you will be able to assist us further?'

Bernice shook her head. 'Chief Harkon and Mr Garshak have all the details you need. My associate Mr Cwej will help as well. Personally, I think it's time I went home.'

She headed for the door, followed by Garshak, Chris and Harkon.

Mayor Ramarr hurried to intercept them. 'Many congratulations! I hope I don't have to say how shocked I am by all this.'

'You'd getter not say anything at all, you treacherous creep,' said Bernice. 'You shopped us to Devlin, when he called you, that time in your office. You sent us into a trap.'

'That isn't true!'

'Oh yes it is!' said Chris. 'He knew we were fakes as soon as we arrived. He called us a daring duo of freelance crime fighters, a phrase he must have picked up from you.'

'You're on the police computer files, Mr Mayor,' said Garshak sinisterly. 'Everything's documented. I'd advise you to give Chief Harkon here *very* full cooperation in future.'

Followed by her friends, Bernice swept triumphantly out.

It took Bernice a little time to say goodbye to Megacity.

She had a farewell dinner with Lucifer in his castle by the sea.

'I'd like to ask you to visit my homeworld Gehenna with me,' he said as they said goodbye on his moonlit terrace. 'But you might not survive the experience.' He smiled, touching her cheek with his long clawed hand. 'I'd like to ask you to spend your last night on Megerra here with me too, but you probably wouldn't survive that either.'

'Pity,' said Bernice. 'Mind you, it would be a hell of a way to go.' She rose on tiptoe, kissed him just once on his hot dry lips, and went down the steps to her waiting hovercab.

She had a farewell drink with Sara and Chris at Sara's Cellar. Chris was staying on in Megacity for a while, to help the reformed DevCorp close down the Project – at least, he said that was why.

Sara took Bernice to see her conservatory – and to ask if she minded about Chris staying on.

Bernice shook her head. 'Chris was a great big kid for a while,' she said. 'He formed a romantic attachment for every female he met – first Roz, maybe me a little. Now he seems to have grown up hard and fast. Too fast. He deserves a good time.'

Sara smiled. 'Well, I'm a good-time girl.'

'I hope so.' Bernice hesitated. 'He won't stay for ever, you know. Chris used to be Roz's Squire – now she's gone he's a full-blown knight errant. One day he'll hear of a lost cause or a maiden in distress and you'll find him sharpening his sword and polishing his armour.'

'I'll deal with that when it comes,' said Sara. 'I know exactly what Chris needs right now – the love of a bad woman!'

'Can't argue with that,' said Bernice. 'Let's get back to the bar before he finds one.'

Then she had another farewell drink with Louie and Garshak and Murkar at Little Louie's Hotel and Piano Bar. She made Louie flush scarlet by kissing him goodbye on top of his bald head. Then she left with Garshak, who was to drive her to the spaceport.

When they'd gone, Louie beckoned over Murkar and some other friends, and treated them all to drinks.

'See that?' he asked them. 'Me and the Dragon Lady are real close. I was in her mob, you know. She and Big Chris are heavy hitters, real big-time. Now Chris has moved in with Sara over at the Cellar. Me and them two and Garshak took down Nastur. And I helped all three of 'em do the big DevCorps job, planned it right here. Ain't that right, Murkar? First we snatched the Mayor's chauffeur . . .'

Meanwhile Garshak and Bernice were having a final drink in the spaceport bar.

'What will you do now?' she asked.

'I'm not sure. Harkon wants me to come back as Assistant Chief. Now he's got the goods on Ramarr, he's planning to run for Mayor next election. If he wins he'll give me my old job back.'

'Is that what you want?'

'I'm not sure. I was a pretty bad cop for a very long while. I rather like being a good private eye.'

An amplified voice called, 'Shuttle for Station Alpha now boarding.'

'That's me,' said Bernice. 'You know, I think I'm going to miss you, Garshak.'

Garshak raised his glass. 'Likewise. Well, here's looking at you kid! We'll always have Megacity!'

They finished their drinks and Bernice walked away.

Demoniacs and Ogrons, she thought as she joined the shuttle queue. I wonder if there's something weird about my tastes . . .

EPILOGUE

On a warm summer evening a lot of travel time later, Bernice staggered up to her rooms at St Oscar's, dumped her travel pack and threw herself wearily into a chair.

Joseph, her porter, floated in and brought her a large brandy without being asked, which Bernice saw as a certain proof of machine intelligence.

'Many urgent messages,' piped Joseph. 'Mr Irving Braxiatel was very insistent that you call the moment you return. Activate vidicom?'

'Very well.'

Minutes later the vidicom chimed discreetly and a jubilant Irving Braxiatel appeared on the screen.

'Welcome back, Bernice!' He beamed. 'Well, you've nothing to worry about! Suddenly all the opposition to you collapsed. All charges and allegations dropped unreservedly, formal apology from the faculty, large ex-gratia payment to compensate for any distress and inconvenience – oh, and the Advanced Research Department people want to offer you a substantial fellowship.'

'Do they now?' She yawned.

'Well, aren't you pleased?'

Bernice could see he was hurt that she didn't seem to share his sense of triumph.

'Of course I am, Irving, and grateful as well. It's just I'm so tired from the journey. Thanks for all the good work. We'll talk tomorrow.'

The real good work had been done in Megacity, she thought, but it would be unkind to say that to Irving Braxiatel. The Advanced Research Department's change of heart and their sudden generosity followed a sharp message from Chief Harkon in Megacity enquiring about their precise involvement in the DevCorp Project.

This had been followed by an even sharper one from Professor Summerfield. In this she informed them that she would soon be placing certain facts in her possession, concerning dealings between the Advanced Research Department and the Devlin Mining Corporation, before the Faculty Ethics Committee.

The vidicom chimed again. A tubby, red-faced man with white hair and a neat white beard appeared on the screen.

'Professor Summerfield? I am Jarl Kedrick of the Advanced Research Department. I take it you've heard the good news? I just want to be sure our little misunderstanding has been cleared up.'

'Not quite yet,' said Bernice. 'I intend to clear it tomorrow, though, before the Faculty Ethics Committee.'

She smiled sweetly at him. 'I'd start packing if I were you.'

'But our offer is most generous. I fail to see why –'

'Jeran,' said Bernice.

'I'm sorry?'

'An Ootsoi kid called Jeran. He had a crush on me and my bike and he got swatted like a fly. You don't even remember him, do you, you callous bastard? Well, you're going to pay for Jeran.'

She flicked off the screen and poured herself another brandy.

Just about the time she finished it, and was contemplating a third, the vidicom chimed again. This time a tall, thin, olive-skinned, silver-haired humanoid was on the screen.

'Professor Summerfield? I am Santos Silvera, the Director

of the Advanced Research Institute. I gather you have just had a rather unfortunate conversation with my Security Chief, Jarl Kedrick.'

'Unfortunate for him,' said Bernice truculently. 'Unfortunate for you as well – you can start packing too.'

'It could also be unfortunate for you, Professor Summerfield. We are a very powerful organization, and we shall survive the unfortunate DevCorps affair. We may never be friends but do we have to be enemies? Why not at least make a deal? We offer very generous terms in return for a little discretion. Our full support in the faculty, a cash bonus and an extremely generous fellowship.'

'No. It's payback time.'

'By the way, the lava lamps you objected to have gone from your favourite bar – together with a number of other, similar installations. That operation is now abandoned – it turned out to be more trouble than it was worth.'

'Sorry, it's still not enough.'

'There must be something extra I can offer you. Something you want enough to make you change your mind.'

'If there is, I don't know what it is.'

He surveyed her thoughtfully. 'Then perhaps I do. We may not be so far apart after all. Goodnight, Professor Summerfield.'

The screen went blank. Soon afterwards a mixture of tiredness and brandy sent Bernice off to sleep in her chair.

When the explosion came it was so loud it shook the room and shocked her into wakefulness. She went to her window and saw a fiery glow coming from the direction of the Advanced Research Department building.

After a moment she switched on the campus audio channel. There was a few minutes of music and then an excited voice said, 'Here is a news flash. Reports are just coming in of the sudden and shocking death of Jarl Kedrick, Security Chief of the Advanced Research Department. It appears that when Mr Kedrick got into his groundcar and switched on the drive, the vehicle promptly exploded. Mr Kedrick was killed instantly. The cause of the explosion is not yet known. We'll bring you further news as it comes in.'

The music resumed and Bernice switched off the audio.

The vidicom chimed again and the screen lit up.

Instead of a face there was one word on the screen.

'Deal?'

'Deal!' said Bernice out loud, and the screen went blank.

Pouring herself one last brandy, she raised her glass.

'Cheers, Jeran!'

Then she smashed the glass into the fireplace and went to bed.

ALSO AVAILABLE
IN
THE NEW ADVENTURES

OH NO IT ISN'T!
by Paul Cornell
ISBN: 0 426 20507 3

Bernice Surprise Summerfield is just settling in to her new job as Professor of Archaeology at St Oscar's University on the cosmopolitan planet of Dellah. She's using this prestigious centre of learning to put her past, especially her failed marriage, behind her. But when a routine exploration of the planet Perfecton goes awry, she needs all her old ingenuity and cunning as she faces a menace that can only be described as – panto.

DRAGONS' WRATH
by Justin Richards
ISBN: 0 426 20508 1

The Knights of Jeneve, a legendary chivalric order famed for their jewel-encrusted dragon emblem, were destroyed at the battle of Bocaro. But when a gifted forger is murdered on his way to meet her old friend Irving Braxiatel, and she comes into possession of a rather ornate dragon statue, Benny can't help thinking they're involved. So, suddenly embroiled in art fraud, murder and derring-do, she must discover the secret behind the dragon, and thwart the machinations of those seeking to control the sector.

BEYOND THE SUN
by Matthew Jones
ISBN: 0 426 20511 1

Benny has drawn the short straw – she's forced to take two overlooked freshers on their very first dig. Just when she thinks things can't get any worse, her no-good ex-husband Jason turns up and promptly gets himself kidnapped. As no one else is going to rescue him, Benny resigns herself to the task. But her only clue is a dusty artefact Jason implausibly claimed was part of an ancient and powerful weapon – a weapon rumoured to have powers beyond the sun.

SHIP OF FOOLS
by Dave Stone
ISBN: 0 426 20510 3

No hard-up archaeologist could resist the perks of working for the fabulously wealthy Krytell. Benny is given an unlimited expense account, an entire new wardrobe and all the jewels and pearls she could ever need. Also, her job, unofficial and shady though it is, requires her presence on the famed space cruise-liner, the *Titanian Queen*. But, as usual, there is a catch: those on board are being systematically bumped off, and the great detective, Emil Dupont, hasn't got a clue what's going on.

DOWN
by Lawrence Miles
ISBN: 0 426 20512 X

If the authorities on Tyler's Folly didn't expect to drag an off-world professor out of the ocean in a forbidden 'quake zone, they certainly weren't ready for her story. According to Benny the planet is hollow, its interior inhabited by warring tribes, rubber-clad Nazis and unconvincing prehistoric monsters. Has something stolen Benny's reason? Or is the planet the sole exception to the more mundane laws of physics? And what is the involvement of the utterly amoral alien known only as !X?

DEADFALL
by Gary Russell
ISBN: 0 426 20513 8

Jason Kane has stolen the location of the legendary planet of Ardethe from his ex-wife Bernice, and, as usual, it's all gone terribly wrong. In no time at all, he finds himself trapped on an isolated rock, pursued by brain-consuming aliens, and at the mercy of a shipload of female convicts. Unsurprisingly, he calls for help. However, when his old friend Christopher Cwej turns up, he can't even remember his own name.

GHOST DEVICES
by Simon Bucher-Jones
ISBN: 0 426 20514 6

Benny travels to Canopus IV, a world where the primitive locals worship the Spire – a massive structure that bends time – and talk of gods who saw the future. Unfortunately, she soon discovers the planet is on the brink of collapse, and that the whole sector is threatened by holy war. So, to prevent a jihad, Benny must journey to the dead world of Vol'ach Prime, and face a culture dedicated to the destruction of all life.

COMING SOON

TEMPEST
by Christopher Bulis
ISBN: 0 426 20523 5
Publication date: 15 January 1998

On the wild and inhospitable planet of Tempest, a train is in trouble. And Bernice, returning home on the luxurious Polar Express, is right in the thick of it. Murder and an inexplicable theft mean that there's a criminal on board; the police are unable to reach them; and so the frightened staff and passengers turn to a hung-over, and rather bad-tempered, archaeologist for much-needed assistance.

WALKING TO BABYLON
by Kate Orman
ISBN: 0 426 20521 9
Publication date: 19 February 1998

When an illegal time-travel experiment threatens to start a war between the People and the dominant power in the Milky Way, Bernice is forced to journey back to the ancient city of Babylon to prevent a tragedy. She has one week to stop the experiment, or God, the People's ultra-powerful supercomputer, will destroy the city and all its inhabitants – an action which could mean Benny will never have existed.

OBLIVION
by Dave Stone
ISBN: 0 426 20522 7
Published: 19 March 1998

A man called Deed is threatening the fabric of the universe and tearing realities apart. At the heart of the disruption, three adventurers, Nathan li Shoa, Leetha and Kiru, are trapped. Their friend Sgloomi Po must save them before they are obliterated, and in his desperation he looks up some old friends. So Bernice joins her feckless ex-husband Jason and her old friend Chris on the rescue mission; but then Sgloomi picks up someone who should really be dead.

THE MEDUSA EFFECT
by Justin Richards
ISBN: 0 426 20524 3
Published: 16 April 1998

Medusa, an experimental ship missing for twenty years, is coming home. When one of the investigation team dies mysteriously, Bernice is assigned to help discover what went wrong. But to do so she must solve a riddle. Somehow the original crew are linked to the team put on board – their ghosts still haunt the ship. And the past is catching up with them all in more ways than one.